THE CRONES

ALSO BY SHAWN MCGUIRE

THE WITCHES OF BLACKWOOD GROVE Mystery Series

HEARTH & CAULDRON Mystery Series

WHISPERING PINES Mystery Series

GEMI KITTREDGE Mystery Series

THE WISH MAKERS Fantasy Series

THE CRONES

A BLACKWOOD GROVE MYSTERY, BOOK 2

SHAWN MCGUIRE

CHAPTER 1

*B*asil, lemon balm, and chamomile or lavender flower tea. Steep the herbs and drink to relieve headaches.

A teaspoon of a tincture made of ginkgo, gotu kola, rosemary, and peppermint taken three times a day to help with memory issues.

Rosemary and lemon thyme tea to drink for sheer pleasure.

What else could I create with the herbs in our garden? The options were endless, and my notebook was full of ideas for cures, creams, and spells. And with more than a month to go before the first frost did its damage, I still had time to create with the fresh herbs and plants too. Then I would harvest them and hang them from the rafters to dry.

I'd gotten so much done today, I allowed myself to clock out a few minutes early and take the leisurely route to pick up my granddaughter, Cricket, from preschool. This meant a walk along the Mississippi River. Breathing in deep lungsful of fresh air and watching the sunlight glisten off the water as it slowly made its way south was both rejuvenating and relaxing.

When I came to where a set of stairs led down to the river, I stopped to notice a houseboat docked there. The owner, Harriet

Wong, told everyone who'd give her five minutes about the boat she was having restored. She saw me up on the road now and gave me a beckoning wave.

"Come on down, Dusty!"

Much as I'd love to see it, I needed to get over to the playground.

"Soon, I promise," I called back as I gave her a wave. Then I crossed the street to another short flight of stairs that led directly up to my family's diner. About fifty yards west of there was a large playground that drew children like a magnet. I had yet to see anyone crying or fighting there and suspected some of the town's witches had cast a spell over it. Life was hard enough, even for children, so I approved of a place where things simply went well.

This was the pickup point. We dropped the kiddos off at Autumn Trainor's organic flower farm in the morning and picked them up here in the afternoon, where they ended their day burning off a bit of their seemingly endless supply of energy. I envied their stamina.

"Hi, Lola!" Cricket called out the Filipino word for *grandma* her mother had taught her and waved to me with her whole arm from the top of a forest-green and tan tower. "Can I play more? Please?"

She dragged out the word *please* for about five seconds.

"Sure. Ten minutes." I wasn't in a hurry to get home but did still need to pick some tomatoes before I could call it a day. Cricket could help me with that.

I turned to find someplace to sit and spotted a toddler triumphantly releasing the lock on the strap holding him in his stroller. In a flash, I saw him topple forward and fall on his forehead. Another flash showed me him years older with a jagged scar over his left eyebrow.

I blinked and then reacted, like anyone would; I reached out as though I could stop the fall from happening. Except, I was a witch and, along with being able to see into the future, I could also alter the course of current events by simply reaching out. The child landed back in his seat, bumping his head gently against the padded backrest. The sudden motion startled him, and he burst into tears. I immediately pulled my hand back and clasped it with my left one—partly because of his reaction and partly because my hand had gone numb and tingled painfully. There was always a consequence for performing magic that interfered with a person's life. Even if the spell was cast with good intentions.

"Oh, sweetie," his mother crooned. "What happened?"

One of the women standing in the little cluster of townies pointed at me. "She happened."

The woman had shoulder-length, somewhat stringy dishwater blond hair and looked vaguely familiar.

"You don't remember me, do you?" she accused.

I shook my head. "Sorry, I—"

"That's what happens when you literally run away from your problems."

My spine stiffened. She was about my age, fifty, and very angry at me. There was only one thing this could be about.

"What did you do to him?" demanded the mother, now holding her squirming son.

"He was going to fall."

"So she claims," the blond woman hissed. "That's what she does, you know. She makes things happen and then claims she was only preventing an accident. She's a witch. A *gray* witch."

Gasps of surprise and judgmental glares immediately followed the labeling. No matter how innocent the act, no matter how positive the outcome, non-magical people— *Ordinaries*, we called them—put gray witches on the same level as violent criminals or folks with deadly communicable diseases. We were to be avoided at all costs and shunned if possible.

"Nothing wrong with being a witch," called out an older townie with a thick white Fu Manchu mustache and a massive black dog. "Not in this town. Not in any safe town. She is free to use all the magic she wants here. And I saw what happened." He spoke directly to the young mother. "You wouldn't know it because you were too busy jabbering and sipping your kombucha, but your kid was making an escape and about to land on his noggin. You should be thanking Dusty, not chastising her."

The woman looked at me with big unsure eyes while rubbing her hand over her son's thankfully undamaged *noggin.*

The blond, however, continued her attack on me. "Do you know what this witch did? Thirty-two years ago, she tried to kill me and nine other people."

She *had* been on the boat. The one I stopped from crashing the same way I just stopped the little boy from falling out of his stroller. By reaching out my hand.

The man shook his head and snorted in disgust. "You mean she *saved* your life and nine other people's."

His coming to my defense this way absolutely shocked me. I'd only been back in Blackwood Grove for three weeks and had seen him and his big dog at The Paddle Wheel saloon once but hadn't interacted with him at all. Like many people in this town, including this woman who looked ready to scratch my eyes out, the old man seemed familiar.

I offered him a grateful smile and then told the woman, "It's been a long time. I recognize you but . . . I'm sorry, who are you?"

The blond laughed at me. "Tracy Slayton."

My mind spun back three decades. The Tracy Slayton I knew was pretty and popular and had a huge crush on Nash Kramer, the boy who'd been driving the boat that day. Not to be cruel, but the years had not been kind to Tracy.

"You can't trust her." Tracy pointed at me while directing her comments to the crowd that had gathered. "You can't trust any of them. They're not natural. Touched by the devil, the lot of them."

They. Them. She meant us witches.

"We're born with these abilities," I tried to explain or defend. Maybe both. "It's not like we asked for our powers any more than we get to choose the color of our eyes."

"What's going on here?" a young woman in a police uniform asked as she approached the group. Officer Leezza Chapman.

"That witch tried to hurt this little boy," someone called out.

"No," I insisted, "that's not at all what I was doing. The opposite in fact. He was about to get hurt—"

Officer Chapman shot a look at me that basically said, *stop talking.* Then she stepped closer to the child and, in a soothing voice, asked, "Did you get a boo-boo?"

He sniffled and squirmed. His mother admitted, "No, he's fine."

"What happened?" the officer asked.

The mom's mouth opened, closed, and then she said, "I can't say exactly. I was talking with these other ladies, and my back was to him. The next thing I knew, he was crying." She offered me a softer expression. "Earl says Dusty stopped him from falling out of his stroller."

Officer Chapman met my gaze briefly. "What's all the anger about, then?"

Tracy started down the *she's a witch and can't be trusted* path again. A few people murmured their agreement with her. Others had already backed off.

Three weeks ago, literal minutes after I'd returned to town, a man was found murdered in our diner. It quickly became my mission, much to the frustration of local law enforcement, to catch the killer and clear my cousin's name. I was able to do that, and the traumatized townies were so grateful there was no longer a killer roaming our streets. During the two weeks since then, however, attitudes changed, and conspiracy theories started flying.

"The timing is too convenient."

"She probably set it up so she could be the savior of the town."

"Trying to get us to welcome her with open arms."

"Why is she back anyway?"

I had returned to Blackwood Grove because someone threatened my granddaughter, and the town was supposed to be a safe place for us.

Cricket. My heart raced. How long had I let myself be distracted? I scanned the playground, tensed when I didn't see her right away, and then slumped with relief when I not only spotted her but saw her laughing with the other little witches from school.

"Seems to me," Officer Chapman told the group, "nothing happened, so I don't know why you all are this worked up." Tracy opened her mouth to speak again, and the officer held up a silencing hand. "You're dredging up rumors about something that happened thirty years ago. Those wounds have healed."

"Healed?" Tracy blurted. "You weren't here. Were you even alive thirty-two years ago?"

By the way the officer's lips pursed slightly, I'd guess no.

"Some of those wounds," Tracy continued, staring directly at me, "are still open and oozing."

As empathetically as possible, I said, "I'm sorry to anyone who feels that way."

"As am I," Officer Chapman added, "but this is not the place to deal with that. Although, Ms. Slayton, it seems you might need to deal with it. If you need assistance—"

"This may not be the place," Tracy hissed, "but I assure you, this problem will get dealt with."

CHAPTER 2

*W*hat was all that about? Did Tracy Slayton threaten me—it kind of felt like it—or had old memories simply risen to the surface and boiled over when she saw what I'd done to stop that little boy from falling out of his stroller?

Do you know what this witch did? Thirty-two years ago, she tried to kill me and nine other people.

You can't trust any of them. They're not natural. Touched by the devil, the lot of them.

I assure you this problem will get dealt with.

Just words. Sticks and stones and all that. Right?

Was Tracy still as angry as she appeared? Was this safe town as safe for my granddaughter and me as I hoped?

These were the thoughts whirling around in my mind as Cricket and I walked the short distance home. I let out a long sigh of relief when we got to the blackthorn hedge that surrounded Applewood Farm. The branches rustled and parted to let us through and then creaked and crackled as they twined back together once we were on the other side. My ancestors planted this hedge two hundred years ago to keep themselves safe from intruders of both the human and animal varieties. As a child, I sometimes wondered if it was keeping us safe or imprisoned.

Cricket ran ahead of me and took a sharp left toward the farmhouse's front door. I had planned to stop at The Apple Barn on our right, the shop where we sold the produce we grew alongside a variety of other items. My cousin, Carly, had taken over running the shop about ten days ago. I wanted to tell her what had happened in the park and ask her about Tracy. Had she suffered any long-lasting or permanent effects from the boat accident? Carly knew a lot about many of the townies. It was well after three o'clock, though, and the shop closed at four. Carly always stopped in the house at the end of the day. I'd talk to her then.

I found Cricket on the covered, wraparound deck, struggling to open the front door.

"It won't let me in."

"Did you ask for the password?" The house liked to tease her and make her figure out a password to gain entry. Being only four years old, Cricket couldn't read, but she was smart and could decipher images.

Unamused, she released the doorknob and let her hands drop to her side. "Password, please."

An index card slid out from beneath the door. On it were two pictures: a rain drop and a purple bow. Cricket studied the card for a few seconds, then blurted, "Rainbow!"

The door popped open, and she darted inside, where she dropped to the floor to take off her sandals. Then she gathered up her shoes and backpack and ran with them to her room. Such a good girl.

Along with the two of us, four other witches lived in the house full-time. My aunts Comfort and Gwynne, Uncle Maks (who wasn't a witch), and family friends Pepper and Jett. My mother showed up on occasion, and visiting witches from other safe towns stayed with us sometimes. There were also two ghosts, but they were so quiet I sometimes forgot they were around until they were in front of me. In less than a month, my life had gone from the serenity of living alone to Cricket moving in with me to the chaos of being back with my family. Most of the time, the chaos was joyful. I had missed them horribly during the years I'd been away. Other times, it was full-on *chaos*. Like now. I heard them before I saw them.

In the kitchen at the back of the house, I found Comfort and Pepper wielding weapons. Pepper clutched a cast iron frying pan by the handle with both hands. Comfort waved a set of tongs about like a magic wand.

"What is going on?" I stormed over and disarmed them. Pepper flexed her hands as though in relief. Understandable; that pan was heavy.

"They're arguing about dinner," Gwynne supplied from a chair by the fireplace in the far corner of the large room. "Like they did last night."

Life in the farmhouse had been fine until my cousin and I decided it was time for Comfort and Gwynne to retire. At eighty-two and seventy-eight respectively, they'd earned the right. Except now they were bored and searching for ways to keep busy. And since Comfort no longer went to the diner before the sun rose, and Gwynne didn't cross the driveway to The Apple Barn right after breakfast, Pepper no longer had the house to herself all day. That wasn't a completely bad thing because, with only the house and passel of familiars to talk to, she had become lonely and a bit depressed.

"Who cooked last night?" I asked.

"I did, of course." Pepper pushed her shoulders back and adjusted the turban-style wrap on her head. "This is my kitchen. I do the cooking."

"*Your* kitchen?" Comfort demanded.

I cleared my throat and fixed her with a stare. I just knew

she was going to say something about Pepper only being a visitor here, even though Pepper had been living with them for twenty-five years.

"For the last two years," Comfort began instead, "your version of *cooking* has been to tell the house what's on the menu and then stand back and watch it do the work."

The house made a *ta-da* noise that I believe was meant to be the audible version of a curtsy.

Stung, Pepper snapped her mouth shut, whatever she was about to say trapped inside. Comfort took on a smug look until Pepper found her words. Her Creole accent was thick with the emotions of the moment when she said, "This coming from the woman who entered the diner every morning to find the day's menu on the counter and all the ingredients cut up and pre-measured." She gave Comfort a *go ahead, tell me I'm wrong* look. "Even Cricket could cook under those circumstances."

From the back corner, Gwynne stated, "A four-year-old really shouldn't reach into a hot oven."

"Not the point, Gwynne," Pepper sang out.

"The ingredients were only cut up," Comfort replied, having recovered from Pepper's accusation. "I did the measuring."

The problem, as I saw it, was that after working sixty-plus years in the family diner, Comfort couldn't stay out of the kitchen. And after twenty-five years of being the family cook, Pepper felt her territory was being invaded.

"Can we figure out a way," I suggested in my moderator voice, "for you two to share the kitchen?"

Cricket skipped into the room then and climbed onto one of the stools surrounding the massive kitchen island. "It's nice to share."

I beamed at my little bug and arched an eyebrow at the warring witches.

"Isabella forgot her lunch today," Cricket continued. "She opened her backpack when it was time to eat, and it wasn't there. Miss Autumn asked us how we could fix her problem. We decided to share. Snack, please." As she continued her explanation, her current favorite after-school snack of banana slices with tiny dollops of peanut butter and a small glass of milk appeared before her. "We all gave her a little bit of our lunch. That made one whole lunch for her." She threw her hands in the air, victorious. "Miss Autumn said we did a good job and gived us mini strawberry marshmallows as a reward." Cricket picked up her fork and speared a banana coin. "Thank you, house."

"Schooled by a four-year-old," Comfort grumbled, but pride in her great-granddaughter was evident in the grin she fought with.

Pepper placed a kiss on Cricket's forehead. "We can't keep bickering like this, Comfort. Especially over something we both love so much. It's not good for our auras. How can we make this work?"

While Cricket ate her snack and the two cooks entered negotiations, I went to Aunt Gwynne in the corner. The slightly lost expression that sometimes crossed her face later in the day was present.

"Gwynne? Is everything okay?"

"Hmm?" She looked up as though she hadn't heard me. "Oh, yes, I'm fine. Still getting used to this new routine. Just like they are." She jutted her chin at her sister and best friend. "You were right. Running the barn was getting to be too much for me, so stepping down was a good idea. It's hard to make such a big change, though. And it happened so fast."

I squatted next to her chair, my knees crackling as I did. "You know, I'm sure Carly would love it if you checked in on her now and then."

Gwynne's face brightened. "You think so?"

"I'm sure of it. This is a big change for her too."

Carly left the diner to run The Apple Barn. Carly's

daughter Nina was now in charge of the diner. And I was learning how to manage the farm from Jett, who couldn't handle it all on her own anymore. The changes were good and necessary, but Gwynne was right; it happened fast. After upsetting the apple cart, so to speak, some pieces needed to be put back together, and others no longer fit anywhere. Even the house was in a state of flux since Cricket and I had moved in.

As though on cue, Carly entered the kitchen. "Everyone looks so serious. What's going on?" She looked at me with an expression that asked why I wasn't handling things.

"Come on." I helped Gwynne out of the chair. "Let's go have a family meeting."

We all gathered around the island, and I explained how we needed to come up with some new daily routines. We all understood that routine was especially important for Gwynne.

I turned to Comfort and Pepper. "Did you two come up with a plan?"

"I can't stop making pies," Comfort began.

We all nodded. People made special trips to the diner from miles away for a slice of Comfort's pie.

"And I prefer savory dishes." Pepper was as good a cook as Comfort was a baker.

"Obvious solution," Carly decided. "Mom takes care of desserts, and Pepper makes the main meals." She brushed her hands together in a *there, problem solved* gesture.

Pepper frowned at the declaration.

"What's wrong?" I asked her.

Pepper lifted a thin shoulder in a little shrug. "I like to bake, too, and Comfort likes to cook—"

"Then you'll need to share," Carly interrupted. Her tone was one she probably used on her four children when they were squabbling. "Take turns cooking and baking."

Comfort glowered at her daughter and held up a calendar

she and Pepper started filling in before Carly arrived. "That's what we plan to do."

"As long as you stop fighting," I said, "you two can run this kitchen however you want."

"Yes, great, we're all on the same page." Carly switched her attention to Gwynne. "How are you doing, Auntie?"

Gwynne glanced at me. "Dusty and I were talking about me coming over and helping out in the store now and then."

"Great idea." Pepper clapped her hands happily. "Nina won't let Comfort do any work, but she goes over to the diner every day and checks that things are running smoothly."

"Every other day," Comfort corrected. "Last time, Nina said, 'You handed over the reins; now let me drive the wagon.'"

Pepper continued, "I'll be doing tarot readings at the apothecary on some Fridays and Saturdays. Trust me, it's good to get out of the house throughout the week. That's a lesson I learned the hard way."

"Another problem solved." Carly told Gwynne, "Auntie, you come on over whenever you want. We figured it would be better if you didn't work full-time anymore. You, too, Mom. But that doesn't have to mean no working at all."

By *we*, she meant herself and me. We were co-caretakers of the house and its residents.

"Please remember," Comfort cautioned, "to include us when making decisions about our lives."

"Of course," Carly assured and turned to me. "Anything else that needs taking care of?"

Why was she acting like that? She charged into the house and, within seconds, took over the situation with the aunts I had already addressed. Did she think I wasn't holding up my end of this bargain or couldn't do this on my own? Maybe it's because she was used to being the boss. She had four kids at home, her husband was almost always on the road driving his semi-truck, and now she was running the store. All I had was

Cricket, which was much easier now that she was in preschool, and managing the farm with Jett's help.

"I'd like to talk with you about something else, if you've got time." I pointed toward the back door. "Out on the patio?"

"What's going on?" Comfort asked immediately.

"Something we should know about?" Pepper leaned toward me.

Gwynne, who seemed to have regained her faculties after being told she could pop into the shop when she wanted to, added, "You know you can tell us anything."

It was like having three nosey mothers. Four including Jett, but she had become more like an older sister to me.

"There's nothing for you to worry about," I assured and grabbed two iced teas for Carly and me.

"She's lying." Gwynne crossed her arms.

"I'm not lying. Not every discussion in this house has to be done by committee."

They formed a threesome and started whispering. Probably planning how to conjure some sort of magical eavesdropping device.

"Cricket?" I called from the back door. "Are you done with your snack?"

She hopped off the stool. "Yep."

"You can go play in your room, then. I'll be there in a few minutes to hear all about school today."

"Okay, Lola." She grabbed Gumbo, Pepper's basset hound familiar, by the collar and dragged him to her room.

I pointed at the elder witches. "Don't even think about teaching my granddaughter to snoop."

This resulted in overly dramatic gasps of shock and denial, confirming my suspicion about what they were planning. Then they re-formed their huddle as Carly and I stepped outside.

She dropped with a groan onto an Adirondack chair and, with what could only be labeled disdain, said, "You know, you don't need to wait for me to make these decisions. Sure, we should discuss some things first, but this seemed like an easy fix. Why are you staring at me like that?"

"I didn't wait. I got them to quit bickering and work out a compromise. When you got here, Comfort and Pepper had already started writing a schedule on the calendar. Gwynne needed a little more help. The change to her routine has knocked her off her game. That's what she and I were talking about when you walked in. She still wants to be involved with the store."

"Right. I said that was fine." Ignoring everything else I mentioned about having things under control, she asked, "What did you want to talk to me about?"

Let it go, I told myself. *Her life has turned upside down, too. She's simply trying to regain a little control.*

That was a new personality trait for my cousin. She had always been a bit bossy, but I'd never considered her to be controlling.

"Do you remember Tracy Slayton?" I asked, happy to change the subject to something other than the house, farm, or aunts.

Carly thought for about half a second. "Yep. She was in our class."

"She was also on the boat that day."

"Right. She had a huge crush on Nash Kramer."

I nodded, smiling at a memory. We used to make covers for our textbooks out of brown paper shopping bags. Tracy drew hearts with *T loves N* all over hers. Nash caught her doing it once in chemistry, and she didn't even flinch. In fact, she looked him square in the eye and said, "Friday night after the football game, I'll show you how much."

"Why do we care about Tracy?" Carly asked, attitude still in place.

Carly drank her iced tea while I told her about the scene in the park. The more I explained, the straighter she sat.

"An old man named Earl came to my rescue." I put my hand to my heart.

"Really? Earl hates everyone. Maybe he's a closet witch."

I frowned. "Is that a thing?"

"We wouldn't know if it was, would we?" Then, as though I was either dense or had missed the punchline, she added, "Because they're in hiding. Again, why are you so concerned about Tracy?"

I blinked at her. Was she not listening? Did I not explain it properly? Did she simply not care? "Because she verbally attacked me and dredged up ancient history in front of a crowd of townies. I'm wondering if this is a problem I should deal with or if I should leave it alone."

"Tracy's kind of a loudmouth. Some listen to her; others tune her out." After a bit of thinking, she added, "No one has talked about the boat accident in years. You returning has stirred up the memories." She thought some more. "Gossip topics come and go with the weather in this town. My bigger concern is that you performed gray magic in front of a bunch of townies."

"It was a reaction. The child was going to fall."

"I understand that, but you need to get control. You can't just *react*."

"But I don't want—"

"Yeah, I know. You don't want everyone to know you're a gray witch. Too late, you're out of the broom closet, cousin." She paused for a breath and then the tongue-lashing continued. "That's why you left, right? To escape what you were?"

"Yes, but—"

"Well, you're back, Dusty, by your own choice. This thing with the kid happened more than fifteen minutes ago, so anyone in town who didn't know you were a gray does now. It's time for you to get control. Which isn't the same thing as accepting it, if that makes you feel better. It means that when you react, the result will be the one you want. Yes, you stopped the boy from getting hurt. But what if your reaction had caused something bad to happen instead?"

She was right. I hated this power. My mother had practiced this wrong thing for the right reason *gift* for years, and it had all but killed her.

"How do I get control?" I wondered out loud to myself in a formulating a plan way, and Carly pounced on it.

"There's a very easy answer. Or if you want to complicate things unnecessarily, you could ask The Council for names of other gray witches, and if there are any you could ask one of them for help."

She wanted me to take lessons from my mother. "I'll think about it."

"Don't think for too long. Tracy has outed you." Carly shook her head. "Correction, you outed yourself. Things will get worse before getting better."

Thanks for bringing that down on us was left unsaid but clear in her tone.

For the past three weeks, the half of the residents of this town who remembered me were wondering why I was back. Honestly, there were moments when I questioned that decision. Being back with family was great. Being back in the town where I had *a past*, not so much.

"Find your mom," Carly demanded. "Time for you to finish your training."

Or rather start it. I had known little to nothing about gray witchcraft when I left.

For the rest of the night, I tried not to think about Carly's directive. Dinner was a good distraction. Gwynne talked about helping Carly in The Apple Barn. Comfort and Pepper told Jett all about their plans for managing the kitchen, which Jett praised as being a grand idea.

After giving Cricket her bath and reading her two stories, I settled into the beautiful bedroom the house had created for me. When we first arrived back on the farm, Cricket and I had stayed in the carriage house across the courtyard. She had a little girl's dream room. I got a literal camping cot in an otherwise empty room. The property had been mad at me for being gone for so long and was punishing me. Then it rewarded me with things like a nicer blanket or thicker pillow whenever I did something it approved of.

I sank into one of the two overstuffed chairs in the sitting area of my bedroom, pulled my feet up into crisscross, turned the TV on for background noise, and tried to meditate. Something I'd been practicing every night for the last ten days.

My mind immediately filled with the discussion Carly and I had earlier. Then I thought of the boat accident. Why was Tracy still *so* angry at me? Nash had been driving the boat that day. I prevented people from dying, which I couldn't prove, but he was responsible for the accident and the fallout from it. Such as Nash going to prison for five years and Beau Balinski losing his right leg from the knee down. I didn't know because I left shortly afterward, but did any of the others suffer permanently because of that event? Specifically, what had happened to Tracy?

CHAPTER 3

"*M*anaging the operation is a big job, and we've got plenty of good people to cover all the chores, but if you have a favorite task, claim it." This was one of the first things Jett told me the day she started teaching me about running the farm.

Cricket had claimed egg gathering as her job. Every morning right after breakfast and at the end of each day just before dinner, Cricket and Jett or I gathered the eggs from the coop and sorted them into trays for delivery. Of course we always brought a supply to the kitchen for Pepper and Comfort.

When I was a kid, I loved delivering our fresh produce, eggs, and goat milk and cheese to the local stores. It filled me with such pride to see people's smiles when I'd walk in and hear them exclaim how beautiful everything was. I immediately knew that was a job I wanted to do.

This morning, after dropping Cricket off at the pre-school at nine o'clock, I drove our delivery van to The Paddle Wheel saloon. No one was there to let me in that early in the morning, so I punched in the code for their back door lock and put the order in the walk-in cooler. One of the benefits of living in a small town.

Then I parked in the mall's parking lot and headed to The Sweet Spot bakery. Raul and Kelsey's pastry of the day today was empanadas, either savory or sweet. I chose one filled with creamy chocolate ganache. Heavenly!

Being a small town, Blackwood Grove had more than its fair share of gossip. Usually, it was someone airing their anger or being plain spiteful, but there were many days when the buzz was about happy things.

"Have you tried Rodney and Mildred's sweet corn yet?"

"For sure. I don't know what they did, but this year's crop is their best ever."

Then everyone would hurry over to their roadside stand and buy them out.

After the news of the corn died down last week—the first harvest was always a reason for celebration around here—the gossip turned to me. The townies had been so grateful when I'd helped Officer Balinski catch Ludo Beck's murderer. There were plenty of pats on my back, literal and figurative. After the initial relief that the streets were safe again, the mood changed.

"*How* did she catch him?" they wanted to know.

"The timing is sorta suspicious, don'tcha think?"

"Gone three decades and a body shows up the same minute she steps foot back in town?"

"It *was* pretty much simultaneous."

"She must have been involved."

In a matter of hours, I'd gone from hero to questionable to villain. Fortunately, any time someone suggested to Officer Beau that he should look closer into this possibility, he declared me "absolutely innocent."

That chatter had finally quieted. Maybe because no more bodies were discovered. I was getting smiles and nods again instead of scowls, but it appeared that today I was once again breaking news. As I approached a table of four in front of So Mote It Tea teashop, a group of women cast judgmental looks my way before speaking purposely loud enough for me to hear.

"That's the one."

"Tracy told me all about the boat accident when I was getting my hair done yesterday."

"Tracy told *me* it wasn't an accident." A head jerked my direction. "*She* tried to *kill* everyone on that boat."

"She tried to kill a child yesterday."

"You know they're all the same."

"Witches?"

"Mm-hmm. Mark my words, she's just the start."

"You're probably right. She's been hanging out with that cousin of hers."

"Thinks she runs the town. Just like all those Warrens."

"You know what that will lead to."

"More deaths?"

"There's a reason everyone's complaining about witches' rights again."

"Maybe it's time to round them all up and do a Salem."

I was prepared to ignore them. They could say all they wanted to about me, I could take it, but they pushed it too far by mentioning Carly and my family. And then suggesting barbaric Old-World punishments for innocent witches?

As I propped the door open with my hip and pushed my dolly full of crates inside, I flicked a finger at a glass sitting next to the "Salem" woman's elbow. I meant for it to look like she had tipped it over, but my aim wasn't much better than Gwynne's on a bad arthritis day, and three of the drinks tipped over, spread across the table, and spilled onto their laps. A happy accident, far as I was concerned.

Seconds later, I knocked my elbow hard against the door to the backroom right on the funny bone. ("It's actually the ulnar nerve, Mom, not a bone," Micah had informed me once after browsing through his high school biology textbook.) The electric jolt that shot through my arm from the impact wasn't funny in the least. My consequence for performing the micro spell . . . but it was totally worth it.

"You're the hot topic of conversation today," Russell noted nonchalantly when I came out of the backroom with last week's empty crates. He dropped a lemon wedge and a handful of raspberries on top of ice cubes in a glass. Then he added raspberry lemonade and handed the concoction to me.

"So I've heard." I took a long refreshing drink. Perfect. "I was prepared that word of my slip yesterday would spread quickly."

He grinned. "Is that what that was outside a few minutes ago? A slip?"

I glanced out the window at Maggie, now hosing down the vacated table and sidewalk beneath it. "No, that was purposeful. And more than a little juvenile. Sorry about the mess."

His smirk let me know he didn't care in the least.

I finished the lemonade, picked out the berries, and popped them in my mouth. "Really good. Thank you for this."

"Thank you for the delivery." As I headed to the door, Russell said, "So you know, I'm not tolerating their talk. I ask that they not speak that way about my friend, and if they continue, I show them to the door. This is a safe town. We shouldn't have to defend ourselves regarding our magic."

Russell was a psychometry witch. That meant he gleaned information about a thing or sometimes a person through touch.

"We shouldn't," I agreed, "but they think I've done these things on purpose. The curse of being a gray witch, I guess. Always doing the wrong thing."

"Convenient how they forget the 'for the right reason' part, isn't it?"

I gave him a grateful smile and laid my hand over my heart.

Reinvigorated by the lemonade, Russell's words, and the

glorious late-summer sunshine, I went to the van to put the empty crates from the teashop inside and reload my dolly with the diner's order. That was my last stop, and then I could go home and check in on my crew.

When my niece Nina took over the diner, she carried on the tradition of the new operator changing the name. To avoid patron confusion, the change was never major. Aunt Comfort had given it the slightly confusing title of Comfort's Food Diner. Nina changed it to The Comfort Diner. Her choice received the Granny Sadie stamp of approval. High praise indeed. Despite changing the name on the sign outside and the logo-embellished merchandise inside, most everyone still called it The Diner.

I'd just reached the sidewalk that bisected the park with my refilled dolly when I spotted two women talking outside the antique shop about fifty yards away. One of them was Marilyn Kramer. She was tall with broad shoulders, and as usual, she wore jeans with her shirt tucked in, which made her easy to identify from a distance. It took a moment for me to recognize the other woman as Tracy Slayton. Marilyn owned all of the buildings on the mall, except for the diner and Silver Moon Apothecary, and was a very strict landlady. Before leaving me last night to straighten out my own mess—my words, not hers, but the implication was clear—Carly had given me a little information about Tracy. *Hairitage*, the hair salon and beauty supply shop she operated, was in the mall's farthest northeast corner.

"She says the name is a play on heritage." Carly shook her head. "'Like you inherited this great head of hair,' she had to tell everyone because no one understood what it meant. We're all pretty sure she'd had one too many gin rickeys the night she chose it."

"Good to know she owns the salon," I replied. "I'll need a

haircut soon and was going to go there. Guess I'll find someplace else."

I paused along my route to adjust the crates on the dolly. Really, it was an excuse to watch the two. Marilyn didn't usually come to the mall until after lunch. When she wasn't here bossing her tenants around, she was helping her husband, Henry, run their farm. Far as I knew, Marilyn wasn't a friendly woman. She was unlikely to stop and shoot the breeze with her tenants, so the two must be discussing the hair salon.

Marilyn leaned in close, backed away again, and waved her hands about in emphasis as she spoke. Maybe word of the scene Tracy caused with me by the playground last night had reached the boss lady and Marilyn wasn't happy about it. A few seconds later, though, Tracy appeared to relax from her protective stance of arms crossed tightly over her chest and dropped her hands to her sides. Tracy wasn't my favorite person at the moment, but Marilyn had been on my least-favorite list for more than three decades. I was glad to see Tracy appeared to be holding her own with the bully who thought intimidating people was the best way to keep them in line.

I went through the diner's back door, which faced the park, and was immediately engulfed by the heavenly aromas of breakfast. Toast, bacon, and cinnamon rolls stood out the most. Not to mention pie. My mouth actually started watering. It wasn't even ten thirty, and I'd already had breakfast, an empanada, and all those raspberries in my lemonade. How could I possibly be hungry?

Avery, one of Nina's employees who had been promoted from part time to full-time cook, reviewed the order for accuracy.

"Not that I don't trust you," they said. "Nina has a lot to prove right now, so I'm doing all I can to make this a smooth transition."

"I don't mind in the least," I assured the twenty-something

trans woman who was almost as good a cook as Comfort was. "I'm going to say hi to my niece."

I loved being able to say that. Considering I didn't even know I had nieces and nephews until three weeks ago, we had a lot of getting to know each other to do.

I entered the dining room through the swinging kitchen door and found Henry and Nash Kramer sitting at the counter. Both had cups of coffee in front of them, and Nina was taking away their empty breakfast dishes. Nash looked up and acknowledged me by maintaining eye contact for about two seconds. That was actually a record. He and I had a very complicated history.

I chatted with Nina near the register for a few minutes. After only two weeks, she was settling in nicely with running the diner.

"Even though I've worked here for years, it's different being the boss. I'm starting to find a new rhythm, though." Her head bobbed up and down as a sort of self-encouragement as she spoke. "I'm getting comfortable making small changes to the way Grandma ran the place. Don't tell her I said that."

"Promise." I drew an *X* over my heart. "New topic. How does your mom seem to you?"

Nina stiffened. "What do you mean?"

I thought of how she took over the conversation with the aunts last night. "I don't know. Do you think she's happy running the store?"

The head bobbing returned. "Yeah, but sometimes it's like she expects things to work just by thinking it. You know?"

I laughed. "I do. Are things not working?"

"She said the store isn't cooperating with her."

Ah. "It isn't handling the change well either."

"Right." Nina glanced at me and away, not comfortable talking about her mother with an aunt she barely knew. That was understandable.

"All this switching of roles," I acknowledged, "it's a big deal for everyone."

The bell over the front door at the opposite end of the building jangled. Nina and I both looked to see who had entered. Tracy Slayton.

"Takeout order," Nina stated and pointed toward the kitchen. "Do you want to—"

"Run and hide?" I pushed my shoulders back. "No. I won't let her intimidate me."

Halfway to the register, Tracy saw me standing there, paused mid-stride, which made her stumble a bit, and then completed her route.

"Twice in two days," she said.

"Lucky me." I gave her a tight smile.

She lifted her chin, daring me to challenge her.

"Hi, Tracy," Nina blurted as she exited the kitchen with a large paper bag in hand. "Your order's ready. Do you need napkins or utensils?"

From seemingly nowhere, two women were suddenly standing behind Tracy. They must have been sitting at a nearby table.

"Witch hasn't got anything to say today?" one of the women taunted.

"No one to come to her rescue," the second added, practically pushing Tracy to start another altercation.

To my absolute joy, Nina stepped closer to me. She didn't say anything, just stood at my side, which was all the reinforcement I needed.

"I do have something to say," I replied. "You took me a bit off guard yesterday, so I'll say this one last time. That little boy was about to fall out of his stroller. I stopped that from happening. As for the boat accident—"

"You tried to kill us," Tracy said loudly enough for the entire diner to hear.

I darted a look at Nash, wondering if he'd do more than watch the exchange with his father. Nothing.

"Get over it, Tracy. You're the one going on about how powerful I am. If I'd wanted you all to die that day, you wouldn't be standing here right now." I wiggled my fingers at the trio in a gesture they could interpret to mean hello, goodbye, or *duck and cover, she's going to throw a spell at us.*

Tracy spun to face her backup and the other nearby diners. "You all saw that. She's at it again."

From his stool by the counter, Nash finally spoke up. "Didn't look like she was trying to do anything to me. Other than defend herself."

Tracy's jaw dropped, and a look of pain crossed her face. I remembered seeing it before. Any time Nash showed attention to another girl. More than thirty years later, Tracy was still in love with him. Based on his body language, the feeling wasn't mutual.

After gathering her dignity, Tracy pointed at him. "You know the truth. You were there that day."

Both men stared at her, neither responding.

"That's enough," Nina declared and shoved the bag of food at Tracy. "You should go now before I have to call Officer Balinski or Chapman and report someone causing a disturbance in my diner. I've got your credit card on file. I'll charge your order and add a nice tip. In the future, unless you can be civil, please send one of your employees to pick up your orders."

Nina stood shoulder to shoulder with me as Tracy left the diner and the other two women returned to their table. My niece would do a fine job running this place.

Nash tossed a few bills on the counter. "Thanks for the meal, Nina." He glanced at the window into the kitchen where Avery had been watching the scene play out. "Great eggs, Avery."

Avery pressed their hands together in thanks.

Both Nash and Henry studied me before leaving. Or rather,

Nash studied, and Henry glared. The elder Kramer hated my family. I was actually shocked he even came into the diner. Although, the food was undeniably good.

"You okay?" Nina asked once they'd all left.

I blew out a breath. "I had a feeling coming back to Blackwood Grove would be a challenge. This wasn't at all what I'd expected, though. Think I'll go for a little walk along the river to settle my nerves before heading back to the farm."

"Good idea." She gave me a hug then. Our first one ever.

CHAPTER 4

I left through the diner's front door and descended the short set of stairs to River Road. As I approached the dock stairs on the other side, two young women in running clothes appeared at the top. They were whispering and laughing to each other. When they spotted me, one with teal-colored hair said, "You might not want to go down there."

"Why not?" I'd planned to dangle my feet in the water and watch the boats float by for a few minutes. Then I remembered Harriet Wong and her houseboat.

"Dusty. Yoo-hoo, Dusty."

"Oops." The second girl put her hand to her mouth while Teal Hair said with a giggle, "Too late."

From the dock, Harriet was waving her arms at me as though flagging for help. I sped up in case she was in trouble.

"Harriet? Is everything okay?"

"Everything's fine. Finer than fine, in fact."

She held her hands out toward her boat just as her cat—a Ragdoll named Fluff who seemed to melt into every surface he laid on—stood and stretched. Fluff spun twice then flopped back down on the same spot in the sun on the roof of the long, low house boat. Harriet wasn't showing off her cat, however.

"It's done?" I asked as if I hadn't heard.

"It is!" She clasped her hands over her heart. Harriet had been working on restoring and decorating this boat for more than a year.

"Come in and take a look," she begged.

Feet in the cool water or tour of a cool houseboat. Either was a nice distraction from the business with Tracy. "I only have a few minutes. Then I need to get back to the farm."

"No problem," Harriet assured. "It's not that big a boat."

Had to admit, I was impressed. The vessel was the perfect size for one person and a cat. Two people if they really liked each other or didn't need a lot of personal space. Harriet decorated it in watery shades of blue and green with splashes of white and sandy beige. At one end was a cozy, sunlight-drenched living room. In the middle, a surprisingly spacious U-shaped kitchen. Next to that, a full bathroom. And finally, her bedroom. The wheelhouse, where she drove the boat, was up top along with a sundeck where she could sit and watch the stars at night or her surroundings during the day. It was an absolutely charming floating apartment. She'd even put perches beneath some of the windows for Fluff.

"It's lovely, Harriet. Is your route still the same?" She had stopped in at The Apple Barn and told Carly about her plans many times. I was there for a few of the encounters so already knew them in detail. She took such joy in talking about it, though, so what was the harm? "Still planning to go all the way to New Orleans?"

The Asian woman gave her long ponytail a snugging tug. "I am. If I go straight through, it will take two weeks. I can't possibly do that on my own, so I'm going to stop along the way and explore some new areas. Figure I'm still young enough for a grand adventure. My first reservation is at the marina in

Lansing, Iowa, about fifty miles from here. That's far enough for the first day."

Harriet was sixty-two, had divorced her husband decades earlier, raised their three kids without him, and still worked as a freelance editor, which she could continue doing from her floating home.

"You're very gutsy," I praised. "Regardless of age, it takes a lot of courage to do something like this by yourself."

"I've done my research," she assured me. "While the crew was rebuilding this beauty, I went on plenty of river cruises, both long and short, and talked the captains' ears off with questions about navigating the river and which areas to avoid. A few with boats similar in size to this one let me drive. They were so helpful. Did you know there are river pirates?"

I did because she'd already told me. That still shocked me.

Harriet stepped on a spot in the floor beneath a table-height counter that served as both an eating and working surface. A hidden panel popped open, and she pulled out a case with what looked like a Glock in it. I knew nothing about guns, though, so couldn't swear to it. "If they try to give me any trouble, I'm protected."

The sight of this tiny woman holding that weapon amused me. I sure wouldn't test her. Those of us who had done our time in the single parent trenches were a tough lot.

"Will you be here for a while yet?" I glanced at the clock on her wall. Time to shuffle off.

"Another ten days or two weeks. Unless Beau tells me I have to leave, or the spirit moves me to go sooner. I've got an editing project I'd like to finish first."

"We should christen your home and do a blessing before you shove off."

She clasped her hands in front of her heart. "That's a great idea."

Touring Harriet's boat was the perfect distraction. On my

way back to the diner to grab my dolly and crates, I thought about how brave the crone was. In another dozen years, would I be brave enough to do what she was doing? I'd like to say yes, but there seemed to be a new ache or pain every morning. At this rate, I wouldn't be able to get off the couch when I hit sixty-two.

Back at the farm, I dropped the delivery crates off at the shed on the far side of the garden. We called it a shed, but it was really a smaller version of a barn. This was where we packaged produce, jarred honey from the beehives, and bottled milk from the goats. The shed also had a small commercial kitchen for making goat milk cheese among other things.

After returning the van to the garage, I was on my way to inspect the garden when Carly flagged me down outside The Apple Barn.

"Nina called me," Carly informed. "She wants the three of us to go to dinner at The Paddle Wheel tonight."

"Okay." I liked The Paddle Wheel. "Any reason in particular?"

"She sounded very serious. Even said she'd bring dinner home from the diner for Alex, Emma, and Sebastian."

"Am I in trouble?" I briefly explained the exchange with Tracy earlier.

Carly shook her head. "She didn't say anything about that. We're meeting at five forty-five."

"Works for me. See you later."

Even though we were getting to the end of the growing season, we'd still get plenty more veggies and herbs before the garden was finished for the year. It was time to make plans for winter, however. Making sure we had enough straw for mulching, pruning back what was appropriate, pulling out supports that wouldn't serve a purpose until spring, and dozens of other little jobs I used to help with as a kid but didn't understand why I was doing them. Jett was teaching me the whys. I was also hanging herbs and flowers to dry so I could make beauty and health care products over the winter. I was really looking forward to that.

Every day at two thirty, before I needed to go pick up Cricket, Jett and I gathered with the crew near the pond by the shed. We discussed any issues or problems that had come up during the day and formulated a plan of attack for tomorrow. Which, in this case, would be orchard day.

"The peaches are done," I noted. Jett nodded her agreement. "There are some apples, plums, and pears ready for picking."

The crew was excited about this. They liked being out in the orchard.

Half of what we harvested tomorrow would be left fresh for baking and selling in The Apple Barn. The other half would be frozen, canned, or dried.

"I checked the hives today," Jett stated. "Next week or the one after will be honey harvest time."

I was excited about that. I'd never done a honey harvest before. Turns out the bees were the reason Jett was here. She and her husband, Freddie, were visiting the US from Scotland. They'd heard about the safe towns and made their way across the country staying with hosts. When they got to Wisconsin, they asked to stay at Applewood Farm for a few days. After wandering around, Jett made a comment about adding beehives near the orchard to help with pollination. The aunts thought this was brilliant and, when they learned Jett was a skilled beekeeper, asked if she wanted to stay. Jett and Freddie went to The Paddle Wheel for dinner to discuss the option and found out the saloon was looking for a bartender. Freddie had spent plenty of time in pubs, even worked in a few, so that was all the encouragement they needed.

On the way to the playground, I decided since I wouldn't be having dinner with Cricket tonight, I would spend every minute with her until it was time to go meet Nina and Carly.

"We learned how to make colors today," she told me as we walked home from the playground.

"You already know your colors." Well, the basic ones—red, blue, green, yellow, black, and white.

She looked up at me with an exhausted expression. "*Make* colors. Not *about* colors."

"Well, that is different. How do you make colors?"

She dropped onto her knees next to the blackthorn hedge and dug a piece of paper out of her backpack. It had colored circles all over it and appropriately colored arrows connecting pairs of circles. She traced her finger along a purple arrow linking a red circle and a blue one. "Red and blue make purple. Yellow and blue make green"

I liked that her chart had the names of the colors printed beneath the circles. She was learning to read and make colors at the same time.

"What happens if you mix purple and green?" I asked, figuring I'd stumped her.

"It depends," she began importantly, "if the green has more yellow or more blue. And if the purple has more red or more blue. That's what Miss Autumn said."

I tapped the tip of her nose with my finger. "I think we should do experiments when we get home."

"Yes!" She clapped her hands. "Then I can show everyone tomorrow."

Once she had everything in her backpack again, I turned to the hedge and said, "Open, please."

The hedge was enchanted to know those who lived on the property or were someone on the approved list, such as visiting witches. Normally, all it took was a simple verbal request for it to open and let us through. A special password was required for anyone who didn't live on the farm.

"Why isn't it opening?" Cricket asked and reached for it.

"No, sweetie, don't touch it. See the spiky bits." I pointed out the inch-long thorns covering every branch. Some were closer to four inches long. "They're very sharp and could hurt if you touch them."

"Guess we have to go around," she deduced.

Fortunately, it wasn't that far. The fact the hedge wouldn't respond was concerning, though. When we came to the end of the driveway, we found Jett by the petting pen outside The Apple Barn. She was attaching leashes to halters that went over the goats' noses, under their chins, and behind their heads. She was about to take them back to their regular pen. The petting pen was a big hit with kids and adults alike, because the little goats loved to be picked up and hugged. Not that we let shoppers get that close. Goats also liked to butt their boney little heads into shins.

"Thanks for letting me know," Jett said of the hedge. "I'll go in search of the problem soon as I'm done with these guys."

"Can I do it?" Cricket reached for the leash.

"Not yet, lassie. They're getting better, but this wee man still tugs a lot."

"That's Hank," Cricket told me. "He's learning from the older goats."

"Just like you learn from older people. Let's go do our experiment."

This issue with the hedge might be something simple, but it reminded me of a conversation I'd had with my dad. He assured me Blackwood Grove's wards were securely in place, which meant the town was perfectly safe. (This said before poor Ludo Beck had been murdered.) The hedge offered an extra layer of protection for the family. We were safe in the town. We were untouchable on our farm.

That's what I wanted. For Cricket, and the rest of us, to be untouchable. Now, though, I was worried.

CHAPTER 5

It was early September, which meant the days were still warm and the nights were getting chilly. Carly, Nina, and I were happy to take advantage of the nearly perfect conditions and walk to The Paddle Wheel for dinner. Except when we met at the intersection of the hedge and the sidewalk that meandered through the mall park, the hedge still wouldn't open.

"Why didn't you tell me about this?" Carly demanded.

"Because I just found out about it," I soothed as we walked to the end of the hedge and then back to the sidewalk. "Jett is checking it out."

Carly frowned deeply as she thought and then, as though this were somehow my fault, said, "I don't remember this ever happening before."

It might have been my paranoid imagination, but this seemed to be a common theme for her lately. If anything goes wrong, blame Dusty.

I replied, "When we were young, Granny Sadie would tell us we didn't need to worry about the hedge because the property would warn us if there was a problem."

"Is that what it's doing now?" Nina asked. "Warning us that someone tried to get through?"

Carly and I looked at each other, her waiting for me to answer, and me waiting for her to.

"Let's not jump to any conclusions," I finally said. "Jett will find the problem, and we'll go from there."

We chatted about random topics during the five-block walk to the saloon. Carly filled me in on her younger daughter Emma ("She's planning to run for student council this year."), her younger son Sebastian ("He finished his punishment hours repairing the Kramers' fence and is now working with Mason Kribs on his farm."), and her older son Alex ("He asked to pick up shifts at the diner.").

She looked so proud of them all, then Nina informed, "Alex is only working so he can buy Savannah Kribs a birthday present and take her to prom this year."

Carly blinked at her. "You make it sound like a negative. He's paying his own way."

I told them about Harriet's houseboat. "Stop and take a look if you get a chance. It's actually really cool."

At The Paddle Wheel, we ordered drinks at the bar, and then Nina led us to a table in a quiet corner.

"Why are you two looking at me like that?" she asked as we sat.

"Private dinner," Carly stated, "tucked into a corner, and you're so serious."

"I thought a night out where we could talk would be nice," she replied. "I chose this table because you know how this town is. We'll be bothered every three minutes. Especially with Dusty being the hot topic this week."

"We should have left town if you wanted to get away from the gossip," Carly quipped. She wasn't wrong.

"Hi, ladies," our server, Kayla, greeted as she set our drinks and menus in front of us. "Be right back to take your orders."

When she returned a few minutes later, Nina asked us, "Are we in a hurry? Or can we just hang out for a while?"

Carly looked at me and gave a subtle nod toward her daughter. The meaning: she seems to want to hang out.

I shrugged. "The aunts are watching Cricket—"

"Or is Cricket watching them?" Carly joked.

Sitting and talking sounded nice, so I told Kayla, "How about we tell you what we want but wait fifteen minutes before you place the order?"

Kayla shrugged. "Works for me."

"Okay," Carly began when Kayla walked away again, "what's going on?"

Nina had a list of things she wanted to talk about. How were the changes to the barn and farm coming along? What needed to be tweaked after two weeks? To me, she said, "You asked that question about Mom, and it got me thinking. Oh, and I'd like a little more information about what all that was with Tracy at the diner earlier."

My first reaction was to brush off her concerns about Tracy so as not to upset her, but Nina struck me as a mature twenty-year-old when I met her a few weeks ago and was even more so now. She deserved answers to her questions.

Carly stared at me with her arms crossed defiantly and a tilt to her head that said she wasn't happy about something. Before she could say what, I answered Nina's question.

"You know I left town because of that boat accident, right?"

"Right," Nina replied.

"Tracy was one of the passengers."

"Ah." Nina's face lit up like it all made sense now. "Do you know what happened to the rest of them?"

I shook my head and suddenly felt bad about that. "Only Beau Balinski and Nash Kramer. And now a little about Tracy."

Carly sighed like she seemed to do every time someone brought up the accident. "You were a scared eighteen-year-old kid who had been threatened by Marilyn Kramer. She's always been scary. It's not surprising you'd want to stay away."

Her words were supportive, but her voice held a bored tone, as though she was exhausted by this topic. I agreed with her. I'd love to be done talking about it.

"Working in the diner," Nina said, "we hear everything that's going on in town. Right now, Tracy has everyone worked up about you, and I wanted to know the details. Half the town supports you, by the way. The other half thinks you got off easy and should have paid for what you did." She cringed at her word choice. "You know what I mean. You didn't *do* anything wrong."

"I certainly didn't intend to hurt anyone." I sipped my tasty but very sugary hard cider, then said what I'd been thinking since I got back to town. "As soon as my dad asked me, I knew I wouldn't be able to move back here and not have this come up. Maybe Tracy getting it out in the open this way will let me finally deal with it."

"We're behind you whatever you do." Nina stared at her mother, who seemed to have disappeared into her own thoughts. After a few seconds, Nina pointedly said, "Right, Mom?"

"What? Yeah, right," Carly dismissed. "What did you ask about me, Dusty?"

At least we weren't talking about me anymore. "I asked Nina how she thought you were doing at the store. You seem a little, I don't know, aggressive lately."

Her eyebrows knit together. "What's that supposed to mean?"

"Maybe edgy is a better word," I amended.

"I'm not edgy," she snapped, crossed her arms even tighter, and stared past us.

Nina said nothing.

Now Carly was feeling attacked. That wasn't my intent. "It's understandable if it's because of taking over the store, so I asked Nina about it."

"You could have asked me." Carly took a swig from her wine glass.

Finally, Nina said, "Mom, come on. Dusty's not accusing you of anything. She's just concerned."

"That's it exactly," I promised. "We're all in this together. Or we should be. You and I agreed things needed to change for the aunts, but that means changes for the rest of us too. I'm trying to get used to a much more physical outdoor job after years of sitting at a desk. Everything hurts at the end of the day, but I love this. It's what I always wanted to do."

And one sentence too many. Carly and I would have been doing this work together for the last thirty years if I hadn't left. I just couldn't win. Two small steps forward, two giant ones back.

Whether because I was floundering or her mother was getting upset, Nina took over and shared her woes. "I think Avery and I have had the easiest time with it. We get to show up at the same place every day and do basically the same job. We just have more responsibilities." She paused with eyebrows raised as though realizing her job was similar but not the same anymore. She gave a quick head shake. "Even the townies are having a hard time. They miss you and Granny Comfort."

Carly softened at that and actually smiled. "Send them over to The Apple Barn."

Kayla arrived with a refill for Nina's diet soda. "Ready for me to place your order? It's been about fifteen minutes."

We agreed she could. Carly asked for a second glass of wine.

"Do you have any ciders with less sugar?" I asked, fanning myself with my hand. "This one is delicious, but it's giving me hot flashes."

The twenty-something girl fought with a grin.

Yeah, just wait, sweetie. In about twenty-five years, you won't be laughing about them anymore.

She returned with a wonderfully tart raspberry cider, so I forgave her lack of understanding. After Kayla left again, Nina admitted she missed being with her mom at the diner all day and was nervous about doing a good job.

"Don't struggle." Carly made her promise. "If you're having problems, let me or your grandmother know before something little turns into something big. And remember how much that place means to her. Your granny wouldn't have agreed to you taking over if she didn't think you could do the job. And I don't just mean my mother. Granny Sadie also said you could do it. According to Jett."

Jett was the only one of us who could communicate with the ghosts. Although, Cricket might be able to as well. Cricket's telekinetic power turned on a couple of weeks ago. I told her she could only move things across the floor until she got stronger, because the last thing we needed was for her to send things sailing through the air and smack us in the head. I had wondered off and on for nearly a year if she could talk to animals. Watching her with the familiars, I was almost positive she could.

Carly's words about Granny Sadie made Nina tear up with pride. A blessing from Ghosty Granny was high praise indeed. Once Nina was feeling better about her worries, Carly confessed she was having a problem at The Apple Barn, but our dinners arrived before she could explain it to us.

Our discussion died down, so we could enjoy our food while it was hot, and then things got a little crazy.

At some point while we were focused on Nina's troubles, Tracy Slayton had arrived at the saloon. My back was to the crowd, or I would have noticed her right away. I spotted her when she drunkenly stumbled past us to go to the ladies' room.

"She was sitting at the bar," Nina whispered, "with a drink in front of her and a bunch of guys around her."

I frowned and asked Carly, "Was she like that in school?"

She shook her head. "I don't remember her being a party girl."

"So that started after the—"

"It wasn't your fault," Carly demanded, irritated. "Don't start taking on other people's problems. If you want to find out what happened to the others who were on the boat, that's one thing. But don't going digging into things if you're going to blame yourself for how their lives turned out. They could all be dead." When I flinched, she added, "Sorry, but there's no easy way to say that. You know you saved their lives."

I did know. Carly and the rest of the family did, too, because they understood my visions were never wrong. If I saw it in my mind, it was absolutely going to happen. Getting Ordies to understand my powers was a challenge because they had no proof, nothing to anchor to.

Aunt Comfort soothed people's emotional and mental woes with her magic by baking comfort into her food, especially her pies. Aunt Gwynne blended plants to ease medical problems and sometimes manipulate relationship issues. (She never would explain what "relationship issues" meant. She just blushed.) In both cases, Ordies experienced or felt positive results based on what the aunts gave them.

My nephew Alex could summon things. If he reached out for an object, it would float across the room to him. My father manifested things out of thin air. Their kinds of magic left people wondering what they'd just witnessed, but at least they had witnessed *something*.

In my case, the dreams showed me the truth of what had already happened. The visions showed me what would happen if I didn't intervene. Neither allowed me to provide a feeling or produce anything that could be seen. My magic left too much room for folks to say I was making things up. Or if they did see me *do* something, like stop the little boy from falling out of his stroller or a boat from slamming into a submerged tree, they said I must be evil and "in cahoots with the devil" for being able to manipulate things that way. Never mind what I'd prevented from happening.

On her way back to her bar stool, Tracy saw me and stopped by our table, clutching the edge apparently to keep herself upright. "Can't go anywhere without running into trouble lately."

"Tracy." Carly's voice held a warning tone. "We're just here to have dinner and discuss family things—"

"Family things," Tracy taunted, slurring. "You mean *witch* stuff. Think you own this town, don't you?"

We got that a lot. Because my family was here first and owned two hundred acres—one hundred of which they sold to the Kribs family decades ago—townies accused us of thinking we were better than them.

"We own the land inside the hedge," Carly corrected with what we'd all been taught to say if people made accusations. "The town is outside the hedge."

"Your precious, ugly, black hedge." Tracy faced me squarely. "Black like your souls. Do whatever you want and walk away scot-free."

Tracy was wearing a short-sleeved shirt and shorts. I scanned her arms and legs for any marks that could have come from a blackthorn shrub. Her skin was clear, so unless she had worn thick protective clothing, she wasn't the one who attacked our hedge.

"We don't hurt anyone," Nina said, defending our family and witches in general.

"Such a child," Tracy spat. "You know nothing." Then she raised her voice. "Only the ten of us on that boat know what *really* happened." With index finger pointing, she swung her arm across the room. "You all weren't there. You didn't see—"

Marilyn and Henry Kramer walked in the door at exactly the wrong moment.

Tracy saw them, stopped her arc, and jabbed her finger at the couple. "You saw. You were there. You know what happened."

Marilyn had been standing on the roadside that day and saw me down by the riverbank. She saw me stop the boat. But they had no idea what Tracy was talking about so just stared at her in confusion.

Stella, the bartender and occasional bouncer, strode over and took Tracy by the arm. "That's enough, Ms. Slayton. It's time for you to leave."

"I didn't finish my drink. And I've got more to say."

"We'll give you a free drink next time you come in," Stella promised while pressing buttons on the saloon's phone in her hand. "You've had enough tonight anyway. And you've definitely said enough. Why don't you come outside with me? I'm calling Nash to give you a ride."

"Nash," Tracy purred and gyrated her hips in a way that left little to the imagination and would have made her fall to the floor if Stella didn't have a firm hold on her arm. "He can give me a ride anytime."

Marilyn gasped and looked repulsed. Not a good idea to talk about your landlord's beloved son that way. Tracy likely had just lost her lease on top of her drink.

She jerked her elbow out of Stella's hand and once again nearly fell. How much had she had to drink? "I don't need a ride."

"You can't drive in this condition. You can barely walk." Stella turned her attention to the phone. Nash must have answered. "Yeah, Tracy Slayton. She'll be outside on a bench waiting for you." She hung up. "Nash will be here in two minutes."

"Well," Tracy declared, "my day just got a lot better."

The saloon had gone silent and stayed that way for a good minute after Stella took Tracy outside. I felt eyes on me from every direction, most intensely from Marilyn and Henry. Would I ever just be a member of this community without this cloud hanging over me?

"Maybe you can't come home again," I murmured to myself.

"What?" Carly demanded. "What did you just say?"

I shook my head. Good thing I had eaten most of my dinner before Tracy began her tirade because my appetite had vanished. "Nothing. Don't worry about it."

Stella stopped at our table seconds later. "Dinner's on the house tonight."

"That's not necessary," I insisted.

"It is. My fault. I didn't recognize Tracy's condition when she came in. She's been cutting back, so I purposely mix her drinks on the weak side." Stella frowned. "There's no way the one I gave her put her into that state. She must have had a couple before she came in. I wouldn't have given her anything but water if I'd known."

I wanted to say it wasn't Stella's fault, but it was part of her job. She clearly felt bad enough, though, so I kept my mouth shut.

Nash walked in and strode straight over to Stella still at our table. "Where is she? You said out on one of the benches, right?"

"Yeah, she's not there?"

He shook his head. "She didn't have keys, did she?"

Stella pointed at the bar. "I took them from her before serving her. Can't believe she drove here."

Nash swore. "I'll go look around for her."

What had happened in Tracy's life to bring her to this state? Was it the boat accident, or was there something more?

"I know what you're thinking," Carly said with more empathy this time. "Not. Your. Fault."

"Yeah, well, trust me, you'd be thinking the same thing if you were the one to cast that spell thirty years ago."

CHAPTER 6

*E*arly, Nina, and I decided we should let the aunts know what had happened both at The Paddle Wheel tonight and at the diner earlier today. Better they hear it from us right away because by morning, the whole town would know and the phone would surely start ringing. However, despite it being only seven thirty when we got back to the farm, the house was mostly dark.

"I can hear Cricket talking to . . . something," I whispered, my ear pressed to her bedroom door. She could be chatting with a ghost, a familiar, or her stuffed animals. I never knew. "I should tuck her into bed. How about you come over for breakfast, and we'll tell the aunts about Tracy then?"

"I can't, obviously," Nina commented. She had to be at the diner by five to open it at six thirty. "But you two really should. The gossip is going to be off the charts tomorrow."

"And the diner will be packed," Carly warned. "It's where everyone meets when there's news to share."

Nina nodded. "Tomorrow's Friday. Can't ask Alex to help, he's got school." She took out her phone, and her fingers flew over the keyboard. Seconds later, she sighed with relief. "Cool. Mia's going to come in early."

"You okay?" Carly asked me before she and her daughter headed for home.

"Upset and tired, but fine," I promised. "Think I'll sit in front of the TV for a while after I read Cricket a story, then go to bed."

Carly's eyes narrowed. "What aren't you saying?"

I shrugged. "Don't know what you're talking about."

But the connection she and I had as kids was slowly reforming, and what she sensed was that I planned to go up to the attic and do some spellwork. I wanted to know what had happened in Tracy's life over the past thirty years, and I'd found plenty of ways in the family grimoire to bring on dreams that could show me.

I knocked softly on Cricket's door and opened it a crack. Since starting preschool, she insisted on "privacy," which meant she wanted her door closed even when not sleeping. I agreed that was fine, but she couldn't lock it. Not that a minor's locked bedroom door was a problem in a magical house. Just demand that it open the door, and it would. The adults had done that to us more than a few times. As for my granddaughter, I had instructed the house to let us know if she was ever up to anything dangerous or naughty in there. It responded with the sound of crickets, the alarm that alerted us to go check on her.

"Hi, sweetie."

She glanced over at me. Her purple stuffed elephant lay on the bed in front of her and she was putting pajamas on it. "I can't do this." She held the pajamas out to me.

"Let me help." I sat next to her and showed her how it was easier to put the little shirt over the elephant's big head first and then do the arms.

She had done this herself many times, but at the moment, she was far too sleepy.

"Did you take a bath?" I asked, pulling the tiny shorts over the purple legs.

"Yeah," she said through a yawn. "Auntie Jett gave it to me tonight. She asked if I wanted a story or to play. I said play 'cause you read my stories."

As though hearing her name, Jett poked her head in the room. "Just checking on the lass. Carry on." She closed the door again.

I settled *the lass* under her covers and sat next to her. Three pages into *Goodnight Moon*, she was out cold. School days exhausted her. Considering everyone else had retreated to their rooms, major changes in day-to-day life had the same effect on the older members of the household.

I slid off the bed, nestled the elephant into the crook of her arm, tucked the covers around her, and pressed a kiss to her forehead. Then after changing into my pajamas and washing my face, I crept up the house's two long flights of stairs to the attic.

The farmhouse routinely added rooms to the basement, first, and second floors as needed, but the attic never changed. It still held the witch's knot or loopy plus sign shape of the original structure. Each branch of the knot faced a cardinal compass point. The family grimoire and altar had always been in the north-facing window.

When I came up here for the first time three weeks ago, I got completely turned around. Unsure which direction was which, I wandered around until Pearl, my black squirrel familiar, appeared and led me right to the grimoire. Now I could get where I wanted to go with my eyes closed if necessary. I actually considered doing that a couple of times because at the top of the stairs, my mother had created a weird sort of makeshift bedroom. The space bothered me greatly, but according to the aunts, Mom's actions had gotten stranger and stranger over the years, so they didn't give a second thought to her staying in an unfinished attic whenever she was around, which wasn't often.

Before telling the big thick grimoire what I wanted from it, I had to tell it what my intent was. I touched my fingertips to the super seven quartz crystal at the center of the witch's knot engraved into the cover. The stone enhanced psychic insight, which was basically what a prophetic dream or vision was.

"Clear my mind," I begged the stone. "Make my sight true."

I opened the cover, and the book's pages immediately flipped to the 'How to Bring on Prophetic Dreams and Premonitions' page.

"That's not what I'm here for this time." That had been my plan, to bring on a dream or vision about Tracy, but something else felt more important. "One of the Ordinaries, Tracy Slayton, is sending out a lot of angry energy to the witches in town. To witches in general, for that matter, and I'm concerned for their safety. How can I protect my family and the other witches in Blackwood Grove?"

After a moment's pause, the pages turned and then stopped on *Protection for Family and Friends*. For this spell, I needed a blue candle, a candleholder, matches, one rose quartz crystal, four black tourmaline stones, and salt. I read through the instructions that stated to place the candle in the holder on the altar and set the quartz between myself and the candle. Then I was to envision a square surrounding the two objects and place a tourmaline stone in each corner of the square. Next I was to cast a circle of salt around the candle and stones, and then light the candle. Finally, I was to read the spell's incantation, inserting the proper descriptors as necessary.

"*May the witches of Blackwood Grove be protected and held safe from any person or thing that may cause them harm, danger, or hardship. Allow this flame to brighten their lives with blessings. So mote it be.*"

"Sounds simple enough."

Having recently lost my home to a house fire, the idea of leaving the candle to burn itself out made me extremely nervous, but this house would make sure no unwanted fires started. I had set the candle and quartz on the altar and was about to place the tourmaline stones when I heard a shuffling sound behind me. Turning and expecting to see Pearl, I was surprised to find my mother.

She had first crossed my path while I was walking in the orchard with Cricket two weeks ago. I honestly hadn't recognized her. Her body was twisted, stooped, and all but broken. Her skin was so wrinkled I couldn't imagine even one more crease forming. Yet somehow since I saw her last week, she looked even worse, as though she was now shriveling from the inside. Dehydrating, like the shrunken apple heads we used to make with the inedible apples that lay on the ground because the trees had rejected them.

"Casting a protection spell?" she asked in her dry, raspy voice.

I turned away and continued with my task. "Yes, one of the Ordies is causing problems for witches."

"Not just any Ordy."

I half-turned toward her. "If you already know, why even ask?"

She shrugged her crooked shoulders. "Trying to have a conversation with my daughter."

After thirty-two years of radio silence, she wanted to make amends. Why, was she dying?

I froze momentarily, one of the tourmaline stones still in my hand. Was she?

"You've been here for two whole weeks," I noted.

"More than that. We didn't come face to face for the first week you were here."

And she either hid in the attic or out in the shack in the orchard rather than letting me know she was around. I didn't want to discuss her and her issues right now. The potential problems Tracy was causing for the witches was far more important.

"You could also use obsidian," she noted. "Instead of tourmaline. Just an option."

"Obsidian is better for supporting emotions. Tourmaline offers more protection." Again, I froze. Where had that come from? I must have absorbed more knowledge as a kid than I'd realized. I turned to her. "That's right, isn't it?"

It seemed to take effort, but her mouth turned in a smile and her bent neck nodded her head yes. "Very good, Dusty."

I was fifty years old and hadn't had this much contact with my mother since well before I turned eighteen. Why did her words of praise, even as minor as these were, create a feeling of pride in me?

Find your mom. Time for you to finish your training. That's what Carly said after I told her about the incident in the park with Tracy.

As though reading my mind, Mom looked expectantly at me, waiting for me to ask another question.

"I'm going to cast this spell now." Recentering myself with a deep breath, I set the final stone in place. "You can stay— Actually, I'd prefer it if you left. This is too important and you're distracting me."

"All right. We'll talk about stones and other things later." She spun, slowly, and shuffled away. "Sleep well, Dusty."

Other things? There was nothing I wanted to talk with her about. She was too late.

Forcing myself to focus, I cast the spell. Even though this wasn't gray magic—there wasn't anything wrong with offering someone protection . . . unless I was protecting someone in a harboring a fugitive sort of way—I still felt like I was going to suffer a consequence. That clause about interfering with the course of someone's life could apply, after all. Or maybe I should have added more clarifying words to the incantation.

May the good, innocent witches of Blackwood Grove, who cast spells with only positive intent and are merely trying to live their lives without persecution, be protected and held safe from anything that Tracy Slayton or any of the Ordinaries say or do that may cause them harm, danger, or hardship. Allow this flame to brighten their lives with blessings. So mote it be.

That seemed like overkill, though. Not to mention, it was a mouthful.

I thought about that as I tried to fall asleep. Had I cast the spell correctly? As soon as that question quieted, the interaction with Mom kept me awake. She appeared to be trying to make amends. But why?

Does it matter why?

It kind of did.

Dad knew where I'd been for all those years. He must have told her why I left, that I'd been in contact with The Council for help, and why I was afraid to return. If she had known, why didn't she contact me even once? If something similar had happened to Micah, I would have done anything I could to help my son or at least assure him I was available if he needed me.

These were the thoughts swirling through my mind at two in the morning. Annoying, angsty teenage thoughts. Guess that came with moving back into one's childhood home.

My alarm went off far too early, because Carly would be here for breakfast so we could fill the aunts in on the latest news. Before even getting out of bed, I sent her a text.

I'm awake. Are you still coming?

Yep. Be there in 20 minutes.

I pulled on jeans and a T-shirt then peeked into Cricket's room. She was just waking up.

"Good morning, little bug."

"Good morning, big Lola."

She giggled when I blew a raspberry on her neck. "It's still early if you want to play in here for a while." Really, I didn't want her to hear the negative talk about Tracy and the other Ordies causing drama.

"Okay," she agreed. "I didn't get to finish playing last night. I was too sleepy."

I bit back a laugh. Did the child ever *finish* playing?

All of the aunts and Uncle Maks were in the kitchen when I walked in. Granny Sadie and Freddie, our resident ghosts, hovered in the corner and chatted with each other. Jett was about to head out the door, but I stopped her. "Carly will be here any minute. We need to tell you all about something."

This of course set off a round of, "Tell us about what?" and "You can't say things like that and expect us to sit patiently," and "Sure hope everything's okay."

Then they started guessing.

"Someone's getting married."

"Someone's getting divorced."

"Someone's pregnant."

"You're pregnant."

"Good goddess, no," I objected while mixing oat creamer into my coffee. "First, I'm well past that phase of life. Second, there's no one in my life to help me with that."

"Don't be so sure." Jett winked. "I saw the way a certain police officer was looking at you at the saloon that night a couple weeks ago."

Pepper grinned. Comfort and Maks gave confirming nods. Gwynne giggled. Granny Sadie and Freddie threw their heads back and laughed. Or so it seemed. It wasn't like I could hear them.

"What's going on?" Carly asked, entering through the back door.

"Thank heavens." I pulled her onto the empty chair next to me and addressed the aunts.

"Hang on," Carly complained. "Coffee, please."

A steaming cup appeared in front of her.

"Ready now?" I asked.

"One sec." She reached for creamer from the lazy Susan on the table between us all.

As long as they weren't talking about my love life, I wasn't in a hurry. Once Carly was ready, I said, "You're going to hear about an incident at The Paddle Wheel last night and probably another at the diner yesterday. We wanted you to hear the truth about them first."

"Always appreciated," Gwynne agreed.

"What happened?" Comfort prodded impatiently. "Spit it out. I need to get over there."

"Because you think Nina needs guidance," Carly began, "or because you want to be in the middle of the action?"

Comfort pointed at her daughter. "Respect your elders, little girl."

I was about to begin when an alarm let us know someone was at the front gate.

"Got it," Jett announced and leapt off her chair. She was full of energy in the morning, but by three this afternoon, she'd be dragging.

She returned with officers Balinski and Chapman in tow. I smiled at Beau, blushed, and broke out with a hot flash. The aunts started giggling again.

"Stop it," I hissed at them. "What are you two doing here so early?"

"We're investigating a death," Beau began.

"A death?" Pepper repeated. "Who died?"

Beau looked straight at me. "Tracy Slayton's body was found in the river this morning."

CHAPTER 7

*T*racy was dead?

"Oh, that's horrible," Pepper gasped.

"What happened?" Gwynne wanted to know.

"Why do you need to talk to us?" Jett asked.

Ignoring their questions, Beau turned his attention to me. "Dusty, we understand you had a run-in with Tracy at The Paddle Wheel last night."

"She did?" Comfort glared at me. "And you didn't tell us?"

"That's what we were about to do." It was seven-thirty in the morning. How did Beau and Leezza know about our *run-in* already? Darned small town.

"Where did you go last night?" Beau asked. "After you left the saloon?"

I pointed at my cousin. "Carly and I came here with Nina."

"Straight here?" Officer Chapman asked, notepad in hand.

"Yes. I always tuck Cricket into bed at seven thirty."

"Can anyone confirm that?" Beau's gaze slid over my family.

Why were they . . . Was I a suspect?

"I can." Carly got to her feet and took a few steps away from the table. Away from me. "So can Nina. The three of us were at

The Paddle Wheel from just before six until seven fifteen. That's when we'd planned to leave so Dusty could put her granddaughter to bed. Took us about ten minutes to walk here."

Cricket entered the kitchen then. "Hi, Officer Beau." She rushed over and wrapped his right leg in a hug. She must have felt the prosthetic but didn't react to it.

He laid a hand on her head. "Good morning, little one."

She scanned the room and must have sensed the tension. She released her hug and climbed onto the chair Carly had vacated. "Can I have breakfast now? Oatmeal with peaches, please."

The house responded immediately. If the full bowl of steaming cereal and glass of milk appearing out of nowhere surprised either officer, they didn't show it.

Beau sat in a chair near Cricket. "Your grandma said she read you stories last night."

"Lola reads to me every night."

"Last night too?"

She paused the stirring of her oatmeal and looked at him like he wasn't listening. At four years old, she already had an impressive *don't make me repeat myself* stare.

"Do you know what time she read your story?" Officer Chapman asked.

Cricket was a brilliant child in many ways. Obviously she could carry on a conversation with the best adult. She knew her basic colors and many letters, especially those that spelled her name. She could recite her numbers one through ten, but couldn't recognize them yet. Math wasn't her thing. And when it came to telling time, she knew when she was hungry and when she was sleepy. That was about it. If either officer had kids of their own—

That was presumptive. Maybe they did have kids. I didn't know anything about their personal lives. For all I knew, Beau was happily married and had a passel of kiddos. Without consciously thinking about it, I glanced at his left hand. No ring. That relieved me more than it probably should have.

Cricket held her loaded spoon near her mouth and answered, "She read my story at *bed*time."

All of us, even the serious police officers, smiled at that.

"Thank you, honey." Beau stood from the chair. "Go ahead and eat your breakfast."

"What about the rest of you?" Officer Chapman asked. "Can any of you confirm Ms. Hotte's whereabouts last night?"

The aunts exchanged looks with each other, then shook their heads.

Comfort spoke for the group. "We had dinner here at five thirty."

"Macaroni and cheese, peaches, and brownies," Cricket announced. She really liked fresh peaches. "I got to pick. It was yummy."

Comfort and Pepper glanced at each other and stood a little taller, proud of their co-prepared meal. Comfort continued, "Then we played some games—"

"Hi Ho Cherry-O, Hungry Hungry Hippos, and poker."

My mouth dropped open. "You taught her how to play poker?"

None of them would confirm or deny.

Guess that was one way to help her with her numbers.

"Anyway," Comfort returned to answering Officer Chapman's question. "After games, Jett gave the child her bath, and the rest of us went to our rooms."

Officer Chapman had waited patiently for the answer. "So none of you can confirm Dusty's timeframe."

"I just did," Carly replied, irritation growing in her voice. "She was here with me and my daughter until seven-thirty. It was probably seven twenty-six if you need me to be more precise. Maybe seven twenty-five. I didn't check a clock."

"And where did you go after leaving here?" Beau asked, his own notepad in hand now.

"Nina and I went straight home. You can ask any of my kids. Emma was having a bit of a crisis because she got a *B* on a project she was sure she'd ace and needed to analyze what she'd done wrong. I sat with her regarding that until eight thirty. Alex wanted to know how to make a spreadsheet for keeping track of his money." She paused and smirked proudly. "That took forty-five minutes. Then Sebastian wanted to tell me about everything he did at the Kribs' farm yesterday. You'll be happy to know he's getting his act together and taking pride in doing a job well rather than honing his skills for a career in vandalism."

Beau nodded. "That is good news."

"Then Nina wanted to discuss some ideas she has for the diner."

"Why didn't she call me?" Comfort wanted to know.

"I don't know, Mom," Carly said and sighed. "Maybe she figured, since it was after nine o'clock, you'd be sound asleep."

Comfort shrugged, not denying the assertion.

"Then," Carly continued, still worked up, "I put in the laundry Emma said she'd take care of, washed the dishes Sebastian was supposed to do, and tidied the family room because Alex was too focused on having enough money for weekend dates, birthday gifts, and prom tickets. That took me until after midnight. Ask Sebastian. He'd been following me through the house while giving me a detailed account of how to clean out a horse stall." She blew out a breath. "That good or do you need more?"

Beau had actually taken a couple steps away from her. "No, I'm good."

Officer Chapman agreed with a crisp nod.

"I can confirm Dusty was here at seven thirty," Jett said during the break in conversation. "That's the time I checked on the wee lassie." She winked at Cricket. "Wanted to make sure she wasn't climbing the walls or some such."

"I can't climb a wall." Cricket giggled, then recalled, "I climbed the fence at Miss Autumn's farm. We were playing balance beam."

Dear goddess, let the child remain unbroken until I find her mother and get her father out of prison.

I made a mental note to ask Miss Autumn about "playing balance beam."

Officer Chapman turned her gaze toward Jett. "Do you know if Dusty was here the rest of the night?"

Jett held out her hands in a shrug. "Couldn't say. I went up to my room after seeing she was back."

A piece of parchment rolled into a scroll floated down from the ceiling and landed on the table.

"That's probably for you," Comfort told Beau.

He opened it. "It's from *The Property*. It states, 'The Warren family property hereby declares that Dusty Hotte arrived at the farmstead with Carly and Nina Flasch at seven twenty-three last evening and has not left the premises. After reading three pages of a story, she went from Cricket's room to the attic, then to her bedroom and finally to the kitchen for a cup of tea.'" He rerolled the scroll. "That's great but not admissible."

The house made an outraged huffing sound.

"Are you saying our house lies?" Comfort demanded.

Officer Chapman's eyebrows shot up, the first indication that she recognized this house wasn't exactly "normal."

"I'm saying," Beau began, "a statement like this needs to be written and signed within police presence."

"You think we wrote that before you came?" Comfort pressed. "Even though none of us even knew you were coming to accuse Dusty of something she didn't do?"

"A statement needs to be made by a person," Beau said calmly. "The house isn't a person."

The kitchen lights flashed like a lightning strike, and the sound of thunder sounded all around us.

"Now you've made it mad," Gwynne said in her earthy, airy way. "Hope it lets you out again."

Officer Chapman's eyebrows rose even further. Worried she was about to be held prisoner? We wouldn't let that happen.

"I can verify Dusty's whereabouts," came a raspy voice from the living room. My mother rounded the corner, and audible gasps sounded through the group. Seemed I wasn't the only one who felt she looked worse.

"Who are you?" Officer Chapman asked, pen ready to write the answer.

"Griselle Warren. I'm Dusty's mother."

Cricket stared at her great grandmother, confused by the wrinkly, crooked woman who was Gwynne's twin. She had seen my mom in the orchard a couple weeks ago, mistook her for Gwynne from a distance, and then became afraid of her when we got close. Minutes after we'd walked away, however, she seemed to have forgotten even seeing the gray witch. My theory was that Mom had cast a disguising or forgetting spell on herself. Whenever I asked the aunts about her, no one could give an answer. They couldn't remember when they'd last seen her, where she'd been, or what she'd been doing.

"How about you finish your breakfast in the living room?" I told Cricket. Normally, that was a no-no, but she didn't need to hear any more of this conversation.

Maks scooped up her dishes and moved her to the next room. "Follow me, squirt."

"Squirt," Cricket repeated as though it were hilarious and laughed the laugh that made the rest of us join in.

"What can you tell us, Ms. Warren?" Beau held out a chair for Mom and helped her sit.

"That I ran in to my daughter in the attic last night," she

began. "It was near eight o'clock. She was preparing to cast a spell."

At the declaration, everyone in the room stiffened or released an exclamation of some type and turned to me in unison.

"A spell?" Officer Chapman asked. "What kind of spell?"

Someone had clearly trained her well regarding the goings on in safe towns. Or maybe she grew up in one. Again, I knew nothing about her personal life. Either way, things suddenly appearing on the table, the house making noise in response to statements, talk of spellcasting . . . none of it seemed to faze her.

I cleared my throat. "Tracy made some comments about witches last night that made me very nervous. She was angry at me because of the boat accident"—I shot a glance at Beau, whose jaw clenched—"but she was starting to encompass other witches in her anger. So last night, I cast a protection spell that would prevent any harm, hardship, or danger from befalling any of the witches in Blackwood Grove."

Mom nodded. "That's what I witnessed. I watched her prepare the spell and heard her words."

"Nothing negative," Beau verified, "against Tracy or anyone else?"

"Nothing negative," Mom vowed. "Only words of protection for innocent witches getting caught up in a personal battle."

Beau squirmed a little, presumably from the intense stare Mom had locked on him. I was dying to talk more with him about the boat accident, but this obviously wasn't the time or place. He and I had talked briefly about it a few weeks ago, and he insisted he had no memory of anything that had happened that day but knew the details because people had told him. What did that mean? What had others said? Did anyone tell him I stopped the boat using gray magic? That it was my fault he lost his leg? Was that why his jaw had clenched at my reference to the accident a minute ago?

Carly cleared her throat. When I looked at her, her expression clearly said, *Not. Your. Fault.*

Officer Chapman asked, "Do you know if your daughter stayed on the property all night, Ms. Warren?"

Mom took a moment to think. "We were in the attic until eight thirty, maybe quarter to nine. Then Dusty went down to her room, and I stayed in the attic to create an herbal blend for a customer who was coming to pick it up at midnight."

She made it sound like a special tea. Which, I suppose, she might do for some of her customers. Mom and the aunts prepared spell kits for Ordies that were enchanted to perform a specific spell in a specific way. The Ordies didn't become magical. They wouldn't suddenly develop powers like ours or be able to recreate the spell on their own. Still, these purchases weren't talked about openly. Late at night, the customer would stand at the gate that led into the orchard, and the appropriate witch would meet them with their goody bag. It was all very cloak and dagger.

"You made an herbal blend for a customer?" Beau repeated. "Mind telling us who that customer was so we can confirm your story?"

"I do mind," Mom answered. "It's confidential. If I were to help you with a personal problem, you wouldn't want me revealing those details to anyone, would you?"

"I suppose not." He stared at her for a beat. Did he know Mom had come into his hospital room after they'd removed his leg and put a forgetting spell on him? Surely somewhere in the back of his brain, he must. The look he was giving her right now made me certain there was a niggle of some kind going on in there.

"Can you verify," Officer Chapman asked, notepad still in hand, "that Ms. Hotte was here all night?"

Mom straightened her body the best she could. "I have every

reason to believe she was. I made my blend, delivered it to my customer when they arrived, and noticed a light flickering beneath Dusty's bedroom door when I came back inside ten minutes later. I knocked. She was in there."

Did she knock? I fell asleep while meditating with the television on for background noise. Something woke me up. It could well have been her knocking. "I fell asleep watching TV," I supplied. They didn't need all the other details.

"What were you watching?" Beau asked, sounding more conversational than interrogational. That seemed to be his style. Small town cop who'd known us his entire life. Serious and to the point sometimes. Easy-going at others.

"An investigative journalism show on National Geographic."

"The counterfeiting episode?" he asked. "I was watching that too."

"It was really interesting." What I saw of it at least, which was maybe thirty seconds before I slipped into a deep meditation.

He nodded. "You should be able to catch the rest on their website."

Everyone was staring at us. Beau blushed. I got swamped by another hot flash.

"Okay." He clapped his hands once. "I think we have enough."

Officer Chapman agreed by putting her notepad and pen in her pocket.

"Are you going to arrest her?" Jett wanted to know. She winked at me in a way I assumed meant she had a plan for busting me out if he did.

He shook his head. "This is only a fact-gathering Q&A."

"Really?" Carly stepped closer to me again. "Because that felt pretty accusatory to me."

Officer Chapman looked at her boss, and Beau gave a nod. She said, "Someone told us about the confrontation you had with the victim last night, so we came to you first. We have plenty of other people to talk to."

"I was with Dusty during the *confrontation* with Tracy," Carly reminded them. "To be clear, Tracy started it. It wasn't exactly a pleasant conversation, but nothing was said that would make anyone kill her."

"Well, someone did," Beau stated. "It appears she drowned."

"Hang on," I interrupted. "Tracy was stumbling drunk last night when she left the saloon. Stella called Nash Kramer to take her home because not only was she in no condition to get behind the wheel of a car, Stella didn't feel she could even walk home. Because she harassed me while I was sitting there minding my own business and turned it into a huge argument, suddenly you think I killed her?"

"No," Officer Chapman said flatly. "We didn't say you killed her."

"And we didn't say you were under arrest," Beau added. "Or even that you were a suspect. We have more interviews to conduct."

"Who told you about the argument?" Carly asked.

Beau seemed to struggle with how to answer. Finally, he let out a heavy sigh. "None of this is public yet, so please keep it that way. Harriet Wong heard a noise outside her boat early this morning, went out to investigate, and found Ms. Slayton's body. Nash Kramer was coming up the walking path with his dog, and she flagged him down. He called us."

"So Nash told you about the argument," I concluded, "even though he wasn't there at the time."

Beau hesitated again before stating, "Correct. We may have further questions later, and we will likely need you, Carly, and Nina to come in and make formal statements about what happened with Ms. Slayton at the saloon."

"So don't leave town," Comfort murmured, half joking, half shell-shocked.

"Where could they go where they'd be safer?" Officer Chapman asked.

Three weeks or even twenty-four hours ago, I would have agreed with that statement. Now? I wasn't so sure.

CHAPTER 8

While Pepper led Beau and Leezza to the front door, Jett took Cricket out to the chicken coop to gather the morning's eggs. Mom disappeared to . . . wherever she went. Comfort and Gwynne sat across from each other at the table, hands wrapped around cups of coffee, exchanging glances and knowing nods. I'd seen them do that since I was a kid. If something tense was going on or they had a secret they didn't want to reveal, they'd have full conversations without saying a word. It was either telepathy or some kind of sister super power. And they weren't even the twins. What were Gwynne and Mom capable of?

"I'm going to The Apple Barn," Carly informed.

"Right behind you," I said, following her.

"We need to have a family dinner tonight," Comfort demanded as we left the kitchen.

Outside, Carly glanced over her shoulder at me. "What's on your mind, Dusty?"

She walked so fast I practically had to run to keep up with her. "Beau said Nash told him about our argument this morning. How did Nash know about it?"

She stopped, halfway between the house and store, and slowly said, "Stella called Nash to give Tracy a ride home. He said she wasn't outside on the bench so went to look for her. When he didn't find her, he returned to The Paddle Wheel, told Stella he couldn't find her, and Stella told him about the argument. There's no mystery here."

"And he happens to be the one walking past this morning minutes after Harriet found Tracy's body?"

Her eyes narrowed in consideration, then she continued along her route to the barn. "Maybe it bothered him that he couldn't find her and he went looking for her in the daylight."

"Hmm. I'm not so sure."

"Good gods, Dusty. Maybe he was just walking his dog. Don't turn nothing into something. Isn't there enough trouble going on around here without you stirring up more?"

She could be right. "In my defense, being paranoid and suspicious isn't an unreasonable response when any of the Kramers are involved with my world."

Carly grumbled something incoherent while unlocking The Apple Barn's front door. Inside, she slid behind the checkout counter to our right and flipped on the lights. It didn't look any different than it had when I'd been in here a couple of weeks ago. Carly had been fully on board with taking over the shop from Gwynne because she had ideas for turning it into something that more closely resembled the store we'd dreamt about as kids. Looked like she hadn't had time for that yet.

"How have things been going here?" I asked as casually as possible. If it sounded like I was questioning her in any way, it would set her off. Didn't take much to do that lately.

She sighed and pulled a three-ring binder complete with tab dividers from the tote bag she brought from home. "These are all my ideas for things I want to do here."

The tabs were labeled *Food, Housewares, Clothing, Health Care,* and *Beauty.* Repositionable sticky tabs further divided

the sections. Food included *Fresh, Frozen,* and *Freeze-dried.*
Clothing had tabs for *Men, Women, Unisex,* and *Kids.* There
were plenty of scribbled notes, hand-drawn sketches, and
pictures printed off the internet. Since blending herbs for
health and beauty products had been my dream, I opened the
Medicinal section, curious to see what she planned to include.
I swore I saw a tab labeled *Dusty* before she snatched the
binder away from me.

"Every night when I finally have time to sit and relax, my
mind floods with ideas for this place. I spend an hour before
going to bed writing them down or they'll keep me awake."

That reminded me of her mother's way of getting her
customer's emotions out of her head. Any magic any witch
performed that interfered with someone's life resulted in a
consequence. Comfort could ease a person's troubles with her
pies. One bite and the person would relax. By the end of a slice,
their troubles were much more manageable. Comfort's
consequence was that she would then hold those troubles in her
mind, sometimes simply knowing how the person felt, other
times feeling what they felt. She released the troubles and
feelings by writing them down at the end of every day to get
them out of her head. Then she burned the paper, destroying
the troubles.

Wonder if that would have worked for Mom. Her wrinkles
and crooked body were the result of nearly sixty years of
performing gray magic. Maybe I should try it. That protection
spell I cast last night, even though positive, interfered with the
lives of the witches in Blackwood Grove. I suffered awful
heartburn because of it. Although that could have been another
gift from menopause.

Carly shoved the binder beneath the register. "I've got so
many ideas and nowhere near enough time to implement them."

A voice in my head warned me to proceed with extreme
caution. "Summer and fall are so busy. You'll have tons of time

over the winter. And I won't be busy with gardens then. I can help."

She relaxed a skosh. "That's true. My problem right now is that the customers constantly mess the place up. Gwynne used telekinesis." Carly flicked a finger at the nearest display mimicking our aunt. "All she had to do was point and everything went back to the way it should be."

"Well, I've seen her point recently and send things flying across the room." I wiggled my fingers. "Arthritis messes with her aim. I understand what you mean, though."

Carly sighed unhappily. "Guess I'll have to hire someone. That would mean keeping track of time and running a payroll."

"What about Gwynne's barter system?" She let people take goods in exchange for working here.

"Yeah, turns out they were basically shopping the whole time and doing very little actual work."

Two thoughts came to me as I looked over the rack of Gwynne's natural remedies. First, I wondered if she'd share her recipes and process with me. Second, "What if we let the aunts help?"

Carly shook her head. "Love them dearly, but I do *not* want them roaming around in here all day."

"That's not what I mean. What if we give them an assignment to work on together? They could create a self-cleaning spell. They could enchant the barn to tidy itself when it got messy."

Carly considered this for a long while. "That could work. I like the working together part. They each have different skills, so this would force them to listen to each other's ideas." She thought a little longer. "Okay. Mom said she wants a family dinner tonight. We'll tell them then."

And there *we* just worked together on a problem. Carly had been dominating lately. Or trying to.

I swiped my hands together, mimicking her *task complete*

gesture. "I need to find Cricket and get her over to Autumn's. Have a sparkly day, cousin."

She grinned at the thing we used to say to each other when our paths would separate at school. "You too."

After dropping Cricket off at school, I went directly back to the farm to organize my crew for the day. Most of them went to the orchard to pick the next batch of apples that were ready. One worked with Jett and the animals. Nicola worked with me in the garden. We harvested veggies and brought them to the shed, where we cleaned up some for direct sale in our shop. Others we dehydrated, canned, turned into apple butter or jelly, froze, or gave to Nina to use in the diner.

I was sorting cherry tomatoes into paperboard packages—we used compostable products whenever possible at Applewood Farm—when my phone buzzed with a message from Kelsey at The Sweet Spot bakery: *Would you drop off bundles of rosemary, thyme, and sage next time you're over here? And two pounds of goat cheese. And make that two bundles of thyme.*

Some of our herbs were getting tired by this time of year, but I had plenty to fill Kelsey's order. Along with the garden plants, we also had racks with grow lights in the shed to keep our customers supplied with the most popular herbs year-round. Once used to cooking with fresh, it was hard to go without. Or so I'd been told.

A little while later, Russell asked if I could drop off two quarts of goat milk. Then Nina asked me to set aside four trays of eggs. *We've got enough for today, so I'll grab them on my way to work tomorrow morning.*

"Everyone was off on their orders this week," I told Jett when she came into the shed later that afternoon.

"Lots of activity in the mall," she explained. "I heard from the crew that townies are gathering to discuss the events of late."

Meaning my interactions with Tracy and her death. "Great. Suppose they're blaming me for what happened to her."

"Not all of them. Sounds like it's an even split."

"So I've divided the town."

From the way she stared at me, she either felt sorry for me or was annoyed with my self-pitying responses. Couldn't tell which. Either way, I kept my mouth shut about it.

"Would you like me to deliver those orders?" Jett nodded at the insulated tote bag sitting on the work table.

"No, I'll do it. I've got to pick up Cricket at the playground anyway." I glanced at a nearby clock. Almost two thirty. "Can you handle the crew gathering today? I'll go now if that's okay."

"Off with you. I've got it." Jett was so happy to have help running the farm. Understandable, it was a ton of work. What would I do when she stepped down?

I stopped at the bakery first, and as I handed them their package, Raul handed me a piece of lemon thyme pound cake.

"Oh my goddess," I gushed after the first bite. "Is that whipped goat cheese on top?"

"Goat cheese, cream cheese, thyme, and honey," he stated proudly.

"That's why we needed more thyme and cheese," Kelsey said.

"Well, it's fantastic." I headed for the door. "Not to eat and run, but I've got another stop. Thanks for the cake."

"Thanks for the quick delivery." Raul raised a hand in a wave. "See you Wednesday if not before."

The mall was closed on Sundays and Mondays, so the shops placed their orders on Tuesday mornings for delivery on Wednesday. Fortunately, it was a simple three-block walk if they needed more of something. I might change my mind about the *simple* part come mid-January when the temperature was below freezing, but for now I enjoyed it.

At So Mote It Tea, Russell told me goat milk lattes were trending and handed me a small mug with a golden liquid inside and a piece of star anise floating on top.

"Is there tea in here?" I asked after my first sip.

He shook his head. "Goat milk, cinnamon, turmeric, ginger, black peppercorns, and honey."

"It's tasty." I drank more. It wouldn't make my favorites list, but it wasn't horrible.

Maggie, Russell's wife, came over to me and laid a hand on my arm. "How are you doing? With all the hoo-ha, I mean."

No one else had asked me that. Not even Pepper or Gwynne. "I feel awful for Tracy. I'm wondering if something happened to upset her before she went to The Paddle Wheel last night. Or was it common for her to drink before going to the saloon?"

The couple shrugged in unison, and Maggie replied, "I didn't know her very well. She sort of steered clear of us."

"Because I'm a witch," Russell added.

Then I remembered seeing her talking to Marilyn yesterday. I mentioned it to the baristas. "They could have been discussing Tracy's shop and that upset her. Or it was something completely unrelated and was a simple conversation."

"Simple conversation." Russell snorted. "Marilyn can upset people without saying a word, but whatever they were talking about, it wouldn't have been Tracy's salon. Not out in public where shoppers could hear. Marilyn only talks business in her office or during surprise visits to shops. She likes to take people off guard. Thinks it gives her the upper hand."

"It only annoys us." From the way Maggie rolled her eyes, she'd never be on Team Marilyn.

"Something personal, then," I mused. "I was just thinking that Tracy starting all this *hoo-ha*, as you called it, Maggie, might have upset the landlady. Not good to have a tenant creating drama. And that's all it was. Drama. I didn't do anything to that little boy."

"Talia, our daughter, fell out of a shopping cart once." Maggie shivered. "I still remember the thump of her head hitting the floor."

"Fortunately," Russell assured, "the girl has a head as hard as her father's, so she was fine."

Maggie took the mug from me when I'd finished the latte. "You didn't do anything to either the boy, Tracy, or the kids on that boat. We know that. And you know how this town gets. Might be ugly for a bit, but it'll settle down again before long."

Yes, but how long? I said goodbye and headed to the playground. No one was there yet, so I sat on a bench in the sunshine to enjoy a moment of stillness before they arrived.

Glancing around, my gaze landed on the spot where I'd seen Marilyn talking to Tracy. What *had* they been talking about? Marilyn did all the talking, at least for the few seconds I saw them, and while Tracy—

The sound of laughter came from the parking lot behind me, putting a halt to my analysis. I turned to see tall, redheaded Autumn Trainor surrounded by her class. Actually, she wasn't that tall, but she looked like a giant surrounded by three-foot humans.

One of the boys pointed at me, then said something to Cricket, who crossed her arms and turned away from him. Autumn pulled the boy aside to speak to him.

"Is there a problem?" I asked the young woman in loose overalls when she came over to me.

"Kind of, but I rank it at the low end of the trouble scale." Autumn pushed her round glasses up her nose, then leaned closer and whispered, "Some of the kids have been saying you're a bad witch." She winced. "Sorry."

In order for a child to be enrolled in Autumn's school, they had to have at least one parent who was a witch, or the child had to display powers. Sometimes powers skipped generations, so both things weren't necessarily true in a magical house. Autumn had mentioned that every kid in this particular class had a witch parent. Was that where these kids heard I was bad? From their parents? It bothered me tremendously for a witch to not be accepting of another witch. They knew we couldn't choose our powers. I couldn't do anything about being a gray.

I looked at my granddaughter who was laughing, running, and playing like always. I grumbled, mostly to myself, "Cricket doesn't seem upset to have an evil grandmother."

Autumn squinted at me, confused, then brightened. "Oh! No, wrong definition. The kiddos think it means you're not good at casting and need to practice more."

Bad as in unskilled. That probably should have given me more relief than it did. "Well, they're not wrong. You know I lived in an Ordinary town before coming back here. I couldn't use my powers there, so I am horribly out of practice."

"I've been nipping that in the bud as soon as I hear it," she insisted. "I explain it doesn't matter how old we are, if we don't practice our skills, we won't be as good at them."

And now my woes were a teaching point. I tilted my head toward Cricket. "That's really all this is? She's okay?"

Autumn held her pinky high in the air. "Pinky promise. May my hair turn pea green if I'm lying."

She was *very* proud of her beautiful red hair.

"Thanks, Autumn."

I made my way over to the slide to catch Cricket on her way down, dodging the looks coming from the other four-year-old eyes. Not that I thought Autumn was lying or even embellishing, but she was very good at smoothing awkward situations. I imagined the kids' parents discussing me being gray, and their son or daughter overhearing. Some might make up an explanation. Others surely told their child the truth. That even in the witch world, being gray was looked down on.

A couple of the parents avoided me and rushed their kids away. Some offered me weak smiles. Others came up to me and told me to stay strong.

"This will pass," one man assured. "Hot topics change with the wind patterns here."

Maybe. But I wasn't so sure that this would simply pass. If it did, something would inevitably happen to make me the hot topic again.

Carly was right. I couldn't wait for these things to fade away. I needed to get control of my powers. My only other option was to leave Blackwood Grove again and return to a life of completely denying my true self. But with Micah still incarcerated, Josie still missing, and the person who threatened Cricket still out there, my troubles were the least of my concerns.

CHAPTER 9

"What are you doing, bug?" I walked in to Cricket's bedroom to tell her it was almost dinnertime and found her surrounded by her toys. Every one of them.

"Miss Autumn said we have to practice or we'll be bad witches."

While that was the truth based on Autumn's alternate definition of *bad*, I wanted my granddaughter to understand the full truth about what my mother and I could do. I sat on the floor close to her and explained what it meant to be a gray witch.

"You're like the police," Cricket decided. "You punish bad guys."

That was a good way to look at it. "Kind of. I can do other things with my magic too."

She frowned. "The police put my daddy in jail. Is he a bad guy?"

A piece of my heart broke off. "No, sweetie. Your daddy is not bad. He didn't do anything wrong."

"Then why is he in jail?" Her voice rose with indignation.

"Because sometimes the police make mistakes. I'm trying

very hard to help them fix their mistake, so he can come home to you."

She stared down at her hands in her lap, her little fingers worrying together. "They think he hurt Mommy."

And there went another piece of my heart. "He didn't. Your daddy would never hurt anyone."

She thought about this for a moment. "Is Mommy dead?"

I knew she'd ask this question, or a version of it, at some point and had prepared an answer. "Do you know what it means to be dead?"

She nodded. "You fall asleep and never wake up again."

"That's right." Or close enough for now at least.

"Then you get to be like Granny Sadie and Freddie."

Ah-ha. She could see them. "Can you hear them talking like Jett can?"

She narrowed her eyes until they were almost shut like she was concentrating. "If I listen really hard, I can."

"Can you hear the familiars?"

"Yes." She nodded and laughed. "They're so funny." Then an idea lit up her face. "If I practice, maybe I can hear Granny Sadie."

Such a brilliant child. "Maybe."

I waited to see if she'd bring up the topic of her mother being dead again. She let it go, so I did too.

"You should put your toys away so we can go eat dinner. Emma will be here tonight."

"Yippee!" She adored Emma.

"Should I help you?"

She shook her head. "I can do it."

She held her open hands up by her shoulders, palms facing the toys, and slowly pushed her hands away from her. My mouth dropped open. All the toys slid slowly across the room.

"Wow, Cricket. That's very good."

She beamed with pride. Then she pointed at a specific toy,

elevated it into the air, and it immediately fell to the ground. Her hand dropped to her lap. "I still can't lift things."

"You will. It takes time to learn new things."

We found everyone in the kitchen gathering around the table by the fireplace, which was lit and crackling for ambiance but not generating any heat. Thankfully. It wasn't quite cool enough for that yet.

Comfort made dinner tonight: a soul-satisfying meatloaf with mashed potatoes and roasted veggies from our garden. Since her specialty was comfort food, she claimed those dishes. Pepper preferred dishes that skewed more toward the gourmet side. They agreed to stay in their lanes and that whoever wasn't making dinner that night would make dessert. Pepper prepared individual mixed berry tarts with whipped cream and a drizzle of honey from our bees.

"This was amazing," Alex complimented after eating two servings of everything.

"Yes," Carly agreed, "I think your arrangement will work well."

"I'll have you know," Pepper announced proudly, "I made one hundred percent of that tart."

We all cheered, and she took a little bow. During the worst of her depression, she let the house do half or sometimes all the cooking for her. They were her recipes, but the love a cook puts into their food was missing. It seemed after the bumpy start over territory, she liked having Comfort in the kitchen with her.

"Time for the farm report," Maks announced once we were all done eating and the house was washing dishes and cleaning up. "I figured out the problem with the tractor. Short in a wire. Good as new now. Dusty? Tell us about the gardens."

I loved the farm report. We could call it the family report because even those who didn't work on the farm updated everyone with what was going on in their lives.

"Blueberries are done for the year, as are peaches," I

announced. "Cabbage looks great, and the broccoli is coming along nicely. Something got into the greens, but we fortified the chicken wire around the patch before they ate too much. Squashes and melons look good. Chickens are producing as always."

Jett agreed. "That's because Miss Cricket tells them how beautiful and special they are every morning when she gathers the eggs."

Cricket sat taller in her chair.

"What about the orchard?" Gwynne asked in the dreamy, mystical way she'd adopted.

"The early apples are ready," Jett stated, "and we'll have loads of pears this week."

"Did you figure out the problem with the hedge?" I asked her.

Jett tilted her head side to side in a *sort of* gesture. "We found a weak spot on the far side of the orchard where it borders the Kribs farm. We don't appear to be in any danger, whoever or whatever was messing with it didn't get through, but we need to repair it. Then I say we do a spell to reinforce it."

"Good plan. I'll whip up a salt and pepper blend." Pepper began listing the ingredients, and the house removed them from the huge spice cabinet on the other side of the room. "White pepper to expose the truth. Black salt for banishment. Gray salt for binding. Rainbow pepper for self-preservation. Long pepper will give the blend lasting strength. Red pepper provides bloodline or ancestral protection. Szechuan pepper and a bit of Himalayan pink salt for ass-kicking warding."

The kids all laughed. Sebastian, who had been scribbling non-stop in a small notebook he'd taken to carrying with him, found it especially funny. "Pepper said ass."

"This is serious," Carly scolded but couldn't help laughing at her youngest. She cleared her throat. "A break in the hedge could be disastrous."

"No break," Jett promised. "I bet whoever did this got gouged up pretty well from those thorns. Unless this hedge has red sap, there were blood drops all over the ground."

"Eww," Emma complained. "That's gross."

Cricket, sitting in her lap now, echoed, "Eww."

"How will you fix it?" I asked. Hopefully I'd never need to worry about it, but just in case, I'd note it in the journal I'd been keeping on how to run a farm. Big job. Thick journal.

Jett wiggled her fingers. "I've got ways to mend splits in wood."

"I don't have those kinds of powers." I wiggled my fingers back at her. "Do you have a more practical kind of magic?"

She nodded. "I've got a concoction. Ask me about it later."

"What else?" Comfort asked.

Emma, Alex, and Sebastian told us about school.

"They're actually teaching something fun this year." Emma looked pleased while Alex said, "Boring as always."

"When did school start?" Sebastian asked as though he'd missed a memo. Since helping Mason Kribs on his farm, his entire attitude had changed. Now he was a little jokester. "Just kidding. It's school. Nothing more to say."

Nina reported that the customers were settling in with the changes at the diner. "Thanks for coming in and checking on us, Grandma. Every other day is perfect."

Comfort shot her a side-eyed glance. "For about ten minutes, right?"

Nina shrugged but didn't say anything more.

"Dusty?" Maks asked. "Are things okay for you? With the whole Tracy thing."

Everyone knew what he meant, but I appreciated the gentle way he asked. "Could be better." I explained the situation at the preschool the same way Autumn explained it to me.

"She needs to practice," Cricket concluded.

Carly held my gaze and arched her eyebrows at me.

"What you need," Comfort began, and I cringed internally over what I figured was coming, "is ears to the ground."

Okay, not what I expected. I was prepared for another directive to work with my mother.

"Oh, I know," Pepper added. "We could set up an apple stand inside the diner and listen to what the townies are saying."

Gwynne clapped her hands. "That sounds like fun."

"Listen to," Carly repeated. "You mean eavesdrop."

Pepper swatted a hand. "Details, details. Jett? You want in on this?"

She considered, then shrugged. "Sure, why not."

"*Not* inside the diner," Nina insisted.

"Outside, then," Comfort replied, disappointed. "If we set up in the grass near the sidewalk, it's still our property and the land baroness can't yell at us."

I did love to see them working together. "Fine if you want to, but Carly has something she needs your help with."

Carly told them about her problem at The Apple Barn.

"An organizing spell should work," Gwynne said. "What do you think, girls?"

"We're going from not enough to do to too much," Pepper noted.

"Not enough to do has never been my problem." Jett sank back in her chair. Freddie stood behind her and pretended to rub her shoulders. Too bad she couldn't feel his hands. "I can't relax until the last apple gets picked and the animals' food stores are ready for winter. Then I still don't get to relax because I have to take care of the animals."

"But you've got help this year." I winked at her, and she tipped her head in a bow of thanks.

"Anything else?" Maks asked.

Granny Sadie said something. Jett interpreted, "She says she's happy to see us all working together to keep the family business alive and well."

We all acknowledged her with smiles, heart hands, or words of acknowledgement.

"With that, I declare the meeting adjourned." Maks rapped his knuckles on the table.

Later, after I'd given Cricket her bath and read her two stories, I went for a nighttime walk around the garden. On peaceful nights like this, I could hear the water of the Mississippi River washing against obstacles in its path—fallen tree limbs, the shoreline, the dock where Harriet's houseboat was moored. I also heard creatures of the night scurrying around. One of them was my all-black squirrel familiar, Pearl.

"Haven't seen you in a few days," I told her. Then I worried, "Is something wrong?"

She circled me then stopped behind me and chirped, forcing me to turn if I wanted to see her. Along with my animal advisor, I found my mother.

"Holy shizzle, Mom. You scared me half to death."

"Apologies," she said in her dry voice. "I came to check on you."

Check on me? She hadn't done that since I was Cricket's age. Why were these troubles worth checking on but all the others over the past three decades weren't? "I'm fine."

"I doubt that. I remember what it was like when everyone discovered I was a gray. Ordies and even other witches can be extremely judgmental. Especially regarding situations they don't fully understand."

The last thing I wanted was to bond with my mother over this gift that was anything but a gift. I did have one question for her, though. "Did you really know I was in my room Thursday night? Or did you lie to Beau and Leezza?"

She stared at me. Her face was so wrinkled and her body so twisted, I couldn't glean any sort of reaction from her.

"I saw the light beneath your door," she stated. "I also heard your television. I did knock and probably implied that I looked inside but I did not."

"Why come to my defense? And don't say because I'm your daughter. That hasn't mattered for the last thirty-two years. Or even before that. Aunt Comfort and Aunt Gwynne raised me."

Her head dropped. Finally, a visible reaction. But what was she feeling? Sorrow? Regret? Annoyance? Disinterest?

"I know you didn't kill Tracy Slayton. Even if I hadn't run into you last night, there would be no doubt in my mind about that."

"Why?" She didn't know anything about me. Maybe I kicked puppies and pulled the wings off flies.

"Because you're not tainted by the power." Implied but unspoken was, "Yet."

Gooseflesh covered my body. I waited for her to say more. When she didn't, I pressed, "What does that mean?"

She turned to walk away. "I'm willing to help if you want me to."

CHAPTER 10

*a*fter thoroughly picking over the garden and orchard yesterday, Jett and I decided we could all take the weekend off. The animals still needed tending, so I would help her with that, but otherwise, I had two full days to reintroduce myself to the joys of working with plants. I could hardly wait to put the gardens to bed for the winter and spend every day doing this.

The late-summer morning was perfect for leaving the shed doors wide open and letting in the sunshine and cool air. Cricket was happy to play with the familiars and *help* me by sorting the jars of dried plants into order from tallest to smallest. I'd return them to alphabetical order later, but the job kept her busy and allowed me to focus.

While drinking an infusion of lemon balm to calm my ragged nerves, I read through a few of our family recipe books. We'd collected a huge bookcase stuffed full of volumes over the years, and I planned to go through all of them during the dark months. For today, I wanted to rebuild my skills by trying a couple of the simpler recipes.

I started by making smudge sticks. Jett had pruned the

blackberry bushes last winter and set aside the cut canes to dry. Wearing heavy-duty gloves, I cut off the sharp bits, then snipped the twigs into eight-inch pieces. Using red string, I tied one end of the twigs into bundles that resembled small brooms. The smoke from the blackberry broom smudge stick banished negative energy from spaces. I used one right away to smudge the shack.

Since ragweed was about to release its pollen and make many of us miserable, I made an herbal steam for clearing sinuses. In a large ceramic bowl, well-scratched from the decades of blending my ancestors had done, I added equal amounts of dried mugwort, chamomile flowers, sage, and peppermint and half amounts of dried thyme and ginger. While combining it all with a hand-carved wooden spoon, I envisioned myself and other allergy-miserable folks adding the blend to steaming water and breathing in the vapors, our symptoms easing as the magic of plants took effect. After spooning the blend into labeled glass jars and pressing on a wooden lid, I held each jar in my hands and whispered, "As I intend, so mote it be."

Finally, I made a simple lotion bar using equal weights of coconut oil, beeswax pastilles, and cocoa butter, and a few drops of vitamin E oil. I melted it all together, then poured the concoction into muffin tins, small jars, or lip balm tubes.

"I don't need my mother for this," I muttered to myself. "Like always, I can teach myself."

"I'm hungry, Lola." Cricket had lined up all the jars perfectly and was now carrying Jett's black and white cat familiar, Oreo, like a baby doll. "Is it snack time yet?"

Glancing at the clock on the wall, I saw it was nearly noon. I smiled contentedly. Hours flew by whenever I immersed myself in something I loved. "We missed snack time, bug."

"What?" she demanded, outraged.

"How about we go to the diner for lunch?"

An excited smile replaced her furious frown. The diner had pie and ice cream. Not that the house couldn't produce whatever she wanted in a blink, but the pies made by a human were so much better. I'd never tell the house that, however. It might take away my beautiful bedroom.

I placed the tins, tubes, and jars on a tray and set the tray off to the side so they could finish hardening without being disturbed. Then we headed for the diner. The hedge still wouldn't open, so we went to the end and doubled back. We could have walked along River Road, but the traffic was heavy during the day and some people drove like maniacs. Too dangerous. I wouldn't risk it with Cricket.

We waved at Silver and Moon as we passed the apothecary and hadn't gone another twenty feet down the mall's sidewalk when I knew something wasn't right.

A crowd, growing larger while I watched, had formed in the park near the diner.

"We deserve the truth," a man hollered.

"We deserve to be safe," a woman replied.

"We *all* deserve to be safe," another woman shouted.

As promised, Comfort, Gwynne, and Pepper had set up an apple stand. Jett had planned to help with the snooping efforts but still had the hedge problem to deal with. Cricket and I skirted the crowd and went to the aunts' table.

"What's going on?" I asked.

"They're upset," Gwynne said seriously.

I sighed. "I can see that. What are they upset about?"

Comfort looked at me like I'd slipped a cog and began ticking items off on her fingers. "Ludo Beck's death a few weeks ago and now Tracy's. And she was one of our own, which makes it worse. Beau hasn't charged anyone yet or even made an announcement about how they're proceeding . . ."

"He's on the way." Pepper pointed over her shoulder at the

diner. "I went inside and called the station. That crowd gathered fast."

Just then, Emma appeared from the far end of the park with shopping bags in hand. "I was over at the General Store. None of them were here when I walked past twenty minutes ago."

Cricket clung to my leg, the crowd upsetting her. "Emma, would you do me a favor? Cricket would like some lunch. Would you take her inside and get her settled? I'll be in as soon as I can."

Emma looked down at Cricket with a joyous smile. "Can I eat with you?"

Cricket immediately released her hold on me, took Emma by the shirttail, and pulled. "Let's go."

Scanning the crowd, I saw the group was divided into three. Witches literally in one section, Ordies in another, and apparently Ordies who supported witches in a third. Some of the Ords were from Blackwood Grove and others from out of town.

"You witches get away with everything," a woman accused. I wasn't sure if she was a townie or visitor. "Perform your evil deeds at will and no one does a thing about it."

"This is a safe town," one of the witch supporters responded. "That's the whole point."

"We're free to use our powers here," a witch added. "It's our right."

"Well," an Ordy man said in a clearly threatening tone, "maybe it shouldn't be."

"Shouldn't be what?" the supporter challenged.

"Maybe it shouldn't be their right." He raised his voice. "It's not natural. They shouldn't have rights we don't have."

The supporter shook her head. "So it's their fault they were born with a gift that you weren't?"

"It ain't a *gift*!" he shouted. "A gift is something good. These people, if that's even what they are, are freaks."

Winnie Monroe, a member of The Council, the governing body for both sides, had stayed with us for a few days three weeks ago. We'd had a hushed conversation late one night outside on the patio.

"You've already sensed it," she'd told me, "and your instincts are correct. There is something going on in this town, but we're not sure what yet."

"Something to do with the witches?" I'd asked.

"As the saying goes, everything old is new again. Even backward thinking and hateful beliefs."

"You think someone wants to harm the witches here."

"And elsewhere. Maybe. Like I said, we're not sure what they're up to yet. There are only quiet rumors at the moment. There could be a group of folks getting ready to act, or simply one unhappy someone with hurt feelings. We're hoping it's the latter. Either way, Blackwood Grove was the first safe town. If it falls—"

"—the others will go down like dominoes."

Looking in horror now at the crowd gathered before me, I wondered if this was part of what she'd been worried about. Townies turning on the witches in safe towns.

They continued arguing.

"Our powers," one of the witches stated, "aren't evil."

"Tell that to Tracy Slayton's family," an Ordy hissed.

"You all know who's guilty of this." The voice rose above the chaos, and everyone turned to see Henry and Marilyn Kramer approaching the crowd. Henry pointed at me. "There's your guilty party."

My heart raced as some of them moved toward me. Angry people who had never even met me but were still sure they knew who and what I was. My head filled with images of innocent people being tied to chairs and dunked into lakes or pools, pressed beneath boards with stones, or burned at the stake hundreds of years ago. We'd gotten good at hiding it for the most part, but had we truly progressed as a society at all?

Thank the goddess for the witches and witch supporters who formed a barrier between them and me.

Marilyn stepped in front of her husband, practically pushing him out of the way. "We saw her fighting with Tracy at The Paddle Wheel Thursday night."

Just that fast, my fear turned into anger. I silently pleaded with whichever goddess might be watching over me at the moment to *not* let me perform any accidental gray magic. I faced Marilyn and stared her in the eye while speaking loudly enough for the crowd to hear me. "You walked in at the last moment and saw Stella removing Tracy from the premises, because she was drunk and causing a scene. You don't have a clue what the fight *Tracy* started was even about."

Someone murmured something about speaking disrespectfully of the dead.

"All right, everyone to your corners," Beau ordered as he and Officer Chapman made their way through the throng from the parking lot side of the mall. My racing heart rate dropped dramatically.

"Why haven't you charged her yet?" Marilyn demanded.

"Dusty? Because she hasn't done anything," Beau said in his patient, light-hearted way.

"Lies," someone in the crowd shouted.

"Do you all want to hear what we've learned about this situation?" he asked.

Nods of agreement and plenty of yeses came from the group.

"Then you all need to settle down and be quiet. I'm not going to shout, and I don't have a bullhorn." He waited until the grumblings stopped. "Officer Chapman and I have spoken with everyone we can find who was at The Paddle Wheel during the incident. Were any of you there but haven't spoken with either of us yet?" A couple of hands went up. "If you have anything different to report after I'm done, come talk to one of us. What we've learned is that Ms. Slayton became highly inebriated soon after entering the saloon Thursday night. This led the bartender on duty—"

"Stella," someone supplied.

Beau stared them down. They shut their mouth. "I won't continue if there's going to be interruptions." The crowd remained silent. "Stella admits to misreading the situation but said she routinely mixed Ms. Slayton's beverages on the weak side. This led her to believe that Ms. Slayton must have consumed some beverages before entering the premises. At one point, Ms. Slayton went to the restroom and, on her way back to her seat, saw Ms. Hotte at a table with her cousin and niece. According to numerous statements, Ms. Slayton started an unprovoked argument with Ms. Hotte that quickly escalated to the point of causing a disturbance. Stella called Nash Kramer to drive Ms. Slayton home and then escorted her outside.

"When Nash arrived, Ms. Slayton was nowhere to be found. He looked around town for a while, driving different routes to her home, but was unable to find her. At 0500 hours on Friday, Harriet Wong heard a thump against her houseboat. When she went out to investigate, she discovered Ms. Slayton's body."

"Who did it?" someone demanded, and this time, the crowd silenced them.

"Officer Chapman and I believe Ms. Slayton fell into the river and drowned. Many people, including Officer Chapman and myself, have witnessed Ms. Slayton walking along the river in an intoxicated state in the past." He paused, then said, his voice thick with emotion, "To put it simply, we believe this was an unfortunate accident."

The crowd erupted with outrage and expletives.

"The police are corrupt," someone shouted. Sounded like the same man who was complaining about witches before. "Witches get away with literal murder."

"Perhaps not corrupt." Henry strode over and stood at Beau's side, immediately attracting everyone's attention. "Did you speak with Dusty, Carly, and Nina about this incident?"

Beau confirmed he had. "Officer Chapman and I went to the Warren farm Friday morning after discovering Ms. Slayton's body. We spoke with both Ms. Hotte and Ms. Flasch at that time. Nina Flasch was already at work, so we spoke with her later that morning."

Anger seemed to radiate off Henry as he asked Officer Chapman, "You believe everything Officer Balinski has said?"

"I do," she answered simply.

"There's only one thing that makes sense, then," Henry told the crowd. "The good officers here are under a spell."

And he didn't mean the one Mom put on Beau all those years ago. He meant that when they came to the farm Friday morning, we spelled them to bow to our wishes.

"I assure you," Beau said, "my mind is perfectly clear. The Warrens did not hex us or curse us or put a spell of any kind on us."

Officer Chapman nodded in vehement agreement.

But Henry continued, his voice raw with emotion, "Officer Beau is friends with Dusty and Carly. Has been most of his life. They went through school together with Nash. Someone spelled my boy after that boat accident." He turned slowly and looked pointedly at me. "It's the only logical reason he doesn't hold you responsible for ruining his life, Dusty."

I couldn't respond. He could be right, after all. Except I hadn't put a spell on Nash like Henry was implying. Had someone else? Mom? Dad? One of the aunts? Or was Henry bluffing? He couldn't know what we were capable of or about what my mother did to Beau all those years ago. Could he?

Other than a few murmurs, the crowd was dead silent. Approximately half of the townies present, and that was being generous, lived here then. This meant most of these people didn't have a clue what Henry was talking about. So now they'd go home, Google *boat accident Blackwood Grove*, and tomorrow morning fresh rumors about me would be flying. With a couple of carefully worded sentences, Henry introduced my nightmare to a whole new group of people.

Beau looked over his shoulder at me, his eyes narrowed, questioning . . . and slightly glassy. What was he thinking?

"You have no idea what you're talking about." Comfort stepped forward now. "Only the kids who were on the boat that day know the truth about what really happened."

"Them and the witch who tried to kill them," Marilyn accused, taking over for her husband again.

Finally, Beau spoke. "This is all rumor and speculation about something that happened a long time ago and isn't what's important right now."

"Right. You need to find out what happened to Tracy," a townie demanded.

"That's exactly what we need to do." Beau's shoulders drooped. "And because there seems to be doubt about my ability to remain impartial in this case, Officer Chapman will continue this investigation."

Without another word, he stepped back to let her address the crowd.

Her eyes were wide. She hadn't seen this coming and had to clear her throat a few times before she could speak. "To, uh, reiterate, I agree with everything Officer Balinski has said. Dusty Hotte has solid alibis for her whereabouts from Thursday night until Ms. Slayton's body was discovered on Friday morning. This is why we have not and do not intend to charge her with anything. I will continue to look into any legitimate leads that come my way. If any of you would like to speak with me, I'll be across the park at the picnic tables between The Sweet Spot and So Mote It Tea. One at a time, please."

Beau stepped forward again. "I have one more thing to say."

The crowd was becoming agitated but remained quiet.

"Regarding the witches who live here," he began, "this is a safe town. I'll say that again. This is a *safe town*. Whether you like that the witches have powers or not, they have them. The law states that they have the freedom and right to live here or within any safe town without persecution. If I find out that any of you are harassing them or infringing on their rights in any way, I will press charges against *you*. You knew what Blackwood Grove was when you moved here. If you're no longer comfortable living by safe town laws and regulations, you're free to leave. Those laws are still the same."

"For now," someone said just loudly enough for us all to hear.

Beau had his back to me, so I couldn't see his expression, but I did see his spine straighten.

Carly and I had talked about Winnie's and The Council's fears about possible trouble brewing after Winnie left Blackwood Grove. That led to a discussion about what it would mean if the wards fell or the laws changed.

"Where does that put cops like Beau?" I had asked. "Do they defend lifelong friends or uphold their careers?"

That question held an even deeper meaning now.

Those laws are still the same.

For now.

Exactly how safe were we here?

CHAPTER 11

Those who had joined the crowd only to watch the show left quickly. The rest dispersed slowly. Almost too slowly. Ensuring there would be no more trouble from angry townies or visiting shoppers, Beau stayed near me and my aunts. Most of the witches, at least those who didn't think we were freaks as that man had called us, and a few of the witch-supporting Ordies hovered nearby as well. It had to be the most slapdash contingent of bodyguards ever. And they were wonderful.

"Glad some of you are still on our side," I told them, grateful, but saddened that Beau wouldn't look at me.

June Stafford clutched her wooden knitting needles like magic wands. "Don't you worry, Dusty. Plenty of us are."

Maybe they were wands. That had to be some powerful magic she worked into her creations.

I waited in case Beau decided to say anything to me and even debated approaching him. Probably shouldn't *if* he still had no memory of the accident. I wished I knew what he was thinking. My feelings of guilt were getting worse by the day.

After another minute without so much as a glance from him,

I slid into the diner through the back door to check on Cricket and grab some lunch.

"Hey, Dusty." Avery was tending burger patties on the griddle while also creating gorgeous healthy salads . . . with vegetables from Applewood Farm. "Have things settled down out there?"

Just the sight of Avery standing there comforted me. Being trans, they could empathize with us witches about not being accepted. "Yeah. Beau and Leezza are sending everyone on their way."

I thought of Winnie again. Were all of the townies in on this together? Was a small group quietly forming a coup? Was it just one of them who had the ability to incite a mob and was trying to create something?

My anger flared. Whatever the answer was, how dare they. Unless we could get nationwide protection, this was, unfairly, the best we had. It was a huge country, and the Ordies could live anywhere. If they didn't like us and our ways, like Beau said, they were free to leave.

I smiled and wondered if we extended the wards well past the town limits. Maybe halfway through Wisconsin. What could they do about it? Demand we take them down again? And if we chose not to? I was suddenly really glad I'd cast that protection spell for the witches.

"Dusty?" Avery was looking expectantly at me. "I asked if you want lunch."

"Oh, yes, please." I was ravenous. "Those burgers smell so good. I'll take a double with cheese, avocado, lettuce, and salsa on the side. Sweet potato fries, too, please. And a vanilla malt."

They nodded approvingly. "Nice twist on the classic. I'll get it ready for you."

I found Cricket and Emma sitting at a booth near the register. They were coloring on the back of their paper placemats.

"All done eating already?" I slid in next to Cricket.

"I was starving." She clutched her stomach dramatically. "I'm still starving."

"What did she have?" I asked Emma.

"A hot ham and cheese sandwich—"

"On a bun, not bread," Cricket clarified.

"And she tried some of the cold peach soup."

Cricket made a face. "Cold soup is yucky. I eated fruit instead. Can I have dessert now?"

"Nina made apple cake," Emma said. "I guess that decision caused a bit of a controversy because the diner didn't have it on today's menu. Nina insisted, and people are loving it so much it's almost all gone."

"Please, Lola."

"Since you ate all of your lunch—"

"Except the yucky soup." She made the same face.

"And because I forgot about snack time today"—this earned me a scowl—"yes, you may have some apple cake."

Cricket leapt to her feet on the bench seat. "Mia! She said yes!"

Other diners laughed at this, but I pulled her back down immediately. "We don't stand on furniture, bug."

Mia brought over a child-size portion of cake with a tiny scoop of vanilla ice cream and my malt. "Glad your grandma said it was okay. I had it waiting for you, and if she said no, I was going to eat it myself." She set my malt in front of me. "Avery says your burger is almost ready."

The aunts entered the dining room from the kitchen then. Comfort bumped Emma further into the booth, and Gwynne and Pepper pulled up chairs.

"Did you sell anything?" Emma asked.

"We did well," Pepper said.

"Half of the peach preserves went," Gwynne explained, "and a third of the apples."

Comfort frowned. "Then the crowd gathered, and they forgot about us. Are you okay, Dusty girl?"

I was going to dismiss the question with an *I'm fine*. But something like this shouldn't be dismissed. What was I feeling? "I'm disappointed, especially with some of the witches. Am I seeing a new side of Blackwood Grove, or was it always like this?"

"It's always been there," Comfort reported, "but usually it's hidden in the shadows. Over the years, people would squawk now and then and think they were going to change things, but the town always banded together and nipped it. Like they did today."

"Momma used to tell us about The Angry Times," Gwynne said. "Remember that, Comfy?"

Comfort nodded. "That was when she was young. Since women started demanding liberation and Ordies think witches are only women, things actually got better for witches as women gained more rights. I don't recall ever seeing the anger, not like this, so it must have skipped a generation. Not sure what's stirring the pot now."

"I blame the mall," Gwynne decided. "All these people coming to our town to shop and gawk at how we live."

"You told me you had to stop letting the diner clean itself," I said to Comfort.

"We did. The Ords were either so mesmerized they wouldn't leave or horrified about evil being on display that they caused a ruckus." She gave a slightly wicked grin. "I told the scaredy-cats they should leave, then showed them to the door."

"Scaredy-cats." Cricket giggled at that.

"That man called us freaks." Gwynne waved her hands about as she spoke. "That's how they treat us. This is our home, not a sideshow attraction where we'll 'do some magic' because they want to be entertained. Come and shop but don't expect us to perform. We're just people."

Pepper put an arm around Gwynne's shoulders to calm her, knowing if her friend got too worked up, she could lose control of her magic. As in plates and tables might go flying due to the way she tossed her hands about as she spoke.

Maybe it was time to talk about something else. "Did you hear anything about Tracy's death?"

The trio shook their heads.

"Not much more than you heard from the crowd," Comfort said. "A few sort of fished for details, asking us what you did to make her so angry."

"Perhaps," Pepper interrupted, "we should head home now. We still have Carly's spell to work on." She gave a subtle head tilt at Gwynne who was now folding and unfolding her hands.

Emma and Cricket went with them. I promised to be there as soon as I'd finished my lunch, which Nina delivered shortly after they left. She dropped into the seat across from me.

"I heard. You okay?"

I took a bite of my burger, and my eyes closed involuntarily while I savored the flavor. "I'm better now."

"I imagine living in an Ordinary town for so long made you tough."

That was an interesting statement. "I suppose it could have, if I'd wanted to fight for my rights. Being the only parent responsible for Micah, though, I flew well under the radar." I studied the beautiful young woman across from me. So full of spunk and determination. Like her mother. "You know I regret staying away for so long."

"I do." When I first got here, she was angry at me in defense of Carly. Thank heavens we got past that.

"We should never just roll over and let others walk on us or take what's rightfully ours."

A proud, rebel smile turned one corner of her mouth. "What are you going to do about it?"

"First of all, I won't let them accuse me of murder. I didn't do anything." To Tracy or to the boat full of my classmates. Or to that little boy. "And I'll defend every witch's right to use their magic."

"And what about you? What do *you* want?"

I jabbed a sweet potato fry at her. "That's an excellent question. Which I don't have an answer for. My life has turned completely inside out in a matter of weeks. I haven't had time to think about it."

My niece arched an eyebrow at me. "Considering people are accusing you of murder, you may want to start thinking about it."

She returned to work, leaving me alone with my thoughts . . . and dozens of patrons staring at me from across the diner. I switched to the other side of the booth so my back was to them.

What did I want? I knew I loved working with plants from seed stage to final product, whatever that turned out to be. I loved how quiet Blackwood Grove was. It was wonderful to be back with my family. But that ever-hovering question about my powers always cast a shadow. Unlike in the Ordinary town, there was no hiding the fact I was a witch here. But would I ever be able to fully embrace my gray side?

Once back at the farm, instead of going straight into the house, I turned toward The Apple Barn to fill Carly in on what happened at the park.

"Holy shizzle." The place was a total disaster inside. Frozen food items sitting on canned goods shelves. Jars of health and beauty items were in complete disarray, some perched precariously on the edges of the shelves, about to tumble and smash to the stone floor. Clothing items were unfolded and left in a heap, which reminded me of Micah's bedroom when he was a kid. I immediately started organizing the displays.

"See what I mean about not being able to make any progress?" Carly was nearly in tears.

"I do. The aunts are working on your spell right now."

"Thank the goddess it's Saturday."

The Barn and most of the stores in the mall were closed on Sundays and Mondays. Two days to get things in order and prepare for the new week.

"What are you doing here?" Carly snapped.

She was understandably upset, so I let her rude tone go. "Thought I'd let you know about the angry mob in the park."

This caught her attention. "Were there pitchforks and torches?"

"Not yet, but if we don't find out the truth about Tracy's death, it could come to that."

"We? You want to investigate this death too?"

I answered with a slow shrug.

Carly sighed. "Didn't you say we were only going to dig around in Ludo Beck's murder?"

Did I? "I think I asked how many investigations *you* thought we'd have to do."

She thought about that for a moment. "Right. You were taking notes on the back of a used piece of paper, and I asked if we should have a notebook."

I grabbed a small spiral-bound book from a nearby shelf. The cover had the Applewood Farm logo—an *A* and *F* in a font that looked like tree branches. I followed Carly around the shop, helping clean in between writing down notes. I also told her about the accusations being thrown about by the angry Ordies.

"It was scary, Carly. If Beau and that group of witches and townies hadn't formed a line between us and the crowd . . ." I shivered. "I'm not sure what would have happened."

"You're right, we need to find out the truth. This could tear the town apart."

CHAPTER 12

*W*e agreed to start our investigation at the crime scene. Carly had to check in with her kids first, and I wanted to take care of Cricket's normal bedtime routine.

"Besides," Carly said, "it's probably better if we do this later at night when the townies won't be wandering the streets."

"True. Especially if they decide to take up their pitchforks and torches."

The echoing of her earlier words was part serious, because some of them really had scared me this afternoon, and part meant to ease the awful tension coming off my cousin. It didn't work. Carly didn't react at all.

"If you don't want to help," I offered, "I can do this alone."

She sighed. "No, I'll help. My mind is just on other things. There's a lot going on."

I was trying to be understanding. Things weren't going smoothly at the shop, and dealing with four kids and a house on her own had to be a constant struggle. She didn't have to watch over the aunts by herself anymore, though. And if I was being honest, this *my life is all turned around* attitude was getting on my nerves. She chose to make the move to the store. She chose a life with a traveling husband. My life was inside out too. Josie was missing, my son was in prison, I lost my job, my house burned down, and my granddaughter's life had been threatened all within the same month. Not that this was a competition, but I think my bad news column was longer.

Saying any of that will only result in Carly getting angrier and feelings being hurt. You don't want that, so let it go.

Decent advice. I decided to listen to me.

I asked Carly about using scrying or divining, her magical ability, to figure out what had happened to Tracy. She always considered her power to be worthless because it wasn't active; she couldn't make things appear or move across a room. I always thought it was cool because she could *divine* the questions that would be on tests, which meant we could spend less time studying and more time planning our shop.

"I haven't used my powers in years." A longing look came over her. "Too busy with life, I guess."

"You could try it tonight," I nudged. "It's still in you."

She wiped her hands on her jeans as though the thought made her nervous. "All right, I'll try, but this would also be a good time for you to try your new thing."

Since I'd had good success with bringing on dreams and visions by drinking a rosebud infusion with a pinch of pink salt before bed, the aunts suggested I try using meditation to gain more control over my powers.

Actually, what Comfort said was, "If you're not going to let Griselle help you with the gray stuff, at least try to do more with the two powers you already understand."

"Meditation could help you with that." Gwynne sat cross-legged with eyes closed and her thumbs and forefingers touching.

"You've got such a strong brain," Pepper agreed. "Give it a try."

"If that doesn't work," Jett added, "I've got a good strong Scottish whiskey that'll make you see loads of things."

Freddie gave two thumbs up to his wife's suggestion.

So every night for the last two weeks, after putting Cricket to bed, I sat in my room and meditated. That's what I'd been doing when Mom knocked on my door Thursday night. The television was on for background noise because I fell asleep if I sat in total silence. I focused on something that brought me joy not distress, things like a flower in the garden that caught my attention or the river when the sun or moonlight glinted off the ripples. Every morning, before getting out of bed, I wrote about any dreams I'd had in the journal Gwynne recommended I keep.

My dreams of the truth behind past events occurred while I slept. My visions of what would happen in the future occurred while I was awake. I hoped my experiment would merge the two and bring on visions of past events while awake. It might have been wishful thinking, but I felt like I had already gained a little more control. Would it work to help solve the Tracy situation? Would I be able to see what had happened to her by slipping into a meditative state rather than trying to bring on a dream? I had no idea. It was worth a try, though, because the only other way we'd learn the truth was to catch the killer and force them to confess all. I labeled that Plan B.

Instead of meditating tonight, I drank a small amount of the rosebud infusion and took a short nap so my brain wouldn't be tired when I met with Carly. At eleven o'clock, I went outside to the courtyard and waited for her to arrive. We figured the streets would be vacant by then.

"Did you bring your crystal?"

"I wasn't sure which one I'd want." She pulled a handful of them out of her sweatshirt pocket. "Clear quartz, amethyst, obsidian, tiger's eye, black onyx, and super seven."

I reached out for the super seven, and she slapped my hand. "Don't touch. I charged them for my use."

"Sorry." I was so drawn to the beautiful stone, though.

She stuck her hand in her other pocket and pulled out something wrapped in a tissue. "You can play with this one."

I opened the bundle and found a hexagonal-shaped crystal about the size of a baby carrot.

"Clear quartz amplifies," Carly explained. "The points at both ends means the wand both gives and receives energy. Hold it in your receiving hand."

I was right-handed so held it in my left.

We walked in silence the few blocks to the dock where Harriet's boat was still moored.

Our plan was to sit quietly near the spot where Tracy's body was found, think about the interactions we'd had with her over the past few days, and see what images we could bring up with our respective powers. Best-case scenario was that one of us would see who killed her. Other possibilities were we'd get a clue that would help, one of us would connect with her spirit, or neither of us would get anything and this would be a complete waste of time and energy.

"Where do you suppose Harriet found her?" I whispered.

Carly pointed toward the back of the boat and matched my low tone. "The current would have taken her south, so she probably got caught against the stern."

"We should have asked Granny Sadie to come," Carly whispered as we settled on the dock near the boat's stern. "She might be able to contact Tracy's spirit."

I groaned. "You're right. We should have."

As though waiting for her cue, Granny appeared and hovered above the water, presumably near *the spot*.

"That's pretty cool," I said, meaning her being out over the water.

"Totally. I'm going to assume that's where Harriet found her."

Granny nodded and gave a thumbs up.

Carly took a deep focusing breath, then chose the amethyst, obsidian, and onyx stones. The onyx immediately fell out of her hand. She put it back, and it fell again. "Guess it doesn't want to play tonight." She put the onyx back in her pocket, placed the super seven on her palm instead, and all was well.

After laying my dream journal and pen at my side, I sat with the little quartz wand in my left hand, fixed my gaze on Granny until she became a fog-like blur, then I closed my eyes and bid my mind to show me what had happened to Tracy. I heard the river water sloshing up against the side of the boat and Carly's deep, even breaths. After a couple of minutes, my breathing synced with hers. Another few minutes passed, and I felt a gentle vibration around my body. Then, as though I was looking through a small hole in a piece of black paper, a scene filled the center of my forehead, my third eye: I saw Tracy, what was directly behind her, and maybe a foot to either side of her.

It was dark, so either late Thursday night or the wee hours of Friday morning. She was walking fast, stumbling as she did, still intoxicated. She appeared to be in fight-or-flight mode and was desperately trying to get away from whoever was following her. Adrenaline would be flooding her body. Her brain would have engaged an animal-like need for self-preservation.

She scurried, half falling, down the bank to the river's edge. This wasn't happening here near Harriet's houseboat. I could see the river behind Tracy, but the boat wasn't there. She stopped at the river's edge and turned, but I couldn't tell what, or who, she was looking at.

Let me turn with her, I begged my mind. *Let me see what she sees.*

No luck. The hole in the paper remained firmly focused on her alone.

She leaned forward, staring, her head tilted, and then her whole body slumped a fraction. With relief? Or resignation?

Her legs appeared to buckle, and she dropped to her hands and knees on the small sandy shore. She looked up, and terror spread across her face as a pair of gloved hands reached for her neck.

No! I screamed in my mind, breaking the trance.

I immediately grabbed my journal and began blindly writing. I didn't think or censor, just let my hand write whatever my mind dictated. After a few minutes, I turned to Carly who was watching me, waiting for me to finish.

"I saw hands around her neck," I told her.

"I did, too." She tapped the center of her chest. "And a knee holding her under the water."

Glancing around the best I could in the darkness, I decided, "This wasn't the spot. I saw her drop onto sand. There's no sand here, so it must have happened upriver a bit, and he or she let her float down river. The hands were gloved, so I can't guess at their gender."

"I didn't see gloves, but you're probably right. Your powers are stronger right now. I'm pretty rusty." She stared sadly toward the houseboat. Granny Sadie wasn't there anymore. "Considering what's been happening in this town, I think I need to make practicing the craft a daily habit."

"Good idea."

"Would you two like to come inside?"

Startled half to death, I let out a little scream. Harriet was standing with her head poking out of the doorway.

"It's a bit more private," she offered.

I turned to Carly. "We should question her."

"True," she agreed and stood with a groan.

Since Carly hadn't been inside the boat yet, Harriet gave her the two-minute tour, and then we sat in her living area. Carly and I took the loveseat; Harriet sat in a chair across from us, her cat in her lap.

"You found Tracy," I began.

Harriet frowned deeply, stroking Fluff's fur. "I did. Very

upsetting." She described how Tracy was face down and obviously deceased. "I didn't know who it was at that time and wasn't about to touch the body. Nash was walking Lady like he does most every morning. And some evenings. He waved at me, and I called him over. As soon as he understood what he was looking at, he pulled his phone out of his pocket and called the police. You probably know the rest from there."

"Did you hear anything that night?" Carly asked.

"Not a thing," she said too quickly as though prepared with an answer to the question she knew was coming. She indicated her open laptop on the counter attached to the back of the kitchen cabinets. "I've been staying up late, well past midnight. Those are my most productive hours, and I've been putting more urgency into getting this editing job done. Something is going on in this town, and I don't like it. I was able to change my reservation at the Lansing marina to Friday, so I'm pulling out earlier than planned."

She was talking too much. Trying to prevent us from asking a question she didn't want to answer? I noticed her open laptop and papers scattered across her counter. "We disturbed your work. Sorry about that."

"That's all right. Sometimes whispers can be more distracting than loud voices." She tapped her ear. "You tend to strain to hear what's being said."

"How long were we out there?" Carly asked, searching for a clock.

"I first heard you about a half hour ago," Harriet reported. "I thought you left. May I ask what you were doing?"

We told her about our attempts at using our admittedly weak powers.

"Very creative," she approved. "What did you see?"

She paled as we told her. I concluded, "Of course, we could be completely wrong."

"But you both saw basically the same thing." She gave us a wise nod. "Don't discount your abilities, girls."

We chatted with her for a few more minutes. She had nothing helpful to add to our investigation but encouraged us to keep digging.

"Don't leave without saying goodbye," I pleaded as we climbed out of her boat.

She winked. "Stop over early Friday morning, then."

When we were back to the road, Carly snorted and said, "She called us girls."

"I suppose a dozen years from now, fifty will seem young." I checked for oncoming cars, and we crossed the road. "She also told us to use our magic."

Carly paused. "Is that what she said?"

"That's what I heard." Gwynne had told me something similar. That we were born with our abilities, which meant we were to use them. "You keep scrying and divining, and I'll keep working on blending my dreams and visions."

"And?"

I sighed. "I'll consider working with my mother."

By the time we were at the spot where Carly would head to her house and I'd go to mine, we had agreed to go to the station tomorrow and tell Officer Chapman what we saw.

I slept fitfully, fighting off images of those gloved hands around Tracy's throat. The poor woman. She had to be terrified. Who could have done this and why? Did Tracy have an enemy? Had she done something to upset the wrong person?

The next morning, when Carly came inside the house to pick me up after breakfast, Comfort asked, "What exactly do you want this spell for the shop to do?"

"Oh, you know." Carly waved her hand around randomly. "A self-cleaning spell. Something that will put the displays to rights after the customers mess them up."

"They are a messy lot," Gwynne agreed. "I was grateful for my telekinesis every day."

When Carly shot her an envious frown, Gwynne wrapped her in a hug, petting her head as she held her. Carly stared at me over Gwynne's shoulder with a *help me* expression, then softened and settled into the embrace.

"We shouldn't be long," I promised Cricket and the aunts.

"It's okay, Lola." Cricket bounced on the balls of her feet. "Auntie Comfort is going to teach me how to make apple pie."

And the tradition continued. She'd taught each of us how to make pie. Carly said Nina immediately showed talent, which was why she was now running the diner. Maybe Cricket would be the next, although considering her attraction to animals, I expected her to become a veterinarian or open a pet shop.

In the police station's interview room, Officer Chapman sat across from us with an open case file in front of her. She listened patiently to our statements, added a few notes to the file, and then closed the folder.

"Thank you for the information." She obviously didn't find any of this important.

"What about the knee?" I reminded Carly. "You didn't mention that."

"Right," Carly answered with a small gasp. "Like Dusty did, I saw hands around Tracy's neck and a knee on her chest."

Officer Chapman opened the folder again and flipped a few pages. "On her chest?"

Carly sat straighter. "Whoever did this to her, held her under water by kneeling on her chest."

Carly and I cringed at that detail. Officer Chapman appeared unaffected.

"So?" I prodded. "What do you think?"

The officer cleared her throat. "I think that's a detail we haven't revealed."

Carly pushed for more this time. "Meaning?"

"Meaning," Officer Chapman said, "that the coroner found bruising on the victim's chest." She held her fingers together in a circle the size of a grapefruit.

"A knee." Carly was happy that her ability had worked properly and then she winced as the reality of Tracy's awful death set in again.

"Do you know what it means," Officer Chapman began, "when someone knows a detail the police haven't made public?"

We waited for her to tell us.

"It could mean one of you is the killer. Or that you worked together on the crime. Or with someone else."

"Whoa, hang on," Carly objected.

"You and Beau both agreed I have multiple, solid alibis," I reminded the officer. "Carly does too."

Carly shifted in her seat again. "It could also mean our powers worked and showed us the killer."

"You saw hands and a knee," Officer Chapman said. "We all have those. Well, most of us. That doesn't give me much to go on. Do you have any other details?"

Carly reached into her pocket and took out the same crystals she'd held last night. "I could try again."

It took the officer a moment to realize what she meant, then her face lit up with what could only be excitement. "Here? Now?"

I looked around the rather large room. "Will anyone else come in here? She shouldn't be disturbed."

Officer Chapman scribbled *Do Not Disturb* on a sheet of paper, taped it to the outside of the room door, and locked it. "What else do you need? A candle? Music?"

I couldn't help but smile at her enthusiasm as Carly said, "I just need a focal object."

She retrieved a coffee mug from one of the cabinets. "Will this work?"

"How about a bowl of water?" Carly requested. "That's better for scrying. A dark color if possible."

Officer Chapman put the mug back, filled a black plastic food container with water, set it in front of her, and then dimmed the room lights.

"Maybe don't sit there and watch me," Carly requested a minute later.

"Oh, sorry." She pointed across the room. "I'll stand over there."

So we couldn't be accused of putting on a show, I stood next to the officer. I cautioned her, "This could take a while, so be patient."

We waited in silence while my cousin slid into a trance state. After almost ten minutes, Carly opened her eyes and reported, "It was a man. I saw yellow or tan work gloves." She touched the outside of her wrist. "There was something here, but I couldn't make out what it was. A mark of some kind, like a stain maybe. He wore jeans or dark canvas pants."

Officer Chapman sat again, adding more notes to her file. "Considering all the farms around here, work gloves and pants like that are standard attire." She closed the folder. "I guess it does at least narrow the suspect list to farmhands."

"I'll try again later," Carly promised. "See if I can make out anything else."

And I'd try to bring on more in a dream. Before we left the room, I asked, "You haven't put us on your suspect list, have you?"

Officer Chapman shook her head. "No. I don't think either of you killed Tracy Slayton."

"And you believe us?" Carly asked. "About what we saw?"

She waited a beat before saying, "I want to. Time will tell, I guess."

CHAPTER 13

*C*arly and I were almost to her SUV when someone called my name from across the parking lot. I turned to see a teenage girl.

"I was going to go in and talk to the police," she said, "but I don't think they'll help me. You're Dusty Warren, right?"

My first reaction was to brace for some new attack. Then I noticed her body language: shoulders rounded, hands shoved deep inside her jean jacket pockets, eyes downcast.

"I'm Dusty Hotte. Who are you?"

"Adrianna."

"Sweetie, if you're a minor—"

"I'm twenty-seven."

An extremely young-looking twenty-seven. I would have guessed seventeen. "What did you want to talk to the police about?"

Her voice was so low I had to strain my ears to hear her. When I did, I gasped internally, trying to remain strong for her.

"I was assaulted last night." Her body began to tremble, and she lowered her voice even more. "Sexually."

People were entering and leaving the station. She didn't need

THE CRONES 113

them to hear this. "Do you have a car? Somewhere we can talk where there aren't so many ears?"

She shook her head. "I walked here."

"Come with me." I led her to Carly's car and climbed into the backseat with her. Fortunately, Carly didn't say a word other than, "Should I leave?"

"She won't tell anyone what you say," I told Adrianna. "Maybe she can help too."

Adrianna shook her head again. "She can stay, but I think only you can help."

For a few seconds, I wondered what she meant, then a feeling of dread flooded me.

"I tried to get in touch with your mom. Griselle Warren, right?"

My stomach flipped. Please don't ask what I think you're about to ask. "Yes, Griselle is my mother."

"Someone gave me her phone number a few nights ago. I'm not supposed to say who. They told me to text her for help. I did, but she hasn't gotten back to me."

I pictured my mother's hands and couldn't imagine her crooked fingers typing on a full-size keyboard let alone a cell phone's tiny one.

When I didn't ask what she wanted me to do, Adrianna begged. "This wasn't random or sudden or whatever."

She explained, in sickening detail, how this man sat next to her at The Paddle Wheel a couple of months ago. He didn't believe her when she told him her age but then took great interest in this woman who looked like a child. Weeks passed, and she came across him again in town. He started by touching her innocently on the shoulder, then her arm. He reached for her breast the next time, and she swatted his hand away.

"It was a reaction, you know?" Tears and terror filled her eyes. "He grabbed my wrist, tight, and asked if I like to play rough. This was over by the vet's office. Nash Kramer saw the guy grab me. He ran outside and the guy immediately let go. Then I came across the man again two nights ago."

She pulled her hands out of her pockets to reveal scratches on them. Deep-purple bruises were immediately visible on her thin arms when she pushed up her sleeves. "There are more on my stomach, back, and legs."

The whole time she spoke, heat that had nothing to do with a hot flash started to grow in my chest. My breaths came short and fast. She was sure he put something in her drink, which blessedly meant she didn't remember a lot after he approached her. I clenched my hands.

"Why—" My voice broke. "Let's go inside and talk to the police."

She shook her head rapidly. "The police won't help. This guy did this to another woman, Dusty. Her story is nearly identical to mine. She's the one who gave me Griselle's number."

"Did she contact my mother?"

"She did. Your mom gave her some kind of potion, but she was too afraid to use it. She was scared that if it didn't work, it would make things worse."

The rage in my belly intensified. "Does she still have the potion?"

"She threw it in the river." She took my hands in hers, and my breath caught. I swear, they weren't much bigger than Cricket's. "Please, I need your help. *We* need your help. I think the other woman will talk to you, too, if you want. She's just afraid to confront this jerk." She pushed her shoulders back, her hands still in mine. "I'm not afraid. We have to stop him from doing this again, because if he did it to us, he'll do it to others. Maybe he already has."

What was I supposed to do? I glanced at Carly. In the rearview mirror, her wide eyes were locked on mine. "I'll be honest with you, Adrianna—"

"Please don't say no."

"The thing is, I've never done this before."

She looked confused. "But you're a gray witch. You help people who need it."

My breath caught again. This time, from the new light this strong young woman had just shined on my ability. I could *help* people. Not do the wrong thing for the right reason. I could do the right thing when no one else could.

"This is important," I continued. "I think the police might help—"

"The other woman told them. She didn't have proof, though, because she waited too long." Adrianna glanced down between her legs. "If you know what I mean. I did too."

She was starting to shake again, and the hot rage in me felt like it was cooking my insides. "Okay, I'll do what I can."

"Oh, thank you." She began to sob with relief.

"Give me your phone number." I dialed it as she dictated so she also had mine. "You understand how important it is for this to be done correctly, right?"

She sniffed. "I understand."

"I don't know how long it will take me, but I promise to work on this. In the meantime, please don't walk around alone at night. Stay with crowds during the day. Call someone . . . call *me* if you need a ride somewhere. All right?"

"I promise." She looked me dead in the eye. "He won't touch me again. His name—"

"No. I don't want to know. It doesn't matter who he is; his punishment will be what it should be."

Not sure where that decision came from. I was going with my gut on this.

Carly drove Adrianna home and then pulled around the corner from her apartment. Her hands shook as she shoved the SUV into park. "Oh my gods, Dusty."

"I know."

"This is huge."

Still stunned, all I could do was nod in agreement.

"Dusty." She waited until I faced her. "If you do this, it has to be perfect. This is a whole different level from the other gray spells you cast. This one can't go wrong."

I wanted to be insulted, but she was right. For Adrianna's sake and the sake of the other woman this man hurt and any future women he might try to hurt, this couldn't go wrong. "I'll talk to my mother."

"Thank the goddess. It's time you—"

"Not me. It's too important. She needs to do this."

Carly slumped in her seat. "If you're going to—"

She cut herself off, but I heard the unspoken words loud and clear. If I was going to *help* people, I needed to know how to do it right.

By the time she dropped me off at the farm, we'd agreed not to discuss Adrianna anymore. I would take care of her problem one way or another. We also agreed to keep trying to see more than yellow or tan work gloves and dark pants on the person who killed Tracy. Hair color would be great. A distinctive T-shirt could help. A face, obviously, would be the ultimate.

Maks was coming out of the back door as I walked up to it. "Everything okay, honey? You look upset."

"A townie asked for my help." He understood immediately what I meant. "Do you know where my mother is?"

"She's on the farm somewhere." He pointed at the carriage house. "I saw her not too long ago going up to the apartment."

"I'll check there first. What about Cricket? Do you know where she is?"

"With Jett. They were going to check on the goats."

Good, she was occupied. "Would you do me a huge favor?"

"Keep the little miss busy for a while?"

I gave him a hug. "You sure you don't have telepathic powers?"

He kissed the top of my head. "Only the kind that comes from knowing my people well. Go do what you need to do."

I crossed the courtyard to the Apple Blossom Cottage, where Cricket and I lived for our first week in Blackwood Grove. As soon as I entered the front door, I could tell something was different. The stairs up to the apartment were no longer carpeted. They were old, worn wood plank boards, which looked to have come from a two-hundred-year-old home. The walls were now painted a neutral ivory instead of garish baby pink and near neon turquoise. Maybe the property was redecorating. It liked to do that. I hurried up the stairs to see what else had changed and found the main apartment was completely different. The interior walls were gone, creating a single room instead of a kitchen, living room, and two bedrooms. The walls were lined from floor to ceiling with mismatched scuffed shelving and chipped cabinets in shades of red, purple, teal, jade, and plain wood. Dried plants hung from beams in the ceiling. A huge wooden worktable dominated the center of the space and was covered with mixing bowls, mortars and pestles, a grimoire-style notebook on a bookstand, and empty jars in various sizes waiting to be filled.

"What did you do?" I asked the property. What had been an adequate apartment was now a witch's dream apothecary. Or at least this witch's dream. I immediately envisioned spending hours and hours in here preserving and blending plants and essential oils.

From the far corner, I heard a toilet flush. Seemed the bathroom was still in the same location. My mother shuffled around the corner.

"What do you think?" she asked.

"I think . . . What are you doing up here? Is this yours?"

She shrugged a shoulder, which made her whole body lean to one side. "I hope you'll let me use it."

I jabbed a finger into my chest. "That *I'll* let you use it?" She must be talking to the carriage house.

"We designed it for you, Dusty. Me and the property." She gave a hopeful smile. "Do you like it?"

Like it? I never wanted to leave this room. First things first, though.

"What's going on, Mom? A young woman named Adrianna asked me to help her with a gray spell because you weren't replying to her texts. It's an important request. A man sexually assaulted her and another woman. Possibly others."

Mom eased herself onto a rocking chair and sighed as she settled. "Looks like we got this room ready for you just in time."

I pulled a low stool over near the rocker and sat facing her. "What are you talking about?"

She met my eyes and seemed to see into my soul. "I know you think I wasn't a good mother—"

"Mom, this is important—"

She held up a gnarled hand. "So is this. I admit the magic took over my life, especially after you left, but I know you better than you realize." She motioned at the room, in general. "This is what you always dreamt of, isn't it?"

Even after I left, years after Micah was born, I had actual dreams of working in a room like this. No, in *this* room. How did she know? "The property did this?"

"It followed my instructions. I know what was in your heart, Dusty."

"Only Carly—" I froze. "Did you spell her to find this out?"

"I talked to her, years ago after she dropped out of college. She told me about the dreams the two of you had and how they never happened. I remembered every word she said, wrote them down, and held on to them for the day I knew would come. This day."

I gazed around in awe. It was like she and the property had a direct line into my brain. "But why now? What's so special about today?"

"You just said it." She settled back in the chair as though getting ready to take a nap. "You got your first request."

I shook my head. "This one is too important."

"They're *all* important. First lesson, you can't let your personal feelings, beliefs, or morals interfere with the customer's request. You give them exactly what they ask for. Nothing more, nothing less."

"Don't go against my own beliefs and morals? Did you make that mistake?"

She hesitated before saying, "I may have learned the hard way, but you don't need to. If a request is too big, you have the right to refuse it. Just know there is a positive for every negative and vice versa. The problem you refuse to fix will likely continue. Sometimes, when the bad guy has done something so heinous, when the victim or a loved one of the victim can't take any more, they'll handle it on their own. You can surely guess how that ends. Whereas if you handle it for them, justice is sure to be served." She patted her wrinkled face. "This is a far better consequence, I think."

She rocked peacefully in her chair. There was no judgement in my voice when I asked, "That's what it's always been about for you. Restoring justice."

Her lips twitched, but I couldn't tell if they formed a smile or a frown. "Superheroes aren't real, Dusty. We gray witches are the closest thing available."

"Surely we're not the only two."

Mom didn't reply. Of course, I hadn't asked a question. Did I want to know? Maybe, but not right now. Because if I was the only other one . . . "Will you teach me how to do these gray spells? If I decide to do this."

"It's a bit late in the game, but I won't be here forever." She put emphasis on those last few words. Or maybe I just heard them that way. "Someone needs to take over."

Was she dying? To anyone who didn't know her, it looked like she might drop dead at any moment. Heck, that was true for those of us who did know her.

"You make it sound like I don't have a choice in this. What if I don't want to be a gray witch?"

Her eyes flew open. "You *are* a gray witch, Dusty."

"You know what I mean. What if I don't want to do what you do?"

She settled back into the chair. "Because after I'm gone, the alternative is far too dangerous."

"What is that supposed to mean?"

A soft snore answered my question this time.

While she rested, I looked around my haven. According to the labels, the filled bottles contained individual dried plants and herbs. The empty ones, presumably, were for me to fill with my blends. One entire case held both modern and ancient plant and herb books. A few witchcraft how-tos were in there as well. While I was happy to use others' recipes as a starting point, I preferred to tweak and create my own. The grimoire on the waist-high table was blank. My place to note every attempt, result, and final outcome. My fingers literally itched to start mixing. Adrianna needed help, though. What I could do right away was flip through some of those books and start coming up with a plan.

I looked around for another chair but found only the hard, backless stool.

"Could I have a second chair, please? A wingback next to a fireplace would be the perfect spot to sit on cold winter days or nights."

I'd been joking about the fireplace, but the property seemed to think this was a good addition. The entire cottage shook, and all I could do was gape as an old hearth-style fireplace complete with a hanging cauldron and ten-inch-thick wood beam mantel emerged from the wall. I took a step back and bumped into a wingback chair covered with fabric that resembled a crazy quilt in colors that coordinated perfectly with the cabinets and shelves. A well-worn wood table with a cast-iron lamp stood next to it.

"That's perfect. Thank you."

The cottage made a happy humming noise that sounded somehow like a curtsy.

I made a cup of tea at a cart loaded with beverage and snack options, then sat in the chair with a few books in my lap. The question was, what was I looking for? Which of the plants, crystals, stones, and oils surrounding me was I supposed to mix together to help Adrianna and the other woman? I had so much to learn.

I glanced at my mother, who was sound asleep in the rocking chair. How much time did I have?

CHAPTER 14

$\mathcal{A}$t some point, Pearl found her way into *The Sanctuary* as I'd decided to call my room. She perched on the back of my chair and listened to me mutter about not knowing what to use for Adrianna's problem. Then she scampered up the shelves loaded with jars of dried plants and laid one of her little hand-like paws on the jar of belladonna. Next, she shuffled down the row to the dieffenbachia. Finally, she scurried back to me and tapped one of the books in my lap. Guess I was supposed to read about them. Turned out both plants could cause forms of paralysis. That could be helpful.

I looked up to ask my mother about this, but she had slipped out without me noticing. Must have been the cloaking spell because although the room was spacious, it wasn't so big that people could come and go without my knowledge. Unless I'd simply been that engrossed in my research.

"Dusty?" Sounded like Jett's voice.

"Yep, I'm up here."

She stood at the top of the stairs and gaped. "Would you look at this. The property made you a proper workshop, did it?"

A proper workshop. I smiled at that. "My mother told it what to do."

"Griselle did? Never would've guessed she could be so thoughtful. Pepper asked me to track you down. Dinner will be ready soon." She made a slow lap around the room. "The others are going to lose their heads over this."

They would. "As long as they don't mess with an experiment in progress or try to redecorate, I can share."

She paused before saying, "You're a better woman than I am, then." The comment was part respect and part *what's the matter with you, girl.*

She was right. I'd been sharing too much of my life recently. Townies wanted to know where I'd been and why I was back. The Council wanted me to give up my privacy to take care of the aunts. Moving into a house with five people and two ghosts. And there was having to step back into a parenting role after I'd been long free of those responsibilities. Although, I didn't have to think twice about taking care of Cricket. It's not like I'd let my granddaughter go into the foster system when I was fully capable of providing for her. But between all of my new responsibilities, my free time was minimal. So really, the last thing I wanted was to have to share my precious alone time in this beautiful space with anyone.

"I get dibs, always," I told Jett, rethinking my statement. "A sign on the door will mean they need to stay out?"

Jett blinked at me, a smirk playing at her mouth as we started down the stairs. "Did you forget who you're talking about? A sign stating no trespassing is a sure way to make them storm the fort."

She knew them well. "Any way I can keep this a secret?"

The smirk turned into a chuckle. "You do like a challenge, lass."

At dinner, the aunts reported the self-cleaning spell for The Apple Barn was ready.

"We're going to cast it after dinner." Gwynne clapped her hands excitedly.

When Pepper asked how my day went, I decided not to tell them about my new space in the cottage—and gave Jett a nod of thanks for keeping my secret—but did tell them a bit about Adrianna's problem.

Gwynne started crying during my abbreviated retelling. "The poor child."

Pepper became outraged. Turned out, her ex-husband was abusive. Not physically, but there were plenty of ways to ruin a person's life that didn't involve fists.

Comfort fixed a look on me that was as concerned and serious as any I'd ever seen from her. "And how are you planning to handle this?"

They all were equal parts relieved and apprehensive about me asking for Mom's help.

"It's the best way," Comfort decided.

"The only way," Jett interpreted for Granny Sadie. "You made the right choice."

Freddie raised a fist, which I guessed meant *you've got this*. Or he wanted me to fight with my mother, but I doubted it was that.

"Say what you will about Griselle's ways," Gwynne mused, "but she is very good at what she does."

Cricket hadn't shared anything about her day. Highly unusual for the child who rarely stopped chirping. I asked her about it during bath time as she drew stick figure ballerinas on the tiled wall with bathtub crayons.

"Is something bothering you tonight, bug? You're so quiet."

After a long moment, she admitted, "My friends said I don't have a mommy and daddy."

Today was Sunday. Had she been sitting with this thought for two days? Had I been so wrapped up in my own issues I hadn't noticed?

"Of course you have a mommy and daddy. They love you very much."

"How come I don't get to see them?"

I never knew how to respond to this question. Saying *I don't know where your mother is* would only lead to more questions I couldn't properly answer. As for her father, I wasn't about to tell her the police thought he had either killed or kidnapped Josie. Micah hadn't done a thing to her.

It felt like someone had set up my son. But who would do that, and why? And where the hell was Josie? In answer to Cricket's question, I did what I always did. I deflected.

"Tomorrow is Monday. You get to talk to your daddy."

This usually cheered her up . . . until it was time to end the call and she sobbed herself to sleep.

"But when do I get to *see* him? Why don't I have a *real* family?"

She threw her crayon into the water, making a huge splash. Normally, I'd scold her. Not this time. Instead, I chose her stories tonight. One about being angry and having a bad day, and another about how all families are different. She liked the first one but insisted the second wasn't true.

"A family is a mommy and a daddy and a little girl."

Nothing I said about me, the aunts, and Carly's group also being her family mattered. Understandably, she just wanted her parents. I had to do something about this. Another week had passed, and tomorrow I'd once again have to tell my son I hadn't made any progress on his release.

I was in my bedroom, wondering if there were any spells in the grimoire that could help me find Josie, when my phone rang with a video call alert. Vic, my friend from the Ordinary town we moved here from, texted often but rarely called.

"I needed to see your face and hear your voice," he said the moment I answered.

"Is something wrong?"

He put a hand to his chest. "You wound me. Must there be something wrong for me to call? Are we only allowed words typed on a tiny screen that you can't read until you locate your glasses?"

If that last bit wasn't true, I'd be offended. "I'm sorry. How are you, Vic?"

He slumped in his recliner. "Missing you and Bug Girl *horribly*. Give me details." He twirled a finger in the air. "Beautiful room, by the way. Where are you?"

I took him on a video tour of my bedroom.

"Fabulous," he approved. "What else is happening in witch town?"

I told him I'd taken over running part of the farm and what that entailed.

"And you like all that digging in the dirt?" He made a disgusted face. Vic was a neat freak and a bit of a germaphobe.

"I love it. From planting the seeds to harvesting and then drying everything to blend into various products, this is what I've always wanted to do." I didn't mention anything about gray magic. In fact, I hadn't told him about me being a gray witch at all.

"And what will you do with all your wondrous creations?"

I settled deeper into one of the cozy chairs in my sitting area. "Carly has taken over running the family store. I'll sell my products there."

"Very enterprising." He leaned closer to the camera. "Now, tell me, are you still happy with this move?"

That was a complicated question. "It wasn't really a choice, Vic. You know that. I needed to take Cricket somewhere she'd be safe."

"And is she?"

"Physically, yes. Emotionally, she really misses Josie and Micah. The kids at preschool, who she adores overall, have been saying she doesn't have a real family." Either he was too choked up to comment or we lost connection because it appeared the screen had frozen. "Vic?"

He shook his head and tapped his fingers against the base of his throat. His sign that he was *verklempt* and needed a moment to pull himself together. Finally, he said, "Poor little bug. I never dreamed this would affect her that way."

"I didn't either. I need to fix this."

He cocked his head. "What are you going to do?" He looked down at something on the side table next to him.

Unbelievable. "Are you taking notes? You promised me you wouldn't write about this."

"Not verbatim."

"Victor!"

He gasped and placed his hand over his heart. He hated when anyone used his given name. "There's some good stuff here, Dusty. I promise I'm not writing *your* story, but that truth is stranger than fiction thing is in full force right now." He dramatically set down his pen. "Fine, I'm not taking notes. Now for the most important question. When can I come and visit you? I'm available next weekend."

"Why? So you can dig up more details for your novel?"

His hand went to his heart again. "That hurts."

"Not as much as you using our trauma for your best seller."

He smiled and took on a faraway expression. "Best seller? You really think so?"

"I can't believe you."

"That's not why I want to come. You know how much I love you and Bug Girl."

I wanted to believe we were the reason he wanted to come. The way he oozed enthusiasm for this novel he'd been talking about for the past year, however, I knew we weren't the only reason. Or even the main one. Could I trust he wouldn't inadvertently give our location to the wrong people? Should I? Someone had set up my son, burned down my house, and threatened my grandbaby. As far as I was concerned, until I figured out who that was, I couldn't trust anyone completely. Except my family. Which included the property.

"Now isn't the best time," I said. "There's a bit of trouble going on in witch town at the moment."

"Trouble?" His eyebrows arched to his hairline.

I swear, he was like a cat with a rat. "Someone died."

"*Another* death?" He waited for me to say more. When I didn't, he pressed me for details. Subtly. "I assume this wasn't death by natural causes then."

He wasn't going to let this go. What to tell him? As little as possible was best. "The police think it was an accident. A woman drowned in the river. Unfortunately, that happens near bodies of water."

"The *police* think. But you think differently."

Time to change the topic. "I'd love you to come for a visit. If you come next weekend, you can help pick apples."

I forced my expression to remain neutral. Picking apples would require being outside, potentially getting dirty, and possibly working up a sweat. Three things Vic despised.

"I could keep an eye on Bug Girl."

"Sure. She's excited about picking apples. You could help her."

He sighed hard. "When *can* I come?"

"The last weekend of October is Harvest Fest. There will be hay bales, cornstalks, and pumpkins everywhere. Very Hallmark. You'll love it."

He pointed at me. "That sounds promising. But if I decide I can't survive another day without a Dusty and Cricket fix, I might show up sooner."

Why the sudden fascination with us? Vic and I had been friendly for a while now, but we never did anything together outside of work. It had to be the inside track to a safe town. A burning sensation flared in my chest again. Nowhere near as powerfully as when Adrianna was telling me her story, but if Vic was using our friendship for personal gain . . . I wouldn't stand for it.

CHAPTER 15

*a*fter dropping Cricket off at Autumn's farm, it took all my willpower to not scurry up the stairs to The Sanctuary. There were still plenty of garden chores to take care of. Bamboo support stakes and tomato cages to pull out, clean, and put into storage. The weeds never seemed to stop growing, even in the cooler months. And Jett insisted we plant a cover crop in the garden, which needed to be done now if it was to have enough time to establish before the weather turned.

"A cover crop protects and amends the soil. In the spring, it will be so loose planting will be a breeze."

Despite the still long list of work to do, all I could think about was making my way through the books in The Sanctuary's bookcase and reacquainting myself with my passion to blend and create.

The farm will sleep soon enough, I reminded myself repeatedly. *Then you'll be free to do your thing.*

By lunchtime, we had checked quite a lot off our list, so I told the crew they were free to take off early today if they wanted to . . . and silently pleaded they would. Some opted to stay a little longer to finish whatever they'd been working on, but most took me up on the offer. They'd worked hard all summer and were also looking forward to the darker, quieter months.

Before going up to my room, I stopped to see how Carly was doing in The Apple Barn.

"The spell isn't working," she complained the moment I walked in.

"Why?" I asked. "What's wrong with it?"

"It's too literal. Good thing we're not open today. This is a disaster." She pointed at the nearest display, which held apple products. Items carved from apple wood. Dish towels with apples embroidered on them. Small apple earrings. The list went on. "Go ahead. Pick something up."

The dish towels were closest, so I grabbed one. The instant it was in my hand, it flew back to the table, perfectly folded and precisely placed. I tried it again with a jar of apple butter on the next table over. Same thing. The jar was ripped from my hand by some unseen force and returned to the shelf.

"I rearranged a few displays before I left Saturday night," Carly explained. "Placing the display units randomly rather than in straight lines will force customers to wander. I walked in this morning and everything was back in tidy rows. I tried explaining my vision, hoping the store would cooperate, but now I can't move anything." She tried, unsuccessfully, to give the apple product display a shove. It wouldn't budge. "Are you laughing?"

"Well, come on, Carly, it is funny. I mean, we knew their magic was wonky but . . ."

She glared at me, then sighed and joined me in a good belly laugh.

I wiped my eyes. "They must have worked in a kill switch to reverse the spell."

"Mom is on the way."

A literal second later, the elder witch walked in. After Carly repeated the demonstration she'd done with me, Comfort pulled a bright blue pencil from deep beneath the register counter. She snapped the pencil in two. That must have been the kill switch—an item charmed to turn off a spell if the item was destroyed.

Comfort frowned. "Not sure what happened. We used the same enchantment we put on the diner."

"That was fifty years ago," Carly complained.

"Thirty," Comfort corrected defensively. "Regardless, something's obviously wrong. We'll consult the grimoire and make a tweak."

"Maybe we should do this," Carly muttered to me after her mother left. "If it's in the grimoire, all we have to do is follow directions."

I disagreed immediately. "Let's give them one more chance. They seem to really like working on these little projects together. And in the grand scheme of things, this was minor."

"I suppose. Fine, one more chance. But I need to be able to open tomorrow."

"You can open. And actually sell things. She broke the pencil." I picked up the same dish towel. This time the shop didn't take it away from me. Just to annoy, I left it in a heap on the wrong shelf.

"What are you doing this afternoon?" Carly refolded the towel. "Back to the garden?"

I explained we were done early today and almost told her about The Sanctuary. I was dying for her to see it, but considering her space wasn't cooperating, showing off my perfect one probably wasn't a great idea.

"Well, I'm not going to spend my time rearranging just to find the *tweaked* spell still doesn't work," Carly grumbled. "I'll try again after they re-cast. Guess I've got some free time."

"Do you want to do a little investigating?" I asked.

"See if we can figure out who Tracy's killer is, you mean?" She shrugged. "Let's do it."

"Any idea where to start?"

She grabbed her bag from behind the register and flicked off the lights. "At the beginning. We need to know more."

"About what?"

"Tracy's life. In particular, what it's been like for the past three decades. That might lead us to someone who had a beef with her."

"We could talk to her employees. Or friends. Do you know who she hung out with?"

"I do. We'll get to all of them eventually."

"Where are we going?" I asked while she closed up the shop.

"You'll see."

TRACY'S PARENTS lived about ten miles outside of town, tucked into one of the many *coulees* or valleys in the area. On our way there, Carly explained that Tracy had moved back in with them six months or so ago. Her dad had fallen off a ladder while trimming tree branches in the spring. He fractured his right hip and broke his right shoulder.

"Her mom is still super spunky," Carly explained, "but can't handle caring for him and the property by herself. I guess the lease on the house Tracy was renting was about to renew, so the timing was right for her. She had been thinking about moving to a new place closer to her salon anyway so came back here to help until she found someplace she liked."

"Is her mom going to be okay without Tracy?"

Carly waited for an oncoming car before turning left. "I heard he was up and causing trouble two months ago. Tracy moved into her new place about six weeks ago. Except for the obvious, her mom should be fine."

"You're up on all the goings-on around town, aren't you?"

"I was," she agreed. "Then I decided to take over the shop. Now we'll need to rely on Nina for intel."

Tracy's parents' tidy little ranch-style home immediately made me think of my own. The one that burned down. I told Carly that as we pulled into their long driveway.

She gave me an empathetic pat on the knee. "Sorry, Dusty."

Making my awful situation worse, my insurance wouldn't cover arson. So now I needed to decide if I wanted to build a new house on my property or sell the land. The value of the lot, however, wouldn't cover all of my mortgage, and I couldn't afford to pay for a new home out of pocket. It might be time to cut my losses and walk away. At least I'd have the sale of the land to put down on the bank loan.

"You do the talking," I instructed as we approached the front door. "They won't want to hear anything I have to say."

A tiny woman, less than five feet tall, stood on the other side of the screen door. Her nose was red and her eyes bloodshot as though she'd been crying.

"Carly." Her lips pressed into a tight line. As soon as she recognized me, she averted her eyes. "And Dusty. Heard you were back."

It was more an acknowledgement I was standing there than a greeting. Not that I expected to be welcome in their home.

"Hi, Mrs. Slayton," Carly began. "We wanted to stop and pay our respects. And we're trying to figure out for ourselves what happened to Tracy. We understand if this isn't a good time."

Mrs. Slayton. Same last name. Did Tracy ever get married? Married but never changed her name? Or maybe divorced and took back her maiden name?

"You understand," the woman repeated dully, not at all happy with this intrusion, "but you figured you'd come on over anyway. Say what you mean, girl. You want to ask some questions."

Carly shrunk a bit at this. "Yes, ma'am. Sorry. We'll leave."

Mrs. Slayton inhaled deeply. "Go around back to the patio. Richard is resting. All of this has taken a lot out of him."

"You as well, I'm sure," Carly comforted.

She paused and fixed a stare on my cousin. "Go on back. I'll meet you."

"Why did you bring me here?" I complained as we made our way to the backyard. "Awkward doesn't begin to describe this. For her and me."

"Who knows a person better than their parents?"

I tilted my head, eyebrows arched in question.

"Okay, maybe not in your case. You've got to admit this is better than asking random townies in the park about her."

"Fine." I didn't like this at all.

"Hopefully, by the time we leave, Mrs. Slayton will believe you weren't responsible for her daughter's death, and we'll have some answers."

Mrs. Slayton exited the patio door with a pitcher of lemonade in one hand and three plastic glasses stacked together under her arm. The gesture was surely more something that was ingrained in the woman than a genuine gesture of hospitality—offer guests, even unexpected ones, something to drink. It was obvious she wasn't happy we were here. Especially that I was.

"Thank you," I said, accepting the glass she set in front of me on the coffee table. "That's very kind."

"You two think our police officers can't do the job we pay them to do?" she accused as she sat. "Is that what this is?"

"No, ma'am," Carly said immediately. "You may have heard there have been skirmishes between some of the witches and Ordies."

Mrs. Slayton cleared her throat, unhappy with the label as some were.

"I apologize." Carly restated, "Skirmishes between some of

the witches and non-magical town residents. This is personal for us. Folks are saying we witches are bad. I know you don't feel that way."

Mrs. Slayton shook her head. "We don't judge people as a whole. Individuals prove themselves based on their actions."

"You know," Carly continued, "that Tracy has had an issue with Dusty for a long time."

"An issue?" She gave an ironic laugh. "Talk about an understatement. It's been thirty-two years. Tracy was never able to get past that accident."

That was what I'd been afraid to hear. "It affected her that badly?"

Her lips pinched, as though me speaking annoyed her. "Got easier after a few years, but for a while, we didn't think she'd ever stop talking about it." She kept her focus on Carly as she spoke. "It's been, what, fifteen years since Nash Kramer got back from jail, the vet school, and whatever else he'd been up to? That boy was gone a long time, and Tracy pined for him every day." She shook her head sadly. "When he went to jail, it was like the girls the soldiers left behind when they went overseas. Tracy waited for him. Refused to let another man even buy her a drink. Finally, about a year before he showed up back here, she started dating. She said yes to a proposal, then he comes waltzing back into town with all his tattoos. I'll never forget it. We were at The Paddle Wheel, discussing wedding plans. Nash walked in, and with her next breath, she turned to her fiancé and called the whole thing off."

Out of all that, the one thing that stood out to me was the first thing she said. "You said you didn't think she'd ever stop talking about the accident."

She scowled at me, like I was intruding on her memories. "For the first six months, it was literally all she talked about. Nearly drove us crazy. Well, me. Richard got to go to work every day, then busied himself in the garage or yard until bedtime. We seriously considered having her hospitalized because she started in with it first thing when she woke up, repeating the same things over and over. Unless she was eating or something on television caught her attention, she didn't stop. I kept that TV on all day for distraction." She shook her head at the memory. "The doctors were pretty sure that was mostly due to her head injury."

"Head injury?" I asked, fearing the answer.

For the first time, she looked directly at me. "When the boat stopped all of a sudden like it did, she hit her head on the side rail. Ended up with a real bad concussion. Couldn't drive or work or do anything too strenuous for those six months. So she obsessed."

"What did she say about the accident?" I hated making her relive all this. Maybe I could make her forget. The thought had no sooner come to me than I felt a sharp pain in the back of my head. Like a *don't be stupid* smack from the Universe.

Mrs. Slayton went through the minutiae of Nash going too fast, the kids telling him to slow down, the thrill Tracy felt sitting so close to him. She was repeating Tracy's rantings, if I had to guess. Then, "Tracy said there were two witches on the shore."

"Two witches?" Carly repeated.

"*Two witches. Two witches.* She muttered that over and over to herself. Swore she saw you." She jutted her chin at me. "Said, 'Dusty stuck out her hand, then the boat stopped.' That's what she told the police and never wavered from it. Police said a couple other of the kids reported the same thing. That you stopped the boat."

I never claimed otherwise. "What about a second witch?"

"Something about another witch on shore not too far from you." She all but dismissed this as ramblings. "No one else reported there being two of you, so the cops never pursued it.

Because of her head injury, she was seeing double, did for two weeks afterward, so they figured that's all it was."

Or Tracy had seen Marilyn. She had been up near the road, though, not on the shore with me. And Marilyn wasn't a witch.

"Tracy hadn't talked about any of this in years. Thank God. Then she heard you were back. Said you tried to hurt a little boy."

"I did no such thing," I objected immediately. And probably too forcefully. "You're aware that my powers allow me to make something happen or stop something from happening. Right?"

Mrs. Slayton squirmed a little. "You and your mother. That's what I heard."

"You heard right," I stated, trying to keep my anger in check. "That little boy was about to fall out of his stroller and get a head injury of his own."

Challenging me, Mrs. Slayton replied, "If that's the case, then you did a good thing."

If that was the case. She didn't believe me. None of the Ordies did. How would I ever prove my innocence?

She scrutinized me for many long seconds. "Beau says you didn't do anything."

Regarding the boat or the boy? I raised my chin, looked her in the eye, and vowed, "I didn't. Not thirty-two years ago and not Thursday night. At no time in my life have I ever purposely done anything to hurt Tracy or anyone in any way."

The woman's hazel eyes glistened, and when she blinked, her lids pressed out a couple tears. Her voice, however, remained strong and unwavering. "He and that new lady officer came and told us what happened to our girl Friday morning. Early. We hadn't even had our second cup of coffee yet. Richard wanted him to lock you up and lose the key. Beau said he couldn't do that because he didn't have even a hint of a piece of evidence that you'd done anything." She stared blankly into the distance. "That's what he said. Not even a hint of a piece. And now here you are, looking me in the face and telling me you didn't do anything to my girl."

My spine relaxed. I thought she was going to say she believed me. When she didn't, I tensed up again. "Mrs. Slayton, I admit I used magic I wasn't yet in control of that day, but it was completely unintentional. It was a reaction to what I knew was coming. If I hadn't stopped the boat, it is highly likely that your daughter and many of the other kids on that boat would have died. I was only trying to prevent that."

A range of emotions skittered across the woman's face, but she didn't reply.

Carly took over. "Do you know anything about any of the others? We know what happened with Nash and that Beau became a police officer. There were ten in total."

Mrs. Slayton set down her lemonade, held up a finger to indicate she'd be right back, and went inside the house.

"You okay?" Carly asked me, a genuine look of concern on her face.

"Do you suppose there's a way to make an entire town forget what happened?" Mom spelled Beau. Could she do it on a grand scale? "Maybe . . ."

"Maybe what? I don't think I like your tone."

I sat straighter. "Maybe Mom could teach me how—"

"No," Carly insisted, shaking her head. "You don't mean that. Think of the consequence you'd pay."

"Couldn't possibly be worse than everyone treating me like a killer and a pariah. I'm not sure how long I can deal with this, Carly."

Like putting on a mask, the concerned look vanished and an angry one took its place. "How long until you—"

Mrs. Slayton returned then with a spiral-bound notebook, the thick kind with tab dividers. It was swollen to twice its normal size with pages that appeared wavy from water damage and other loose ones that had been stuffed inside. She sat, rested the book on her lap, and placed her hands on top of it.

"Tracy kept track of all of the kids on a regular basis. She kept notes on every conversation they had. She printed out every email or text and taped them in here." Mrs. Slayton pressed her lips together, as though trying to control her emotions. "You'll note that three of these sections are very small. Those three kids died years ago. Natural causes and a car accident, I understand. Two others moved across the country, which explains all the printed-out emails. They said they're doing fine and stopped responding to Tracy's questions years ago. The last two still live in the area." She held the notebook out to us. "I'd like this back, but if you think it'll help, you can look through it."

Carly took the book from her and held it in a way that made it clear she wanted to review it before she'd let me see it. Maybe that was a good idea.

"I appreciate you trying to figure out the truth. Not that I think Beau and this Chapman woman can't do it without you." Mrs. Slayton was obviously done answering questions and reliving horrible events. "Dusty, I appreciate your honesty. I wish I could believe you."

I dug a fingernail into a knuckle and willed the tears prickling my eyes to not fall in front of her. "I wish you could, too, ma'am."

"Like I said, I want that notebook back. And I want to be done talking about this now. It's consumed far too much of my life. I'd like whatever time I have left to be peaceful." She gasped, trying not to cry herself. "As peaceful as it can be without my daughter."

CHAPTER 16

*T*hankfully, Carly didn't say anything to me on the drive back to town. It felt like a ball of red-hot energy was swirling in my chest, and I was afraid if I spoke or moved too quickly, or goddess forbid sneezed, a bolt of gray magic would shoot out of me.

What was I supposed to do? How would I ever get the townies to believe me? Would I ever be able to just live my life in Blackwood Grove without this hanging over me? Because if this was how it would always be, maybe I needed to check out a different safe town.

Was this why Mom was gone all the time or cloaked herself and stayed in the attic or out in the orchard shed when she was here? Maybe I should seclude myself in that shed. Wonder if she'd teach me her cloaking spell.

Except I had to watch over Cricket. She wouldn't like living in a shed. Speaking of whom, it was a little after two when Carly pulled into the mall parking lot. Not enough time to do any more investigating—which, at the moment, was a good thing—and too early to pick up Cricket at the playground.

"Think I'll stop in at the diner," Carly announced. "Want to join me?"

She was trying to be sly about it, but I knew she wanted to check on Nina. And she missed the place. "A cup of coffee sounds good."

Being the gathering spot in town, especially when there was something juicy to talk about, The Comfort Diner was packed with primarily townies when we walked in. As though eager for more gossip, all eyes turned toward the front door. Then they all homed in on me. Some of the casual glances became glares. Tablemates leaned closer together and whispered. Some hid their mouths behind their hands, in case I could read lips, I guessed. Others spoke boldly. And loudly.

"Some nerve."

"She needs to go back to wherever she came from."

"She *needs* to be locked up."

Carly slowed our trip across the building to a turtle's pace. Loud enough for all to hear, she asked, "If they're so afraid of witches, why do they come to a witch-owned business? Don't they realize what we could do to their food?"

When she wiggled her fingers dramatically, eyes bulged and faces paled.

"She's joking." Nina was at our side in a blink. "The Comfort Diner is a neutral establishment. *All* are welcome." She grabbed her mother's arm and ushered us to a tiny table near the diner's retail section. "What's the matter with you? Are you trying to kill my business? This is the best day we've seen here since I took over." She pointed a scolding finger at her mother. "Shush!"

Granny Sadie floated over from the corner near the kitchen door and stood by her young protégé, copying Nina's angry finger pointing. Nina had told us the other night that Granny had been hanging out here almost every day and that she liked it because her ghostly grandmother could guide her without being able to actually speak to her.

"Sorry, honey," Carly said. "I understand your feelings, but perhaps you should reconsider that neutral thing. Sometimes it's important to take a firm stance."

"And remember," I added, "despite the equally divided crowd out back on Saturday, this is a safe town. Most of the people here are witches. Something the Ordies appear to have forgotten."

I envisioned *us* with pitchforks and torches, spewing hate and threatening to take away rights. How would they feel if we turned the tables on them?

I blinked and found Carly staring at me, worried. "What are you thinking about?"

"Nothing," I insisted too quickly. "Is Nina bringing us coffee? I need to keep an eye on the time."

"Dusty—"

I dismissed the warning tone in her voice. "There's nothing wrong with thinking something. The problem comes when you act on it."

"Yes, but if you think something often enough, it starts to make sense, and the next thing you know, you *are* acting on it."

At a nearby table, a customer who was too busy watching me to pay attention to what she was doing knocked her hand against the full glass of water Mia had just set in front of her. I reacted, my fingers spreading wide in a stop gesture. All she saw were my hands.

"Did you see that?" she demanded, standing and pointing at me. "She did that thing with her hands, and she was looking right at me."

Murmurs slowly filled the dining room as people turned to watch every move I made. What none of them saw was the woman's tablemate. She pulled her friend back down to her chair as she mopped up the water that had spilled. Then she tapped the now partially full glass and gave me a small smile. Obviously, I had stopped the whole thing from spilling. The first woman's fear turned to embarrassment. In fact, she mouthed *"Sorry"* at me. But she didn't let the rest of the patrons know about her mistake.

I closed my spread fingers, placed my palms together, and bowed my head at her. "One at a time. That's how you make a difference. Right?"

"Right," Carly echoed. She had seen the exchange.

By the time I'd finished my coffee, the tension coming off the crowd had grown. Like they had on Saturday, the crowd divided into witches vs. Ordies. Once again, they were arguing with each other over *witches are absolutely entitled to equal rights* and *whoever decided safe towns were a good idea had clearly been hexed into believing that nonsense.*

Carly was about to jump out of her skin but said nothing. Instead, she clutched the edge of the table and waited for her daughter to take charge.

Granny Sadie hovered in the middle of the room, not that anyone other than Carly, Nina, and I could see her. She practically glowed red with anger and was vibrating. The patrons must have been able to feel her energy. Not sure what Granny's goal was, but her anger riled them even more.

"You all want to live somewhere together?" someone shouted. "We'll make a big compound for you and fence you all in. Like animals in a zoo. Or freaks in a circus."

He laughed long and loud like this was the cleverest thing he'd ever come up with. The other men at his table fist bumped him in approval.

This pushed Nina to her breaking point. She charged over to the man and literally took him by the collar. "Get out. You three as well. I said we were neutral. If you can't respect that, if you can't agree to play nice long enough to enjoy a meal, don't come back." She faced the crowd as a whole. "That goes for all of you. This is my place, and I make the rules. Abide or go find someplace else to spend your five dollars and occupy a table for three hours while you spread your rumors. And I don't recommend Russell and Maggie's place. They're a mixed couple, remember. Witch and Ordy. The living definition of neutral."

Nina held the door as a few people got up and left. Then she crossed the room and stood by our table like a bodyguard. Her chest heaved, and she propped her fists on her hips in a power pose. "Dang, that felt good."

"I'm proud of you, sweetheart." But Carly's tone made it clear she still wished her daughter had taken a side rather than going the neutral route.

I narrowed my eyes at my cousin. Meaning, *be supportive.*

"Don't worry," Carly said, but to which of us I wasn't sure. "This happens now and then. The Ords get worked up, raise a fuss over something a witch did, and boycott all witch-owned businesses. In about a week, they get tired of having to drive twenty miles to shop, because nearly all of the businesses in town are witch-owned, and they come slinking back. Then you paste a little smirk on your face and in a bless-your-heart way ask, 'How can I help you today?'"

Nina looked at me then. "You need to go."

I checked the time. "I do. Time to get the kiddo."

Nina took my cup. "Refill?"

"How about a cherry lemonade? I can share that with Cricket."

For an instant, I debated sneaking out the back door with my drink, but I'd done nothing wrong. I didn't need to hide.

My confidence got deflated halfway to the playground when Carly came running up to me.

"Just to clarify, she meant she wanted you to leave her diner."

I was so shocked, I literally tripped over my own feet. "She . . . Nina? Why?"

Carly waved a hand at the town in general. "All of this is because of you."

"The anger and fighting? Are you serious? This isn't my fault. Have you forgotten that Ludo Beck was already dead when I got to town?"

She shook her head and laughed in the high-and-mighty way that used to really tick me off when we were in high school. "You think *that's* what started this? Back up a bit." She ticked items off on her fingers. "Josie went missing, your son was imprisoned, your house burned down, your granddaughter was threatened, *and then* a man was found murdered in our family diner. Back up even further. What happened thirty-two years ago that everyone is so worked up about today? What's the common denominator, Dusty? Blackwood Grove has been a great place to live—"

"Really? You were so overworked and stressed out when I got here you looked ready to rock in the corner and suck your thumb. The aunts were causing chaos, and your youngest was vandalizing farms."

She stuck her finger in my face. "Do *not* talk about my children."

"Then don't talk about mine." We stared at each other for a moment, both of us breathing hard. "I'm just saying, don't try and paint Blackwood Grove into a perfect picture. Dad wouldn't have conned me into coming back here if things were perfect."

This time, we both froze.

"Is that what you think?" she asked, stunned. "That he conned you?"

Did I? "I'm not sure what to think, but you said it. Josie, Micah, my house . . . All that happened in a month. One month. And then, when I was desperately in need of help because *everything* in my life was upended, The Council decides the perfect solution is for me to come back here? After three decades? Why now? I don't think it had anything to do with you having a hard time controlling the aunts. Something else is going on."

Carly stood by patiently, letting me vent my frustrations. I expected she'd agree or at least offer a few words of comfort. Instead, she said, "How long until you leave again?"

The question left me momentarily speechless. "As in leave town? Is that what you think?" My anger flared again. "Is that what you've been so crabby about? You still don't trust me. No matter what I say or do, I can't make you believe me. Guess that fits because it seems to be the common theme in this town right now. No one wants to believe the truth."

Again, she stood mutely, her hands hanging at her sides. When I stopped talking, she said, "Get over yourself. Don't tell me you're not thinking about it."

"You know what? You're right. If this is how life is going to be here, with the fighting between the residents and my once best friend not believing anything I say, maybe I should leave." I blew out a slow breath, forcing myself to calm down. "You know, there are times I feel more alone here, with my family, than I ever did in the Ordinary town. Sure, I had to keep my true self hidden, but until recently, my life there had been good. Here, where I should be safe, I'm being harassed every time I leave the farm because people still can't accept the truth about me."

Townies had gathered to watch and listen to us. I spun on my heel and walked away. Fortunately, neither Carly nor anyone in the crowd followed me to the playground. I needed to calm down before Cricket got here. She didn't like it when Lola was upset.

"Focus on your happy place," I told myself when I'd settled onto a bench beneath an oak tree. I didn't have the ability to form a privacy bubble around myself, so it must have been the anger radiating off me that made people keep their distance. "Do I even have a happy place?"

I closed my eyes and immediately my sanctuary filled my head. It truly was my perfect place. And despite my threat to leave, I couldn't go anywhere. Whoever had threatened Cricket, and possibly Josie and Micah, was still out there. Until the person or persons who'd done it was caught, I had no choice but to stay. The orchard shed wasn't appropriate, but I could seclude myself in my new space. I'd be perfectly content there.

"Dusty?"

I opened my eyes to see Autumn standing next to me. She told the kids to play and stood where she could see them.

"What's wrong?" I shot to my feet and looked for Cricket. She was laughing with another little girl and climbing the ladder to the slide.

"Cricket is fine," Autumn began. "I'm so sorry to say this, but she's going to have to stay home tomorrow."

"Why? Is there a problem at your farm?" Then I realized she was only talking to me. Why not have a gathering of all the parents?

"Cricket displayed some naughty behavior today." Autumn cringed, clearly sorry to have to say it.

Naughty? Other than a rare tantrum when she was overtired, I'd never seen her be naughty. "What did she do?"

"She flung Cole's art project across the room." She flicked a finger, letting me know this was a telekinetic naughtiness.

Part of me wanted to cheer. Purposely picking something up and sending it flying that way took a great amount of control. Instead, I tried to brush off what had to be a misunderstanding with a laugh. "She's been having a hard time with levitation. We're working on that."

Autumn shook her head. "They sat down to finger paint, Cricket told Cole he was 'so stupid,' then pointed at his picture and then at the wall. It was deliberate. I pulled her aside and explained that what she'd done was not acceptable and almost called you, but there was only an hour left of our day so decided to talk here instead."

It had been years, decades since I'd had to deal with a problem at school. "Okay. What caused her reaction?"

Autumn blinked. "I'm sorry?"

"What did Cole do to make her angry?"

She chewed her lower lip. "He teased her about you being a gray witch." Before I could respond, she said, "Look, I know you haven't done anything, but this is starting to cause a disturbance."

This meaning me. I was causing a disturbance.

The ball of heat in me flared *again*. "Let me get this straight. The other kids are picking on my granddaughter and she's the one who has to stay home?"

Autumn held her hands up. "Only so I can have a discussion with the other parents. I need to gather my thoughts before I say anything, so my plan is to tell each of them at pickup that we need to have a short meeting before school starts tomorrow. I'm sorry. I didn't handle this well with you. I'm trying to keep Cricket from getting picked on anymore."

I looked down and willed the heat inside me to cool. It did by a degree or two. "All right. I'm sorry I snapped."

She winced again. "It would probably be a good idea for you to talk about anger issues with her tonight."

This said to the woman who was dangerously close to making Mt. Vesuvius look like a Fourth of July sparkler.

I thought about the anger story I read to Cricket last night, and despite the seriousness of the situation, I laughed. "Believe it or not, we have been. This is because she misses her parents."

I hadn't told Autumn the truth about Micah and Josie. Only that they were away for a while.

"And that's completely understandable." She took a step away from me. "I'll call you sometime tomorrow and let you know how things went."

CHAPTER 17

*W*e dropped Cricket's backpack and my purse on a chair on the patio and continued walking toward the orchard. Cricket loved to see the apples hanging from the branches, and it seemed like a nice neutral place to talk.

"Are you mad, Lola?"

Why did I bother to try and hide things from this child?

"I'm not mad." Not at her, at least. "I am upset, though. Miss Autumn told me you had a fight with Cole today."

Cricket frowned and stared at the ground while we strolled among the trees. After nearly a minute of no reaction, I asked, "Will you tell me what happened?"

She ran around the trees, picking up apples that had fallen and carefully setting them next to the closest trunk. "Cole said you were bad because you're a gray witch. I said, no, you're not bad, you're like a witch police. He said you hurt people." Her eyes were wide and innocent when she looked up at me. "Did you hurt people?"

Her expression and four-year-old concern tugged at my heart, but I couldn't talk about that damn boat accident again.

Maybe I'd tell her when she was older, when she'd be able to understand, but not now.

"I did not hurt anyone." I used gray magic to help them not die.

She smiled. "I knew it."

"What did Cole's words make you feel?"

Her smile turned into a scowl, and she touched the center of her chest. "I felt hot right here. That's angry, isn't it, Lola?"

Hot. Like me. "That is what angry feels like. What did you do?"

She repeated almost exactly what Autumn had told me. "I pointed at his picture, then I pointed across the room. I was trying to put his stuff on the art cart, but it went too fast."

Because her emotions amplified her power. Like mine did. "We talked about you using your magic. What did we say?"

Her head dropped forward, and she murmured, "Only in my bedroom. I'm sorry."

"You know that was naughty."

"I know."

"What happens when you do something naughty?"

"I hafta do a punishment."

"Right."

She gave a resigned sigh. "What is it?"

I didn't want her to be angry at Autumn. She was only doing her job and protecting the other kids. "You can't go to school tomorrow."

Tears immediately flooded Cricket's eyes. "But I love school and my friends."

"I know you do. But you did something naughty and could have accidentally hurt your friends." My words faded as I said them. Oh, dear goddess. This was hitting way too close to home.

"I don't want to hurt my friends."

I knelt next to her. "I know you don't, bug. Tomorrow, you

can spend time thinking about what you should have done instead."

She wound around the trees. "Can I draw pictures?"

That was her version of journalling or writing an apology letter since she couldn't spell many words yet.

"I think that's a great idea. You can sit in the kitchen with Pepper or Comfort and draw while I work in the garden."

This whole incident seemed to be harder on me than it was on her. That had been true with Micah too. He didn't often do things that required a punishment, but when I did have to issue one, it disrupted my day as well as his.

"Do you remember what day this is?" I asked as we started walking back to the house.

"Daddy day!" She hugged the closest tree, all thoughts of punishment gone.

While we walked, we talked about the importance of not telling him about her magic. I told her, as I did every time it came up, we needed to keep it a secret until he could see her do it. That way it would be a surprise for him. Cricket liked the idea of having a surprise for her daddy.

Honestly, though, the more that I thought about that, the more I thought it might not be such a big surprise. Micah once displayed telekinetic powers as a toddler by summoning a toy helicopter from a high shelf. He knew about witches and some of the things they could do; everyone did. Living in an Ordinary town, I told him every time the opportunity arose that witches couldn't use their magic where we lived or they'd be punished. He didn't understand why. I told him I didn't either but that was the law, and he seemed to accept it. Because we never talked about either of us having powers, I assumed I was either wrong about that one time or he hid his telekinesis from me. He was probably scared to death after all my warnings about punishments, but witches were taken into custody and never seen again for using even minor magic. I wouldn't let that happen to my boy.

And then there was Josie. I was certain she was also a witch, because I saw her use manifestation a year or so ago. Micah had to know about her skills. And hard as I tried to hide it, I must have slipped and inadvertently done something at some point. That was my track record, after all. So, between the three of us, Micah probably expected Cricket would have powers before she was even born. The surprise would be that at four years old, his daughter was already a strong witch.

At dinner, Jett reported, "We've repaired the hedge."

Gwynne clapped. "How did you do it?"

Eager to share her ways, Jett explained, "We grafted branches the hedge donated from other areas to the damaged spot. Once the grafts were in place, we painted on my special paste and wrapped tree tape around them. Should be fine now."

"But we'll need to cast a spell," Comfort advised. "Right away."

"As in tonight?" I thought of our upcoming phone call. "All of us?"

"It won't take long," Gwynne promised.

"We know what happens on Monday night at seven thirty." Pepper winked at Cricket. She blinked both eyes back at her.

While Comfort called Carly and told her where to meet us— at the spot where our orchard met the Kribs farm, which was very close to her house—the house cleaned the kitchen and the rest of us gathered sweaters and scarves. It was chilly in the shade this time of year, and the sun would be low in the sky when we gathered.

At the hedge, Carly and I stood on opposite sides of the half circle of family members and didn't acknowledge each other. Fights between us were rare, but the aunts generally ignored them and let us work through issues by ourselves. As long as there was no bloodshed. Which only happened once . . . no, twice, but neither time was intentional.

"Normally to cast this spell," Jett said, taking the lead on this, "we would walk the perimeter of the property to be protected. Considering our perimeter surrounds more than a hundred acres, we'll make do with casting a re-protection spell around this particular spot. That's the part in question anyway. Start by visualizing a ring of energy rising up from the ground and surrounding us and this section of hedge."

"What does visualize mean?" Cricket whispered to me.

I tapped her forehead. "See it inside your head like a movie."

She nodded. "What does energy look like?"

Good question. What would she understand? "Like a purple cloud shaped like a ring with little lightning bolts zipping around inside it."

"Okay." She squeezed her eyes shut.

"Now join hands," Jett instructed.

I took Cricket's and Pepper's hands. We stood in silence, visualizing for a few seconds. I was happy to see that everyone took this seriously.

"Keep thinking of that energy ring," Jett said, "and repeat after me. This land is protected."

"This land is protected," we said in unison.

"Nothing and no one can harm it."

We repeated her words.

"No evil may get through."

We said those three lines two more times and that was the extent of it. It took us longer to get here than it took to cast the spell. But as Gwynne reminded me a few weeks ago, magic is fifty percent intention.

When we'd finished, Jett raised her voice. "This land is protected. The wards are secure. So mote it be."

"So mote it be," we repeated.

"What's a ward?" Cricket asked when we were given permission to break the half circle.

She was asking tough questions tonight. I knelt on the ground and drew four circles in the dirt. "Pretend the circles are purple energy clouds." I drew lines between the clouds, forming a square. "Now pretend that square is your bedroom. The clouds are the wards, and they protect you and everything inside the square."

"I want that," she said seriously.

"We don't need wards in our bedrooms because we have wards all around the farm." I asked the aunts, "Where are the wards anyway?"

I figured they were special trees, or something buried beneath the ground. But then everyone looked at me like I was joking.

Gwynne pointed at the hedge. "Why else would it be so important to fix the break and cast the protection spell so quickly?"

My face heated with a blush. Of course. We were completely protected within the hedge. What about the town? Were there literal wards around it, or was it simply the law that stated witches were free to practice magic at will within the safe towns that kept us safe? I wanted to ask but also didn't want to embarrass myself further so let it go. Fortunately, the alarm on my watch went off. Micah time.

"We need to get back."

Cricket and I waved goodnight to the Flasch family and speed walked down the path that ran parallel to the hedge and straight to The Apple Barn.

"Start Cricket's bathwater please," I called out as soon as we'd stepped inside the house. We used to talk with Micah during her bath. But that gave her time to start missing him again before I read her stories. Now, using Carly's suggestion, we did her bath using a lavender and mint herbal sachet to help make her drowsy and got her into her jammies before he called. She was warm and cozy when she got beneath her blankets, and by the time they finished the next chapter in the story they were making up together, she was drifting off. This meant I got less time to talk to my son, but if it meant Cricket didn't cry herself to sleep, it was worth it.

"Are you having any luck getting me out of here?" Micah asked after they finished talking. My pause said all I couldn't. "Nothing. Are you even trying?"

"Of course I'm trying, Micah." This was a much harder task than I thought it would be. "Last time, we talked about trying to find Josie first."

"Right. If we find her, it'll prove I didn't do anything to her. Any progress on that?"

I closed my bedroom door and headed for one of my chairs. "There's a lawyer who specializes in this kind of thing. I'm going to talk to her tomorrow."

This was a bit of a stretch. Lucia Valentia was The Council's attorney for witches. If anyone could help me find Josie, she could. I had called her multiple times over the past week, but always had to leave her messages, which she returned, but it was inevitably during times when I was in the middle of something. One night, I finally left her a detailed voicemail. She vowed to look into the situation.

"That sounds promising, I guess." I heard a whisper of hope in his voice. "Where did you find her?"

"My aunts know her." Complete truth with details left off. Would Micah be angry at me when we finally told him my family was all witches, except for Maks, or would he understand why I felt I had to keep it all hidden from him? "How are things going for you?"

This time, his pause spoke volumes.

"Micah?"

"You don't want to hear the details, trust me." Before I could react, he blurted, "I'm physically fine. No one has touched me, but there's pressure to pick a side."

"As in, join a prison gang?"

"More or less. There's one guy here . . . I was able to convince him I didn't do anything to Josie, that I was set up. He believes me, and he's got a little pull around here."

"So he's protecting you."

"I guess, yeah."

The automated voice I'd come to despise announced our one-minute warning.

"Cricket didn't say anything about preschool. How's that going?"

"She loves it and is making friends. A little girl named Isabella is her best friend, I think. That sometimes changes day by day."

He laughed softly. "I say it every time, but thank you for all you're doing for her."

"It's my honor. I promise to have some news for you next week."

"Okay. I love you, Mom."

My voice caught. "I love you, Micah. With my whole"—and the automated system cut us off—"heart."

I took a minute and let myself cry. For the first month, he'd been safe. At least that's what he told me every week, that no one was bothering him. It hurt so much to think of him in that cell. Especially now he was admitting he might not be as safe as he was leading me to believe.

I dried my eyes, blew my nose, and picked up my phone to call Lucia. But it was already after eight and unlikely she'd take my call now. First thing in the morning, I'd summon her. It was a little aggressive, but we'd been playing phone tag long enough.

My plan for after the phone call was to settle in and practice my meditation like I had every night for the past two weeks. But I felt suddenly exhausted from the emotions of the day, and the thought of meditating sounded impossible. Besides, Carly's words kept echoing in my mind. *How long until you leave again?*

As much as I loved this bedroom, I needed my sanctuary. So I pulled on my pajamas, grabbed another piece of the apple crisp Comfort made for dinner on my way through the kitchen, and crossed the courtyard. Before entering the cottage, I told the property, "Keep everyone out, please. But let me know if there's a problem with Cricket."

The sound of chirping crickets sounded in my ear, assuring me the message was received and my little bug was being watched.

My tension eased the moment I stepped over the threshold. My happy place. Or maybe safe place was the better term right now. I wasn't sure anywhere else truly was at the moment.

With my fingers mentally crossed—*please, let the room still be here . . . don't let it have been a cruel joke*—I climbed the stairs. Not only was it still my sanctuary, the fireplace was lit and welcoming crackles bid me to return to the wingback chair. As I sat, a mug of tea appeared on the table with the stack of books I'd been looking at.

I took a bite of the crisp and let Comfort's magic calm me. And then another bite. The warm tea helped soothe me further, and my thoughts drifted to Josie. Up until she went missing, life was good in the Ordy town. I missed my family and was glad to be with them again, but for thirty-two years, I was independent and relatively anonymous. Never once had I needed to defend myself regarding a split-second reaction *to help people.* Sure, there were advantages to performing magic, but I managed to get along just fine without it for all those years.

But what couldn't you do?

I paused, mug to my mouth. Whose voice was that? It sounded like it had layers, like many people were speaking as one. Old and wise . . . Oh! It was the property. The combined voice of all my ancestors who remained here to guide those of us still trying to figure out life. Did the others hear it too?

What couldn't you do, they asked again.

"I couldn't perform magic." I spoke aloud. I didn't like my mind being probed.

Go deeper.

Deeper. Okay. "I had to deny part of myself. But I've dealt with that already. I got along fine without magic."

Your soul too?

My soul? "Was it okay without magic?"

The flames in the fireplace flared for a moment as though we were playing a literal game of hot-and-cold.

Carly and I started mapping out our store in tenth grade. We designed the main area together, and she suggested we should also have our own rooms.

"Space where we can create without distraction or fear of getting feedback before we're ready."

Great idea. My cousin could be a bit opinionated at times.

Along with being the perfect place to create, this room that should have been in our shop, this safe room within the safe town, was also a place where I could speak my truth without fear of judgement.

Holding the mug of tea in my hands and staring into the fireplace flames, I confessed to my room, "Honestly, my soul had been shriveling in the Ordy town. I just can't win, though. Here no one believes me. It's like they're all looking for someone to blame for everything going wrong, and I'm the easy target."

The sound of a crying baby filled my sanctuary. Guess there would be judgement.

"Fine, I get it. Turn that off." The baby quietened. "I'm not feeling sorry for myself, this is a legitimate problem." I drank some tea. "*Am* I the reason things are going wrong?"

The flames shrank to embers. *Getting colder.*

Not the reason. The solid answer provided a glimmer of hope at the end of a very long tunnel.

The fire inside me was heating up again. "You're right; I'll dry up and die if I leave again. Not to mention, Cricket would be in danger, and I'd lose my cousin forever. If I stay, I'll keep facing days like today. What am I supposed to do?"

The flames remained steady, but after a few seconds, my ancestors asked, *What do you want?*

I laughed. "That question has been bouncing around in my brain for the last three weeks."

I drank the still perfectly hot tea and let my gaze scan the room. The books and candlesticks. The jars of ingredients, mixing bowls, and wooden spoons. Crystals, incense, and oils. Baskets and broomsticks. A waiting grimoire, a pot of ink, and a quill. Magic, mystery, and hope. The promise that everything would be all right.

This room was me. I was this room.

Everything I always thought I wanted was right here. Both in this space and in this town. The only things missing were Micah and Josie. There was nothing tying me to the world outside Blackwood Grove. No offense to Vic and my wonderful neighbors.

What do you want? They were getting a bit insistent.

"I want to create. Creams and cures. I want to help people. I want to—"

Say it.

I could reach out and brush the finish line with the tips of my fingers . . . but then the line moved. I couldn't say what I wanted. Not even in this room. Because what if I made the wrong choice again? What if it was too late for me to start over?

CHAPTER 18

The sound of crickets, growing increasingly louder, startled me awake.

"Ow."

My hand went to a crick in the right side of my neck. And then to another in my left hip. The book that had been on my lap fell to the floor when I moved. I'd fallen asleep in the chair while searching for a solution to Adrianna's problem. What time was it?

Light streamed in through the windows. Morning. I slept through the night here in my chair. I stood, yawned, and stretched. Despite the two angry spots, which were already settling down, I felt more rested than I had in months. Was that the magic of my sanctuary or the magic of speaking my truth?

"You can put the fire out," I told the room while I crossed to the stairs.

It obeyed immediately.

With my hand on the railing, I looked around and smiled. "Thank you."

I swear I felt arms surround me in a hug.

"Good morning, Lola!" Cricket leapt off her chair at the table when I entered the kitchen and ran over to give me a hug. Seemed she had slept well too. "Where were you?"

Seven sets of eyes—Comfort, Gwynne, Pepper, Jett, Maks, Granny Sadie, and Freddie—were on me.

I pointed across the courtyard. "I was in the cottage."

Jett grinned.

Comfort's eyes narrowed with suspicion. "In the apartment?"

Gwynne and Pepper stood on either side of her as though completing the wrinkly, witchy version of Charlie's Angels.

"Maybe she's planning to move out again," Jett suggested with a chuckle.

She vowed to not reveal my secret. She never agreed to not be a brat about it.

"She did something," Comfort declared.

"Let's go see." Gwynne stepped toward the back door.

"All right, hang on," I ordered. "Let me get some coffee first."

All of them, Cricket included, gathered around the table and listened while I told them what the property had done.

Maks' eyes lifted to the ceiling and then shifted over to his wife. "I told you they watch us. How else could the property create an exact replica of the room she designed as a teenager?"

Comfort blushed at the *being watched* statement. I did *not* want to know why.

"Will you share?" Gwynne clutched her hands excitedly.

I knew they'd ask. Figured they'd wait longer than five seconds, though.

"I could say no," I answered. "Ask the property to keep you out."

Pepper swatted a hand at me. "We have ways of getting through."

That's what I was afraid of. I'd seen the damage some of their spells had caused.

"There would have to be rules," I insisted, caving to their

pressure despite Jett's stare locked onto me like a cat on a bird. "No rearranging *anything*. If I've got things spread out on the table, don't touch them. If I leave books sitting out, don't move them. And I get to call dibs at any time and kick everyone out."

"Sounds kind of selfish." Gwynne pouted.

But I saw the grin behind the pout. They were baiting me, and I was about to bite the hook. "It is a big space, though, especially since the bedrooms are gone—"

"My room?" Cricket demanded, slapping her outraged little hands on the table. "I loved my room." She giggled when I reminded her the room had been moved from the apartment to where it was now. "Oh, yeah."

"How about this?" I proposed, hoping I wouldn't regret this. "I'm holding tight to the dibs rule, but I could set up a table for you all to use. Maybe back in the corner where my bedroom was."

"We won't be shoved in a corner." Jett raised a rebel fist. Then laughed. "This doesn't concern me. Nice room, but I don't do that kind of magic. Shove them wherever you care to."

"You've seen it?" Comfort asked.

Jett flashed her a smug smile.

"I thought you mixed herbs for the animals," Gwynne stated in a very *not* confused way. "And what about that paste you put on the hedge?"

Jett's grin faded. "I might want to borrow that table in the corner now and again."

"I'm going to get dressed." I waggled a finger between Jett and Cricket. "You two need to collect eggs. And as for the rest of you, you have the attic, which has everything you need. You can go look at my room if you want but no touching. And for the record, I haven't agreed to share anything."

I went to my bedroom to shower and get dressed. Halfway through shampooing my hair, I remembered I was going to summon Lucia. As soon as I was dressed, I called, "Lucia Valentina, I need to see you."

The woman appeared in the middle of my bedroom, toothbrush in her mouth, curlers in her hair, and fuzzy pink pig slippers with curlicue tails on the heels encasing her feet. At least she was dressed in her standard business suit. A beautiful plum color the exact shade of her hair. A pale-pink blouse peeked out from beneath the jacket.

"Good goddess," she exclaimed around her toothbrush. She passed a hand around her head making the toothbrush and curlers disappear. "That was unnecessary."

I stood with my mouth hanging open. "And not what I intended. I'm so sorry. I expected you'd hear me calling and come on your own."

"It was the tone in your voice," she decided. "Or the use of both names. My grandmother would yell that way when we were in trouble. *Please* don't tell anyone. I can only imagine the chaos that could cause."

I promised.

"I assume this is about your son and his girlfriend."

"It is . . . Wait." I twirled a finger at her head. "Wasn't your hair silver gray the last time I saw you?"

She tugged on her jacket lapel. "I like to coordinate. All right, tell me all the details."

We sat in the two comfy chairs in my sitting area. Lucia held out her hand, and a folio notebook and pen appeared on her palm. I started with the day Josie disappeared and told her everything I could remember until the phone call with Micah last night.

"Having a protector, of sorts, in prison could be a good thing," she noted. "We don't want to rely on that for too long, however. Allegiances can change quickly. One caveat before we go any further. According to Council rules, I can only help witches. Micah is your son and therefore has witch blood. That is acceptable. Josie, however . . ."

"I'm ninety-nine percent sure she is also a witch. I never asked her, though, which is why I can't say one hundred percent."

I told Lucia about seeing Josie manifest a toothbrush at my house that time.

She nodded. "That's a pretty good sign. Okay, do you have any ideas for how to proceed?"

The question threw me. I expected her to take charge and tell me what would happen.

As though reading my mind, she said, "I want to see if we're on the same page. I know how I'd like to move forward with this."

I explained my thoughts of finding Josie first. "Trust me, I hate the thought of leaving my son behind bars for even a second longer, but if we find her, there will be no reason to keep him locked up."

"And you're sure he didn't do this?"

Much as I hated that she asked, I understood she had to. "My dreams show me what happened in the past. They're never wrong. He didn't do this."

She finished the note she was writing and closed her folio. "We're on the same page. Since your father is the witch liaison for this town, I will need to share this with him unless you have any legitimate objections."

Did I like him being involved in my life after basically ignoring most of it? No. Did I care? Not really. "Long as this ultimately leads to my son being released, I have no objections."

She stood, straightened her skirt and noticed her feet. Then she scowled at me. "You could have told me I was still wearing my slippers."

I shrugged. "I know people who wear slippers everywhere."

Lucia snapped her fingers, and a pair of plum pumps

replaced the pigs. "I apologize for not getting back to you expediently. There have been some problems with the safe towns."

"I noticed."

"I will talk with your father about this today, formulate a plan, and report back as quickly as possible."

"Thank you. I promise not to summon you that way again."

She placed a hand over her heart, bowed her head in thanks, and vanished from my room.

CHAPTER 19

I opened my bedroom door to find a trio of crones standing on the other side. Pepper raised her hand in greeting. Gwynne looked guilty for having gotten caught doing . . . whatever they were doing. Comfort stood with her head high. Jett must have still been collecting eggs with Cricket.

"What's going on?" I asked.

"We want to help," Pepper announced.

There were many things that could pertain to. "With what?"

Gwynne nudged her sister with her elbow.

"We heard what you and Lucia were talking about," Comfort began.

"Not hard with your ears pressed up against the door," I noted.

Gwynne giggled and then, as though reporting an indisputable fact, said, "We're going to bust him out."

If the past three weeks had taught me anything, it was that anything regarding the aunts and *bust* should never be used in the same sentence. "Him who? What are you going to do?"

Comfort shushed me. "We're going to make a releasing potion that will get Micah out of prison."

A releasing *potion*? I imagined them spraying a smoking, bubbling liquid on the outside of the prison and the wall of his cell slipping off the building. "We can't just break him out. Then he'll be a fugitive, and when they catch him, things will be even worse. You said you heard the plan Lucia and I came up with. We need to find Josie first. She'll explain what really happened, and they'll have to release Micah because she'll provide the alibi he needs."

All three of their backs straightened at this revelation. Then they formed a huddle and whispered softly.

Comfort turned back to me and stated, "We'll cast a revealing spell instead, that will disclose Josie's location."

They could do that? I mean, *could* they? Any number of things could go wrong with what they were proposing. After all, it took two tries to get a simple organizing spell for The Apple Barn to work right.

"How about," I asked, "practicing this on something other than Cricket's mother first?"

"Okay," Pepper decided for the group. "You hide something on the property, and we'll find it."

"Hmm. Not sure I trust the property," I mused.

The sound of an outraged gasp filled the air.

"You know how you get," I told it. "If you're in a mood, you'll either show them without the spell or purposely not let them find it. It would be better to hide the thing somewhere in town."

The silence that followed meant the property agreed with my statement. Or it was busy dismantling my sanctuary.

I thought for a moment longer about their proposal and nearly laughed out loud at the hopeful expressions on their faces. "Okay, let's do the *find the thing* spell before the *find Cricket's mom* spell. What do you want me to hide? Nothing living."

Pepper took a hand thrown ceramic vase from a table in the hallway. "This will work."

"Be careful," Gwynne begged. "Grampy Clay made that."

Clutching the vase closely, I chuckled. It amused me greatly that our grandfather's name was Clay, and he made pottery. It was the little things in life that got you by sometimes.

Before they scampered off, I asked them for clarification regarding gate magic, my label for their dealings with customers at the orchard gate.

"Use your strength," Comfort advised. "Pepper uses salt and pepper for much more than enhancing the flavor of her food."

The Creole woman explained, "I add them to charm bags, witch balls, poppets . . . those kinds of things to help with protection, purification, and banishments. They also aid in reversals, bindings, warding, and elemental magic spells. And they enhance herbs and offerings to the goddesses and gods."

My jaw dropped. "I had no idea."

"Fifty percent intention," Gwynne reminded me. "I create herbal, oil, and crystal blends much like Griselle does. Except I only do positive magic."

Comfort smiled at her cronies. The Cronies. I chuckled. Maybe that's what I'd call them.

"My magic has always involved food," Comfort stated. "Over the years, I narrowed it down to pies, because I love making pies, but my *gate magic* as you call it is almost exclusively recipes for which I supply enchanted ingredients."

Use my strengths. "My magic is dreams and visions. Not sure how to package those and sell them at the gate."

The three of them stared at me.

"You mean blending plants?" I hadn't considered that to be part of my magic. "I could do that."

Gwynne blinked. Pepper raised her eyebrows. Comfort continued staring.

"What?" Oh. My other ability. "I'm working on that. And

before you say it, Mom is helping. She set up The Sanctuary for me."

"Let her do more," Gwynne said with total seriousness and clarity. "Say what you will about my twin's methods, she is a very powerful witch."

After I promised to treat the vase with extreme care, we disbanded. They went off to work on their revealing spell, and I headed to the shed. Jett had told me at the height of summer weeding, watering, and garden tending, she had six helpers scattered throughout the farm: two people working the garden, two tending the animals, and two monitoring and tending the orchard. Now I had one person, Nicola, helping me with the garden while all the others were on orchard duty. Jett had decided to take care of the animals and bees herself.

"How's it going, Nicola?" I greeted my helper.

She was the happiest person, and I absolutely adored her. She loved working in gardens, and was thrilled to take half her pay in fresh fruits and veggies. Her son attended Autumn's school as well, so Nicola empathized with me over Cricket needing to stay home today.

"I spoke with Helios last night," she reported. "Sounds like *the incident* happened exactly as Cricket said. He said if Cricket gets mad again, he'll give her a hug to make her happy." She put her hands to her heart and blinked. Her voice broke as she added, "He's such a good boy."

"Tell him Cricket's grandma appreciates that very much."

Nicola already had all the crates lined up and ready for filling. Preparing the orders was her job. While she did that, I went through our inventory, moved anything no longer suitable for sale to the animal feed bin, and updated our website with inventory counts. I did that every morning. I hated having to tell people we didn't have something in stock when our system said we did.

By the time we were done with our tasks, it was raining.

Hard. Jett had dropped Cricket off with us, and my little bug kept busy playing with the familiars who had also come in out of the rain.

"Okay," Nicola said with an eager exhale, "orders are ready. The packing station is cleaned and sanitized. Anything else you want me to do?"

"The others have probably come in from the orchard, otherwise you could help there. You can call it a day if you want."

She swallowed. "I'm going to miss coming in here every day this winter."

I'd miss seeing her happy face. "Don't get all weepy on me yet. We've still got plenty to do before you're free."

"True. And the dark months pass so quickly. We'll be turning the soil and planting seeds before we know it. Have a good rest of your day, Dusty."

Cricket skipped up to me. "Can we play now?"

"Did you do your feeling drawings yet?"

"Oh, yeah." She shook her head. "Not yet."

"Tell you what, let's have lunch and you can come with me to my new room to do your drawings."

After grilled cheese sandwiches and tomato soup, perfect for the chill-in-the-air afternoon, we splashed through the puddles in the courtyard as we crossed to the cottage.

"Rain boots off," I reminded her as I closed the door.

She blinked at me as though to say, *I know*, and dropped down onto her butt to tug them off. "It looks different in here." She meant the walls were a different color. Wait until she saw upstairs. "No more pink and green?"

I shook my head. "I like those colors, but not where I work."

"I thought you work in the shed and the garden."

"Lucky me." I pulled her to her feet and blew a raspberry on her neck. "I have lots of work places."

She giggled, scampered up the stairs, and gasped. *"Everything is different."*

I couldn't tell if she was entranced or outraged. "I told you it was."

Not caring at all about the rest of the room, she ran to the corner where her bedroom used to be. It now held floor-to-ceiling bookshelves packed full of books, various types of paper, writing utensils, paper bags to hold gate magic spells' ingredients, stickers with witches' knots to seal the bags shut, and so on. One item in particular on the bottom shelf caught her eye. She pulled out the purple cardboard box with ballerinas on it and found *Cricket* painted on the top.

"Why does this say my name?" she whispered.

"I'm not sure. You should probably open it." When she lifted the cover, we found drawing paper, crayons, colored pencils, and water color paints. "Looks like The Sanctuary knows what your job is today."

"Draw my feelings," she said solemnly. "Where will I sit? At the big table?"

"That's where I'll be working. Where would you like to sit?"

She stood and spread her arms wide. "Right here."

Behind her, a child size version of my table and a chair appeared.

"Turn around," I told her with a grin.

She spun and squealed with delight.

"You need to be serious about this now." I set the box on her table. "Using your magic the way you did yesterday wasn't a good choice. Do you know why you did it?"

"Because I was angry at Cole." After a short pause, she added, "And a little scared that they'll make us leave. Then I have to get another new bedroom."

My breath caught. "Why would they make us leave?" Whoever *they* were.

"Cole said you were bad. The police said Daddy was bad and made him go away."

I dropped to my knees and pulled her into a hug. "They won't make us go anywhere."

"But what if everyone is mean to you and you don't want to stay?"

That was a fair question. I wouldn't lie and say we could stay forever, because I couldn't promise that. "Don't worry about that, bug. Today, Miss Autumn is going to talk to everyone about what happened. She's going to call me later and let me know how it went."

She squirmed to get out of my arms. "And then I can go back and play with my friends?"

"I hope so. But you'll have to have your pictures to show everyone."

"I better get busy, then." She pulled out the paper and crayons. After checking inside the little box, she announced, "They're all sharp."

Carly and I were in first grade before we realized Ordinary kids' crayons lost their points.

While Cricket drew one picture after another, I pored over my books, immersing myself in Adrianna's problem. At one point, I had a dozen books open and spread out across the table. Every herb, flower, crystal, stone, oil, or incense that could potentially work for this problem ended up written in my grimoire. I jotted down note after note in the huge book but didn't feel any closer to solving Adrianna's problem. No wonder my mother looked so tired. This was exhausting.

Speaking of my mother, she came up just as I decided I'd never come up with an answer.

"The energy!" she exclaimed. "I could feel it from out in the courtyard. What's going on up here?"

"I'm working on the spell to protect Adrianna from that man."

"Spinning your wheels, are you?" Mom took in the array of books. "Did she ask for protection?"

"Of course—" But did she? I thought back to the conversation we had in Carly's SUV. *I'm not afraid. We have to stop him from doing this again.* "She wants to stop him."

"That will mean a thousand things to a thousand different people. You'll need to trust your instincts to decide what 'stop him' means."

All right. That narrowed the scope.

"Before you do another thing, did you discuss a price with her?"

I shook my head. "What should I charge? A hundred? Two hundred?"

Mom laughed and quoted an amount that nearly made my eyes fall out of my head.

"That's a fortune," I complained. "Talk about taking advantage of someone when they're desperate."

"It's not taking advantage," Mom insisted in her dry voice. "It's ensuring this isn't an emotional or spontaneous decision. The price for a potentially life-altering spell should not be based on the amount in someone's bank account. And undercharging is the same as them taking advantage of you. Set the price. Make it worth your time and the consequence you'll pay afterward." She gestured at her horribly creased face. "If they're not willing to pay, it's not important enough to them, and it shouldn't be important enough to you no matter the situation."

All of that made sense. I sent Adrianna a text with the price, said I'd only accept cash, and asked if she wanted to proceed. Her response came less than a minute later.

Yes, absolutely. When will it be done?

I had no idea. *I can't rush this, it's too important. I'm working on it and will text you when it's ready.*

"Very good, Dusty," Mom praised. "I understand the first one is hard. Now, set aside your feelings and emotions. Your job is to help Adrianna do what she wants to do regarding her situation. What does that mean?"

"To stop this man, this predator, from ever assaulting anyone ever again."

"Distill that to the fewest words possible. It keeps your goal clear in your mind."

"To stop a sexual predator."

"Good." Without another word, she shuffled across the room to Cricket who didn't appear to be at all afraid of her great grandmother anymore. Mom sat next to her, and Cricket immediately started talking to her and showing her the drawings she'd made.

I turned my attention back to Adrianna. Help her stop a predator, keeping my feelings and emotions out of the equation. Considering what my scumbag ex did to me, remaining neutral would be hard. He was a con artist, not a predator. He stole all my college tuition money and left me pregnant and humiliated. All these years later, I was still furious with him. I can't imagine what I'd be feeling if he'd done to me what this man had done to Adrianna and the other woman. Good thing I didn't know who he was because then I might not be able to set my emotions aside.

Help Adrianna stop him. That was the fifty percent of this spell I needed to take care of. I'd provide plants, essential oils, crystals, or whatever else I felt would do the job. Since magic was half intention, the other fifty percent was up to Adrianna.

Before long, the entire second page of my grimoire was filled with options. (I'd claimed the book by signing the first page: *Property of Dusty Rose Warren Hotte.*) I could give Adrianna a few of the options and let her choose the one that would best fit her intent. I liked that idea. Some of the plants were deadly, though, and even though I was supposed to keep my feelings out of this, I'd have a hard time living with myself if I gave her something that would kill the man. There were countless ways to do that without getting me involved if death was her goal. I wasn't a hit woman.

So, what should I do with all these options?

Distill that, Mom had said.

Okay. The best way to stop someone from repeatedly doing something was to either incapacitate them or make them learn a lesson. I was a big fan of learning lessons. Like my dear little Cricket was doing today. She liked drawing but didn't especially like thinking about her feelings. Hopefully, this drawing exercise would teach her a lesson about using her magic inappropriately.

What would teach a predator a lesson?

I again scanned all the open pages before me for options. Datura caused hallucinations. Not quite sure what Adrianna could do with that. *Cnidoscolus aconitifolius,* also known as *mala mujer*—which ironically translated to *bad woman*—released a toxin that would drive the man crazy for hours with a nasty case of stinging, burning, and itching. Applied to the appropriate area, that could teach a powerful lesson. A tea made from the same plant reportedly decreased sexual desire, although a sexual assault had nothing to do with desire, it was about control. The seeds from the *cerbera odollam,* or suicide tree, were highly toxic and would likely cause death. Not what we were going for, so I closed that book.

What else?

My phone rang before I could look at anything else. Autumn's name was on the caller ID.

"Hi, Ms. Hotte," she greeted when I answered. "Is this a good time to chat?"

I confirmed it was, and she told me she had spoken with the parents and kids at pickup yesterday. The parents all agreed to talk to their kids at home last night and then they had a group discussion this morning at drop off.

Wonder why Nicola hadn't mentioned that. Of course, she'd

needed time to pull herself together after saying Helios would give Cricket a hug the next time she was mad.

"The parents are on your side," Autumn continued.

"All of them?" I asked.

"You sound surprised." I could hear the smile in her voice. "You shouldn't be. These families all have at least one witch in them. They understand you weren't able to practice your magic for many years and are now getting back into it."

My cynical side told me this sounded like a well-spun way to keep me happy. Goddess forbid, don't make the gray witch angry. My reasonable side decided Autumn deserved a lot of credit for her efforts. She took the time to talk with everyone, and that couldn't have been easy for her. Autumn didn't like conflict. At least not the kind that came from adults.

"Did you talk with the parents about the dangers of saying these kinds of things in front of their kids? We all know how fast words can spread." Like a rash from a mala mujer plant.

"Oh, gosh, I didn't get into that. The kids are my realm, not the parents."

"But one of the kids—"

"Heard it from their parent and said it to Cricket," she completed my thought. "I understand your concern. I told the group as a whole I didn't want that kind of language being used at my school and warned them that any child who said it would have to stay home the next day. And then for two days if it happened again. I'm hoping the parents received and respect my message."

Suppose I couldn't ask for much more. "So, no more teasing, and Cricket can come back tomorrow?"

"The kids are very sorry she got upset and promise not to say anything about bad witches or gray witches again. Isabella and Helios were especially sad Cricket wasn't here today." She paused. "One thing, though. Cricket has to say she's sorry to Cole, and she can't use her magic that way again. Honestly, it took me completely by surprise. I've never had a four-year-old who was so skilled."

"Pretty sure Cricket surprised herself too." I explained that Cricket was making drawings of her feelings today. A decent stack sat on her table. "She'll bring them tomorrow."

"Oh, that's perfect. We'll have a group discussion."

Great. More talk about feelings. Cricket would be thrilled.

CHAPTER 20

*a*fter ending the call with Autumn, I sat across The Sanctuary from my mother and granddaughter and watched them bonding. Mom listened with full attention while Cricket pointed out things on each drawing. When Cricket became too emotional, Mom put a hand on her back. She even pulled her onto her lap at one point and held her. It was an extraordinarily touching scene and not only because of the tenderness she showed my girl. It touched my heart to see Mom be so caring.

Then my warm heart chilled again. Had she ever been that way with me?

Shortly after four o'clock, I got another surprise. Carly climbed The Sanctuary stairs.

"It really does look like what you described as a kid." She wandered the perimeter, her fingertips skimming over items on shelves and on top of cabinets.

"The Apple Barn could match your vision, too, you know. You can do it yourself, or you could ask the property for help."

"I could," she said noncommittally. Then she jutted her chin toward Cricket's corner. "What's going on over there?"

"Cricket is serving out her punishment for using magic inappropriately at school. Mom showed up a couple of hours ago, gave me two minutes of guidance on Adrianna's problem, and has been sitting right there with Cricket ever since. I think she even drew something herself."

"I'd pay to see what it is." She waited a beat, then said, "I hear a bit of irritation in your voice."

I sighed and indicated the mess all over my table. "I'm having a hard time figuring out a solution for Adrianna. This is a big deal for her and me."

"You could ask your mom for more help." Her echo of my words from moments ago held a teasing tone.

My face flushed. Time to change topics. I swept my hand grandly across the room. "Welcome to The Sanctuary. How can I help you today?"

"You make it sound like a store. I thought this room was supposed to be your private space where all your creating happened."

"Seems I can't stop family. The aunts have already requested a table in the far corner."

"Even though they have a whole house and the attic?"

That was basically what Jett said with her *You're a better woman than I am* comment. I was far too nice. "You're right. This is my space. Cricket is the exception. The rest of you can pop up for a visit, unless the door is locked, and then get out." I pointed dramatically at the stairs.

Carly's lips twitched with a smile. "I am here for a reason. Tracy's salon has been closed since Friday, but I heard they're open today. Thought we could go talk to her employees before they close at six. Maybe we can get some more insight into Tracy. Like who she hung out with, was she really cutting back on her drinking, who might have had it in for her. That kind of thing."

I narrowed my eyes at her. "I thought you didn't trust me. Why are you so interested in helping me?"

She shook her head as she spoke. "It's not that I don't trust you. I don't trust you're not going to skip town again. Can you promise you won't leave?"

Honestly, I couldn't. I was fairly sure Cricket was safer here. My life, however, wasn't better. The wood burning in the fireplace released a loud pop, and I remembered my ancestors asking how my soul had been in the Ordinary town.

"There's a lot at play regarding—"

"That's what I thought." Carly stiffened. "Regardless of whether you're staying or going, you're here now. Someone needs to figure out what's going on in this town."

At least we agreed on that.

My mother agreed to bring Cricket to the house and said she'd stay with her. Cricket was excited with this plan.

She whispered in my ear as she hugged me goodbye, "She's not so scary anymore, Lola."

Anymore? "Do you remember seeing her before?"

"Silly, Lola. Inside the house with the aunties. And one time —" Her words cut off, and her smooth brow wrinkled with confusion. "I can't remember."

Must be the cloaking spell.

It was still raining lightly, so we grabbed umbrellas for the walk to Hairitage. Before we left, I stopped in my bedroom and got Grampy Clay's pot, now wrapped in a fluffy blanket and encased securely in a metal ammunition box Maks had in the red barn.

"What's that?" Carly asked.

I told her about the test run for the revealing spell.

"Good plan. Who knows what they'll end up exposing."

I tucked the box between a shrub and the Silver Moon Apothecary building and then stopped inside to let Silver and Moon know it was there.

"It's like being involved in a secret mission," Silver said covertly, tapping her fingertips together. "Thanks for the heads up. I'll let Moon know."

As the rain pattered on our umbrellas, Carly told me she'd done some other investigating. "I talked with the two classmates from the boat who still live in town. Vicki and Duane."

"Cheerleader and football player," I recalled after some thought. "What made you decide to talk to them?"

"Two reasons. The rain made for a very slow day, so I took a break between making changes to the barn."

"How's it coming? The barn."

"It's a work in progress." A small smile flashed across her face. "Every little tweak helps."

I was excited that she was excited about this new venture. "If you want any opinions, let me know. What's the second reason?"

She stared straight ahead. "Because I know it's hard for you to keep talking to people about the accident."

A warm gush of appreciation flooded me. I was grateful she understood.

She continued, "They also saw two people on the shore. Like Tracy supposedly did. It was a little strange."

"What do you mean?"

"It was almost like they were spelled. They used almost the exact same words. Vicki said, 'I saw Dusty and someone else on shore, but they must have been in the shadows because I couldn't say who it was.' Then Duane said, 'I saw Dusty with her hand out, so I knew she stopped the boat. There was someone else, too, but they were all shadowy so couldn't tell who it was.'"

"Sounds like Mom spelled more people than Beau."

"What are you talking about?"

I scanned my memory. "Didn't I tell you about the dream I had? The one where I saw Mom in Beau's hospital room? She put a memory spell on him to forget the details of the accident?"

Her jaw tightened. "No, you didn't. I would definitely remember that."

"Sorry, it wasn't purposeful. There were other things going on then. And Pepper convinced me it was just a regular dream, not a prophetic one."

"Retrocognitive."

"A what?"

"Turns out, the mind wanders through lots of topics while doing menial tasks, like sorting through stockroom inventory. For some reason, I thought about your dreams and then did a bit of research. *Prophetic* by definition means foretelling or predicting the future. Your dreams are of the past. Precognition means knowing that an event will happen. Retro or postcognition means knowing about something that happened in the past you couldn't have known about or weren't there to experience."

"In other words, the power I always thought I had—"

"Is still the same power. Don't be dramatic. It was simply mislabeled."

I mulled that around in my brain for a bit. "I think I like your definition better. We'll need to note this in the family grimoire."

She perked up at that. "Cool. I've always wanted to add something to the book."

"Back to Vicki and Duane. They must have seen Marilyn by the river that day. Another reason for Nash to stay mute about the accident. It's one thing to put the blame on me—"

"But another to admit your mother might have been involved."

I shook my head. "I don't know what Duane and Vicki think they saw, but Marilyn couldn't have done anything. She isn't a witch."

Inside Hairitage we found two customers and three employees. A man with black eyeliner and nail polish sat behind the desk.

"Good afternoon, ladies." He scanned the computer and murmured, "We don't have any more appointments scheduled for the day and do accept walk-ins. Would you like haircuts or another service?"

I glanced at his nametag. "Hi, Ari. We were hoping to talk with someone about Tracy."

He tilted his head to the side in question. "I know you, Carly. Who are—"

"She's the witch who started all this," called out a woman engulfed in a cloud of hairspray thanks to her stylist.

I smiled at her and held a finger to my lips. Her eyes went wide, apparently believing I had the power to silence her. Guess I did because she didn't say anything else, although it had nothing to do with magic.

"We're trying," Carly said, "to understand Tracy better. We went to high school with her, and although she and I crossed paths over the years, we didn't really know each other."

The *silenced* woman stood by the door clutching her bag to her chest while her stylist, a woman with a perfect 1970s Farrah Fawcett hairstyle, charged her card. The stylist asked, "What's your angle? What are you up to?"

"We're just trying to figure out what really happened," Carly stated. "Dusty did nothing to her that night at the saloon except defend herself in an argument." She looked skyward. "May lightning strike me here and now if I'm lying."

The woman by the door yelped and ran outside without her credit card. Her stylist gasped and stared wide-eyed at the ceiling.

"Good gods," Carly muttered under her breath. "We know someone attacked her Thursday night but haven't been able to prove anything."

Farrah ran after the woman, credit card in her outstretched hand.

The other stylist had braided bangs that hung in her eyes

and a silver nose ring with a dangling pentacle piercing her septum. She asked, "Are you two private investigators or something?"

I shook my head. "Just trying to clear my name in the hopes that will help settle things around town."

"Thanks, Zavia." Her customer handed her some bills. "No change. See you in a few weeks."

My spine stiffened as Zavia turned off the *Open* sign and locked the front door once her customer left. Either Ari was pressing a hidden alarm button behind the desk to summon the angry mob or we got lucky and were talking to the exact right employees.

"What do you want to know?" Zavia asked.

"Whatever you want to tell us." Carly took a step away from the desk as though giving them the stage.

"She was a good employer," Ari began respectfully. "Not too demanding. Understanding when personal things came up."

"That's because," Zavia offered, "she needed us to keep the place running for her after a night of too much imbibing."

"Zavia," Ari scolded.

"I'm not disrespecting her. Yes, she was trying to pull it together, but you know she slipped now and then. I'm the assistant manager here . . . Guess I'm the manager now."

"And the owner," Ari pointed out.

I immediately wondered if Zavia killed Tracy to gain control of the salon. Stranger things than that happened in towns this size.

"Tracy's parents were her beneficiaries," Zavia explained, "and want nothing to do with the salon. They told me on Saturday they're going to sign it over to me. They want nothing as long as I agree to take it over as is." Zavia smiled fondly. "Nice of them, but I wish it was under different circumstances."

Glad my suspicious brain was wrong this time.

"You said she was trying to pull it together," I noted. "What does that mean?"

"She could be a little . . ." Zavia looked to Ari.

"Reckless," he concluded, on board with his boss in speaking the truth. "Like Zavia said, Tracy was trying to clean up, but when she drank, it was always one too many."

"Perfect way to put it," Zavia agreed. "One too many, then she'd go for a walk by the river."

Carly and I both straightened at the declaration.

"We know that's where they found her," Ari said.

Zavia shook her head, long braided hair swaying with every move. "I couldn't even guess how many times I told her not to do that. She'd go stumbling out of The Paddle Wheel or the hotel bar and go straight across the street to the river."

Ari was staring at us. "You said someone attacked her. Do you know this for a fact? The police haven't said anything to us."

Neither of us answered.

"If it helps," Zavia said, "we're both witches. Totally on Team Dusty." She mimicked shaking pompoms.

"Truth." Ari held a hand in the air as though taking an oath.

"I had a dream," I told them, "and Carly scried. We both saw the same thing."

Carly nodded, subdued. "Someone held her under the water."

Ari's hands went to his heart.

Zavia's eyes closed. "That's awful. Any idea who?"

"The only thing we know," I explained, "is that the person wore tan leather work gloves."

"With something on the cuff," Carly added, touching her outer wrist.

"Like a logo?" Ari asked.

"A logo?" Carly repeated. "Yeah, that could be."

"Or maybe a brand farmers put on their cattle?" Zavia asked. "Every farm around here has a brand."

My eyebrows shot up. "Very good questions. I'm not sure. I need to try to bring on another retrocognitive dream."

I winked at Carly as I tested my new label.

"You're a retrocog?" Ari practically swooned. "That's so cool."

My ability even had a nickname? How many people knew about this? Clearly not my family or someone would have corrected me. I hoped.

"And you can bring on the dreams?" Zavia gave me the same look of respect. "*Very* cool."

I felt myself stand a little taller.

"Anything else you can think of?" Carly asked.

The two cosmetologists shook their heads but promised to talk it through and would let us know if they came up with anything.

"And let me know," Zavia told me, "when you're ready for a haircut. I've got openings next week."

"And I can help you both put a glow back on your faces," Ari offered. "I do the skincare here."

Now that he'd said that, I noticed he had a flawless complexion. Carly and I touched our faces, looked at each other, and shrugged.

"Monday at four thirty?" Carly asked me.

"Sure. And book something for my granddaughter too. She's four. She could use a trim and would love a bit of pampering."

Ari's fingers flew over his keyboard. "Done. See you Monday."

CHAPTER 21

*W*hen we got back to the farm, we found a shelter tent, the kind with no sides, set up on the patio to protect the chairs and table from the rain. Two glasses, a bottle of wine, and a plate with cheese and crackers appeared as we approached. Apparently, we were supposed to sit for a while.

"Okay," Carly agreed before we were even beneath the structure. "I can stay for one glass. Then I should get home and check on my rug rats."

While we sipped and nibbled, I twirled my glass and watched the wine swirl around inside.

"What are you so deep in thought about?" Carly asked.

"Adrianna," I mused aloud. "She said her attacker put something in her drink. And people keep reporting how Tracy had been trying to cut back on her drinking."

"Right. Stella was surprised Tracy got to that state off of one weakly mixed drink."

"Exactly." I held my glass still. "What if she hadn't had anything to drink before coming to the saloon and someone put something in her drink?"

"You think Adrianna's attacker and Tracy's killer are the

same guy?" Carly wondered. "It's possible. We should mention it to Leezza."

Then I switched topics and told her about my discussion with Lucia that morning. "Up until now, I had convinced myself Micah was okay. The alternative was too hard to think about. But now I'm worried about him. I *have* to find Josie."

Carly sat with her legs crossed and casually kicked her right foot. "I might be able to help."

I nearly leapt out of my chair. "Really? You mean by scrying?"

A little embarrassed, she admitted, "I've done more practicing since the night at the houseboat. And I didn't tell you, but I did some while Beau had me locked up for Ludo Beck's murder. I had nothing to do in that cell and convinced Leezza to let me keep this small stainless-steel bowl my breakfast came in. Add some water and . . ."

"You've got a reflective surface to gaze into."

"Like you with your meditation, I've been trying to train my brain to pick up on helpful information." She swirled her hands around in a mystical sort of way. "We are all constantly putting information into the Universe. It's out here, floating all around, free for the taking if you can latch on to it."

I gazed from my right to my left, wondering what exactly was floating around me. "How's it going?"

She shrugged. "I can put myself into a relaxed state pretty quickly. Narrowing in on my target is still giving me troubles. Don't tell him, but I've been trying to get information on Sebastian. He carries that notebook with him everywhere, won't tell me a word about what he's written or even let me touch it. I don't need to know every detail, but I'd like to know if there's something going on with my kid that I should be worried about."

"Hang on. I'll be right back." I raced up to The Sanctuary and pulled a book titled *Divination: Learn to Connect with Your Higher*

Self, the Collective Unconscious, and the Spiritual World from one of the bookshelves.

"You have a how-to book on Divination?" Carly asked, amused.

"Did you notice all the books up there? I think I've got a book for every kind of magic known to witchkind." I flipped to the chapter on scrying. "Good that you can relax so quickly. That's the literal first step. There are tips for helping with that if you need them. It says to place divination oil on your pulse points. There's a recipe for the oil here. You can light your favorite incense, candle, or herb bundle. Play some music or try a singing bowl."

"Not a singing bowl. I can never make the thing sing and focus on relaxing at the same time."

Smiling, I continued, "Wrapping yourself in a cozy blankie is always worth a try. Unless it's a hot day. Oh! There are recipes for relaxation tea. You can have some of mine if you want to try it."

She held her hand out. "Can I borrow your book?"

"Sure." I watched her flip through the chapter, nodding her head at whatever she read. "You're really going to do this? Look for Josie, I mean."

She closed the book and held it on her lap. "We're family, Dusty. I'm still scared you're going to leave me again, but your boy is in trouble, and we have no idea what's going on with Josie. I might be able to help and am pretty sure my ability won't make things worse."

I didn't know what to say so placed my hands over my heart in thanks.

"I'm going to head on home and practice some more." She stuffed the cork into the wine bottle and held it by the neck. Taking it with her apparently. "Fortunately, Nina is in her room by eight, so she can be up at four. Emma is a studying fanatic. Alex blasts through his homework and then is either over at the

Kribs farm or texting with Savannah all night. Never know what I'll get with Sebastian. He either follows me around the house all night or disappears into his room right after dinner."

I held my wine glass up. "Here's hoping for the latter so you have time alone."

She clinked the bottle against it. "If I don't see you before four o'clock tomorrow, should we plan to talk with the folks at The Paddle Wheel after work? See what they have to say about that night?"

"Sounds like a plan to me."

"And then tomorrow night, I'll try to connect with Josie. Water is my preferred reflective surface. Crystal balls never worked for me, flames bother my eyes, and mirrors freak me out. If I see something reflected in it, I'm always sure it's hovering behind me." She shivered. "I want to try the pond."

The one on the other side of our garden. "Big surface and possibly infused with ancestor energy. Brilliant."

THE NEXT MORNING at the preschool, Autumn flipped through all the pictures Cricket drew yesterday. Every image consisted of mostly circles, straight lines, and scribbles, but the meaning behind each was obvious.

"These are very good, Cricket," she praised. "I can see that you were angry and scared." She held up one in particular. It was of a group of people standing together with a smaller person standing alone off to the side. The lone person had long dark hair and was surrounded by yellow lines that Cricket said were lightning bolts. "Are these people you know?"

She pointed at the smaller figure. "That's me. Everybody else is Lola and my aunties."

I smiled. She drew a picture of her family? Were Micah and

Josie on there? "I don't remember that picture, bug. When did you draw it?"

"This morning before you waked me up."

"Why are you standing way by yourself?" Autumn asked. "Looks like your arms are crossed. And is that a tear on your face?"

What? A sad picture of her family?

Cricket nodded at Autumn's question. "I'm mad and sad. Everyone else gets to do their magic but I get in trouble if I do mine. It's not fair."

I sat next to her on a hay bale covered with a wool blanket. Autumn preferred an all-natural classroom whenever possible. She had a room inside her barn where they could gather if the weather wasn't good.

"Sweetie," I began, "you know you can use your magic at home."

She huffed. "Only in my room. Everybody else gets to do it wherever they want."

I glanced at Autumn. She gave me a cringey smile and leaned back, letting me know this one was mine to handle.

"You know that the aunts and I have been practicing our magic for a long time."

"Nuh-uh. You never did at our other house."

No, because I didn't want to go to jail. Either way, my magic wasn't active. She wouldn't have known even if I had done something right in front of her.

"My point is," I continued, "it takes a long time to get good. Your magic lets you move things. You could accidentally hurt someone."

Autumn stepped in. Thankfully, because I felt like I was floundering. "You are much better at magic than the other kids. Some of them don't even have their powers yet. But your lola is right. Magic is new to you, and you could hurt someone. I have to make rules here, and my rule is that no one but me gets to use magic unless I say it's okay."

"The other thing is," I said, "you should never use magic in anger."

Something I needed to remember. Too many times over the last few days, the feeling of hot rage burned in my belly. If I wasn't more conscious of it, I'd end up performing a spell accidentally. The way Cricket did with Cole. The way I did with the boat, although that wasn't due to anger.

We talked with Cricket a little longer, and then Autumn told me all was well and I could leave.

"I'll talk more with them today about feelings," the young woman assured me. "Her pictures will be the perfect visual aids, and I'll let her talk about how she felt."

I wished I could be there for that, but then Cricket might censor herself if I was sitting there. "You'll let me know if anything concerning comes up?"

"Of course."

My next task was to drop off deliveries. First The Paddle Wheel, and then I headed to The Sweet Spot for my Wednesday pastry. And to deliver their order, of course.

"What happened to your sign?" I asked Kelsey and Raul when I stepped inside. It was sitting on the ground, leaning against the sign post out front instead of hanging from it.

"We're not sure," Kelsey said. "We saw it hanging by one hook about twenty minutes ago. Raul took it down so it wouldn't fall and break."

"Looks like a screw eye came loose. I'll fix it later." Raul was in the middle of dusting what looked like cocoa powder on top of chocolate cupcakes. "Pastries first."

I stepped closer to the work counter, my mouth watering as the smell of deep, rich chocolate hit me. "What have you got there?"

He chuckled. "Mexican hot chocolate cupcakes with dulce de leche frosting."

I pretended to wipe drool from my chin, and he rewarded me with one of their delicacies. The first bite was tender and sweet. When I swallowed, a tiny bit of heat hit the back of my mouth.

"What am I tasting?"

"Cayenne pepper," Kelsey said proudly. "That's where the *hot* comes from in the name."

After finishing my cupcake, I thanked them, took their empty crates to the van, and got the order for Russell and Maggie.

"Good morning, Dusty." Maggie greeted me with a cheery smile. Once I returned from the kitchen with their empty crates, she asked, "What can I treat you with today?"

I told her about the cupcake, and she thought a salted caramel latte would be perfect.

"Sounds delicious." I put a hand to my belly. "I love Wednesdays."

While I waited for her to make my drink, a crashing sound came from behind me. I spun around to find one of their framed pictures had fallen from the wall. The glass inside the frame shattered and scattered everywhere.

"Are you okay?" Maggie asked the customers sitting nearby. They said they were fine. "Don't move. I don't want you to step on any glass. And don't eat or drink anything on your table. Glass gets everywhere. I'll make you new orders after we clean up." Then she turned toward the kitchen and yelled, "Russell!"

He darted out of the swinging door, eyes wide and wild. "What's wrong?"

It took him two seconds to understand. He grabbed the broom, dust pan, and mop.

In the back corner, a wooden sign also fell off the wall. No glass to shatter on that one, but it nearly hit the customer sitting on the leather sofa beneath it.

"What's going on?" Maggie muttered.

I shook my head. "Witchcraft? Is someone mad at you?"

"Everyone's mad at everyone right now," Maggie handed me my drink in a paper cup. "Not that you're not welcome to stay, but I think we should clear the building and figure out the cause before someone gets hurt."

"Good idea. I'll stop back in a bit and see if you're okay."

After getting the diner's order from the van, I crossed the park pushing my dolly. Along with the standard discomfort of various townies glaring at me, I saw more signs of things going awry. An elderly man's belt broke and his pants nearly fell to his ankles.

He blushed fiercely and patted his big belly. "Guess it's time to switch to suspenders."

The handles on a woman's paper shopping bag stamped with a Waste Not Antiques logo broke. The bag fell to the ground and for the second time in minutes I heard the distinct sound of glass breaking. She swore, gathered up her broken purchase, and headed back down the sidewalk. She looked at me as she passed and insisted, "I told Donna this bag wasn't strong enough. I want my money back."

What the heck was going on around here?

Things were chaotic inside the diner too.

"I don't get it." Nina was in the sitting area across from the front door. The walls there were covered with wallpaper depicting iconic diner images. "It's like the wallpaper is just releasing from the wall."

"Releasing," I repeated, and suddenly everything made sense.

I pulled my cellphone out of my pocket and called the house.

Gwynne answered on the fourth ring. "Dusty? Is everything okay?"

"Let me guess. You three activated your releasing spell, didn't you?"

"We did. About forty-five minutes ago. We haven't gotten any hits on Grampy's vase yet, though."

"I don't think it's working right." I told her what was happening around town.

She burst out laughing. "Oh, goodness. No, that won't do. Okay, we'll deactivate it and go back to the cauldron."

Her version of back to the drawing board. I thought about asking her to reverse the spell instead of only deactivating it, but who knew what sort of chaos that would result in.

"Hang on," I told Nina. "Everything should be back to normal shortly."

"Whatever that means around here," she muttered, trying to hold the wallpaper to the wall.

I chatted for a couple minutes with Avery and Mia and then remembered I had a small order to drop off at Grimoires & Gimlets, the bookstore and family-friendly bar. Cricket fell in love with the place the first time I took her there to get some new books. Today they were experimenting with fall beverages, all virgin of course, so needed mint, thyme, basil, and rosemary.

The aunts' releasing spell still hadn't fully worked its way out of the park yet, so bags were still breaking, children slipped away from their parents' grasp, and dogs got off leashes. As though this were somehow my fault, they took out their anger and irritation on me.

"There she is. The murdering witch Beau let walk away scot-free."

"What sort of spell did she put on him?"

"She came back to town to finish off her classmates, you know."

"She came into the salon with her witch cousin yesterday," the Farrah-haired stylist said. "They were trying to dig up dirt on Tracy."

"Probably trying to push the blame for the accident onto the kids who were in the boat."

A loud, strong, male voice roared, "That's enough!"

We all turned to find Nash Kramer and his Pitbull, Lady, standing in the middle of the park. His tattooed forehead was furrowed tightly in anger. Lady looked at him with her head cocked, her tail wagging and pausing, then wagging again, as though she didn't know if she should be her happy self or not.

"It's been thirty-two years," Nash began as the crowd gathered closer to him. "We need to stop talking about that accident. You all want to know the truth about what happened that day?"

Murmurs of agreement spread through the group. My heart rate picked up in anticipation of what he'd say. Should I get ready to run? Could I make it to the hedge before they got me? No, the delivery van was closer.

"The truth is—" He paused, seemingly psyching himself up for whatever he was about to say. "The truth is the accident was my fault. I was driving far too fast and had overloaded the boat with way too many people. It was reckless and irresponsible and completely my fault." He pointed at me, and dozens of people turned toward me. "Dusty saw what was going to happen. Those of you who were here then surely remember the huge tree that washed downriver when the ice melted then submerged right over there." He pointed toward the boat dock. "It was a hazard, and no one was in much of a hurry to get it out of there." He jabbed his finger into his chest. "I was about to run smack into it at more than fifty miles per hour. Double the legal speed limit."

"But she could have killed you all," someone called out.

Nash ran a hand over his bald head. "You're still not listening. *I* would have killed myself and my nine friends that day. Pretty much a guarantee. Dusty saw the accident." He tapped his forehead. "As in, saw it in a vision so knew it for a fact. If she had been able to cut the engine to slow the boat, it might have dropped to forty miles per hour before impact. Still lethal. She reached out her hand in reaction to what she saw coming, never expecting she had the ability to stop the boat." He was emotional by this point, his chest heaving. "I swear on my life this is the truth. And Dusty keeps saying the same thing because that's the way it happened. If you all want to keep being mad about magic and witches and whatever else you're pissed off about, go right ahead. But do not say one more word to her about that damn accident."

He stopped talking then. Everyone was still looking at me but differently now. I didn't expect words of apology or understanding. If they would quit blaming me, I'd be overjoyed.

"Doesn't mean she didn't kill Tracy," someone muttered just loudly enough for me to hear as they passed by.

Catching the killer would prove I didn't, and my resolve to do so doubled. *If* I was going to stay in this town, I couldn't live under these conditions.

After the crowd had cleared, I found Nash sitting alone on a park bench beneath a maple tree, the leaves of which were just starting to turn red. He had a small box from The Sweet Spot in one hand and a big bottle of water on the seat next to him. "Mind if I sit?"

He glanced down and nodded in a *go-ahead* gesture. Lady pressed up against me in hopes of an ear scratch, which I was happy to give her.

At that moment, Granny Sadie and Freddie floated over and stood with their fisted hands on their hips. The world's most ineffective bodyguards. I fought a smile and did my best to ignore them.

"Thank you." I worked my way down Lady's back. "For what you said."

"Did it for myself as much as you. Didn't want you to keep taking the blame, and I can't keep living with the guilt."

Despite what he'd just done and said, tension hovered between us like a storm front. If we were going to live in the same town, we should be adults and talk about our issue.

I sat quietly and let him eat the first of the two hot chocolate cupcakes in his box. When he finished it, I asked, "Can we talk about it?"

He paused while drinking his water, then swallowed. "What do we need to talk about?"

I watched as Lady's tail stirred up a small cloud of dirt as it swept across the ground, trying to decide how to say what I wanted to say. "I've thought about you many times over the years. Wondered how your life turned out. After you'd served your sentence, I mean. I was surprised to see you here. Not sure what I expected, but the tattoos and a veterinarian practice weren't anywhere on my list of possibilities."

He took a bite of the second cupcake, chewed, and swallowed. "Did you have a question?"

"How's your life now? Are you happy?"

He leaned back. "Not sure anyone's ever asked me that. Yeah, I'm happy. I like working with animals and living in a town where the only expectations people have for me are that I keep the farm animals healthy and the pets alive as long as possible." He paused before saying, "The accident changed the course of my life, Dusty, but it didn't destroy it."

I was about to tell him that made me happy, but Nash cut me off before I could.

"Like I said, I take full responsibility for the events of that day. I would have ended up killing myself and the others on the boat. What you did, unintentional as it was, forced me to grow up."

Granny Sadie put her hands over her heart.

"What happened after prison?"

A look of regret clouded his face. "Obviously, I lost my football scholarship, so that changed my plans. When I got out, I came home to help my parents on the farm. That lasted for about forty-eight hours." His eyes took on a faraway stare as he remembered something. "I couldn't handle the constant berating and looks of disappointment from my dad, so I hopped on my motorcycle and roamed."

Freddie gave two *rock on* hand signs.

This intrigued me. Nash roaming, not Freddie's gestures. I told him, "When I left here, I drove until I found what felt like a good place to stop up north. Where did you roam to?"

Nash shrugged. "Everywhere. Anywhere. Worked as a metal band roadie for a couple years. That's when all the tattoos started. That's also where my drug and alcohol problem started."

"Stella told me you're clean and sober."

He gave a crisp nod, staring across the park. Or maybe just looking anywhere but at me. "When I realized my lifestyle was putting me on track to hurt someone else, I quit. Been sober for twenty-six years, five months, and thirteen days. My dad agreed to pay for veterinary school as long as I promised to tend his animals when I graduated. He meant work on his farm but neglected to include that in the fine print. I take care of his animals and everyone else's too. I'm not proud of the road I followed for a while there, but I'm happy with the one I'm on now."

What was this feeling warming me inside? Not pride. I had no right to feel that.

"You've got a weird look on your face," he noted, really looking at me for the first time since I'd sat. "What were you just thinking?"

"That's what I was trying to figure out. You and Beau suffered because of that day. I'm relieved you both have done so well. Sounds like Tracy also had a hard time."

"She did. I tried to be a sponsor for her, but I think her problem ran far deeper than the alcohol." He tapped his head. "I think her brain got messed up when she hit her head that day." Then he shrugged and added offhandedly, "You suffered too. I heard someone told you to leave. That took you away from your family, and I know you all are close. Your life probably didn't turn out like you'd hoped either."

More unidentifiable feelings swirled in me. "I didn't know how much I missed my family until I got back here. As for how my life turned out, like anyone's, a lot was good, and some parts were bad. Recently some truly awful things happened." I didn't want to talk about the events of the past two months right now. I checked the time instead. "I'll tell you sometime if you're interested. For now, I should get back to the farm and let you get on with your day. Thank you for talking to me, Nash, and for everything you said to the townies. I appreciate it more than I can say. We can go back to ignoring each other now if you want."

"We don't need to do that." He ate the last of his cupcake. "Thanks for asking about my life and for unintentionally getting me to admit to what I did. As I've learned, it's not good to hold that stuff inside."

I stood to leave, then sat again. "You know I didn't kill Tracy, right?"

"Never imagined that you did."

"Do you have any idea who might have? Carly and I are trying to clear my name."

"Couple of amateur sleuths, hey?" He shook his head. "I don't know anything, but I'm all over the town and farms. I'll keep my ears open."

On my way to the van to get Tabitha's herb order, I first wondered where Granny and Freddie went and then thought more about Nash. The conversation had gone better than I thought it would. He didn't seem to hold any kind of grudge toward me and even admitted my actions ultimately turned his life around instead of upside down. I didn't know a lot about the AA program but was pretty sure forgiveness was part of it.

The mistrustful part of me, that I couldn't seem to shake lately, wondered if everything he said was above board. Like Beau was, Nash could be under a forgetting spell. Except while we talked, I searched his eyes for any sign of the glassiness that clouded Beau's whenever he talked about the accident. Nothing. Nash's were perfectly clear.

I was in awe of how he was able to get past what happened. Could he help me do the same?

Or was he lying and I shouldn't be quite so eager to look to him for help with anything? He was a Kramer, after all.

CHAPTER 22

"Garden tools are cleaned, repaired, oiled, and organized," I reported, looking over the day's task list.

"So are the supplies," Nicola reported.

"We also have a detailed inventory of what we have and what we'll need for next year." I put a checkmark next to that line. "Last item, what worked well this season and what can we improve on next year?"

My young helper got emotional every time I even hinted at being done for the season.

"We're not done yet," I reminded her. We still had the fall harvest—apples, squashes, potatoes, pumpkins, broccoli. Then a quick turning of the soil. I wouldn't need her every day, though. Just one here and there.

She held her head high and blinked repeatedly. "I know."

I smiled at her, unsure if she'd miss working or having time to herself away from her kids. They were both well behaved, but every mom needed a break now and then. Whether they wanted to admit it or not. Maybe especially if they *didn't* admit it.

"Tell you what," I soothed, "I'm going to ask Carly if she needs help at The Apple Barn for the next few months. Don't get excited about it yet, she may say no, but after only a few weeks, I can vouch for what a great work ethic you have."

Nicola hugged me, bouncing up and down as she did, and thanked me over and over. Then I told her she could take off for the rest of the day. "Since you have time and it's such a beautiful day, maybe you could go for a little hike."

"That's a great idea. Think I'll do that. Thank you, Dusty." She got teary again. "See you . . . when?"

Sweet girl. "Plan on Tuesday. You can put the orders together for me and there may be things ready for harvesting."

I had ninety minutes before I had to go pick up Cricket, so I took a quick shower to wash off the grime, then went up to my sanctuary to work a little more on Adrianna's spell.

"Do all of the gate magic requests take this long to prepare, or will I get faster at this the more I do it?"

The fireplace crackled loudly in response. Whatever that meant.

While searching through my books I learned sniffing camphor or placing it by the bed decreased sexual desire, rubbing lettuce juice on the forehead induced sleep, and vervain was helpful for both banishing malevolent forces and inducing chastity. My witchy senses tingled at each of them, so I figured that must mean something. The rest of my strong possibilities list included the hallucinatory effects of datura, the ability to temporarily paralyze a victim with belladonna or dieffenbachia, and the nasty stinging, burning, and itching that mala mujer would produce.

Now what? Blend them all? Blend a few? Create a few different blends?

According to the books, it wouldn't take much for any of them to produce the stated effects. Since I didn't know exactly what result Adrianna was hoping to achieve, I could give her a bit of each plant along with the instructions for casting the spell, information about what each herb could do, and the warnings about what could go wrong. That way she could decide how she wanted to proceed.

"That makes sense, right?" Even to myself, I sounded uncertain.

Suddenly not comfortable with any of this, I pushed away from the table and then paced the perimeter of the room.

Comfort provided recipes and enchanted ingredients. Pepper used salt and pepper blends to protect, banish, and create numerous other desired results. Gwynne was the positive yang to Mom's negative yin. They all affected lives with their magic.

What was the difference between what they did and what I was about to do? What made their magic positive and mine gray?

Could I learn from them instead? Or was my path unalterable because the gray was in me as much as my blood and bones were? Did I have to follow the negative, wrong-thing path?

Then again, what was *wrong* with stopping a man from attacking women? Especially if the police couldn't or wouldn't help, citizens had to handle their problems on their own. And really, I wasn't actually *doing* anything beyond providing the possibility.

This was where gray magic was, well, gray. I was going to need my mother's input before I did anything else with this spell.

The cricket alarm went off then. Time to go get my girl.

Autumn reported the day passed without further magical incidents. "Cricket gave Cole a very nice, sincere apology, and we had a good conversation about feelings."

"So everyone is happy again?" I asked.

"There were no incidents today," she repeated. A smart answer from a woman who knew a child's emotions could turn on a dime for no apparent reason. Much like a menopausal woman's.

Word of Nash's lecture this morning must have spread, because no one in the park said anything about me trying to kill people. They still gave me sidelong glances because of the *witches are so entitled* argument, but I'd take this as an improvement.

By the time we got back to the farm, I had just enough time to get Cricket a snack, hear her version of how things went today, and find someone for her to hang out with while Carly and I went to The Paddle Wheel.

"How about," Comfort began, "you help me make dessert?"

"Yay!" Cricket clapped wildly. "I love dessert."

Carly arrived just as Comfort was tying Cricket's apron behind her back.

"What's that look for?" I asked. "Remembering her doing that with us?"

"Yes and no." Carly gave a shaky, emotional sigh. "Remembering her doing that with my kids. She rotated through the lineup. Alex always made a fuss when his week came up, insisting he didn't want to learn how to make pie, but he's the only one of them who does it at home now. Nina gets a pass because she makes so many at the diner."

"Alex makes pie?" I loved this.

Carly smiled fondly. "Once a week. Every other week, if he's busy with school stuff. Or sometimes twice a week for the same reason. There's magic in making pie. He claims it de-stresses him. And he's quite good."

As we walked to The Paddle Wheel, Carly reported, "Looks like the aunts figured out the problem with the organizing spell.

Not only could my customers shop without items being ripped from their hands, I was able to move a display without finding it back to its previous position the next time I came out of the storeroom. Although, the paint started peeling off the walls at one point. I thought it was trying to restore the barn to its original interior."

"Early this morning?" I asked.

"Yeah. Around nine thirty or ten o'clock."

I explained the aunts' revealing spell and what had happened around town. "Took me a minute to figure it out. I called them right away and told them to deactivate it."

We walked a little farther, and she said almost sheepishly, "I've been looking through our notebooks to figure out how to best lay out everything in the barn. I have to say, we knew what we were doing."

A wave of nostalgia flooded me. "You have our notebooks?"

She blushed and then tried to shrug off her bout of touchy-feely emotions. "Course I do. They landed in the trash can many times, but I always pulled them out before the garbage truck took them away. I never could get rid of them."

"I'd love to take a look. Does The Sanctuary really look like the room I designed, or am I imagining it?"

She smiled. "It's uncanny."

Happy warmth filled my chest. I could get used to these afternoon meetups.

"Hi, ladies," Stella greeted as soon as we entered the saloon. "Early dinner? Late lunch? Afternoon tipple?"

The saloon was mostly empty with only a few folks sitting in the other room enjoying one or all of Stella's options. Perfect. We could talk with her without being interrupted.

"I'll take a glass of Chardonnay," Carly requested while sliding onto a stool at the bar.

"A greyhound for me, please," I said. "And we need to ask you some questions if you've got time."

Stella checked her watch as she poured Carly's wine. "I've got about twenty minutes before I need to get ready for the dinner rush." We waited while she mixed ice, grapefruit juice, and vodka in a highball glass for my drink and then set it on a napkin in front of me. "Okay. What's up?"

"The topic is Tracy," I began, tapping my glass against Carly's. Then we held them up in a salute to our bartender. "Specifically, we're wondering what happened before she started that argument with me."

"That's right, your back was to the room."

"I didn't notice her either." Carly centered her glass on her napkin. "We were deep into conversation, so I wasn't paying attention to anyone else."

"You want to know if her killer was here," Stella concluded while putting the grapefruit juice back in the fridge.

"That would be super helpful," I agreed, "although if you could ID the person, you probably would have told Beau or Leezza by now."

Stella turned up the volume on the country music coming over the sound system a bit. So the other patrons wouldn't hear our conversation? "I did talk with them but wasn't able to say for certain who might have done this to Tracy. There were a lot of people here that night."

There had been.

"There are three who stand out to me." She shook her head in a disgusted way. "I call them Triple Threat. They're nothing but trouble. Always starts with laughing too loudly. When they head to the pool tables, my radar ramps up to high and I get ready to kick them out."

"Wait." I held up a hand. "I came in here with Maks and the aunts about a month ago."

"I remember." Stella gestured toward the far end of the bar where I'd sat that night. "Henry got in your face."

"Right. There was an argument going on by the pool tables."

"That was them. They've never gotten into a physical fight with each other. I think they're hoping a girl or two will come over and try to break it up." She rolled her eyes. "Guys and their pickup tactics."

"Who are these three?" Carly asked.

"The redheaded White guy is Keefe. Don't know if that's a first name or last. The bald Hispanic guy is Paco. I think that's a nickname. The Black man, Marquis, has the biggest afro I've ever seen." She held her hands a good twelve inches on either side of her head. Then she sighed. "Shame he's such an ass. The man is beautiful."

I smiled at her bittersweet reaction. "Did any of them do anything to Tracy?"

Stella sighed. "Their schtick is to choose someone and circle them. We all know who they are and what their game is, so whoever sees them walk in first puts out the Triple Threat alert."

"Sounds like a lot of work," Carly noted, her anger growing. "Why don't you just ban them from the saloon?"

"Because they've never done anything to anyone that we're aware of. Honestly, plenty of folks come here to meet someone, and they like the attention. Still, when they circle, one of us stays nearby. If the person shows signs of annoyance, we send the boys away. When their pool table antics get loud, Nash steps in. That man is a godsend, I'm telling you."

"So they circled Tracy on Thursday?" Carly went to the pretzel dispenser at the end of the bar, turned the knob, and a serving of twists fell into her palm.

"They did." Stella's jaw set. "Something was going on that night. Like a Mercury in retrograde type thing. Triple Threat was worked up, and Tracy was already halfway to blotto when she walked in, which I realized too late. I'm kicking myself for that now. I mean, I almost always notice that kind of thing. It's my job, after all." She took a moment to shake it off, then said,

"Anyway, I knew the boys were bugging her, as in, more intensely than normal, so I tried to keep my eye on them.

"You're not at fault," Carly said firmly.

The conversation Carly and I had out on the patio last night came back to me. "Have you ever seen them try to put something into their victims' drinks?"

"Oh, yeah," Carly breathed.

Stella's eyes narrowed and then widened as my meaning became clear. "You think that's what they did to Tracy?" She put her hands to her face. "How could I be so stupid? I've never seen them do that. Obviously, if I had, I would have reported them. It would be so easy, especially when it's busy like it was Thursday night. Wait until whoever is working the bar to turn their back, then one or two of them distract their target while the other doctors the drink."

Adrianna didn't say anything about there being more than one man, and I felt like she would have. Was her attacker and Tracy's killer the same man?

"Or," I thought out loud, "one of them could be working on his own."

"This would explain why I didn't recognize her condition when she got here." Stella's slight relief didn't last long. "The other thing bothering me is I don't know if they followed her. She started that argument with you, Dusty, then I called Nash and took her outside because she was making a scene."

"Nash got here a few minutes later," I recalled, "and he said Tracy wasn't outside."

"Right." Stella looked up at the tin ceiling and blinked repeatedly. "He said he'd go look for her, so I basically passed the baton to him and went on with my night." She closed her eyes, and when she opened them again, they were glossy with tears. Her voice broke as she said, "I don't know if they followed her."

Gooseflesh broke out over my body at the implication of her words.

Carly reached across the counter and patted Stella's hands. "Did any of the other employees notice?"

She shook her head. "I asked them all. After they found Tracy's body, I reviewed the events of that night with the staff. No one saw when they left."

"What about security video?" Carly pointed at a camera over the bar area.

"The camera by the pool tables has been broken for a couple weeks," Stella admitted. "We're waiting for a part to come in. Someone decided it was a good place to hang jackets and practically ripped it off the wall. That one also covers the front entrance. There aren't any outside."

"So no help there," I concluded.

"All I know for sure," Stella began, "is Triple Threat will need to take their business elsewhere from now on. I told the owner we dealt with them the best we could but no more."

Carly reached for her glass. "You shouldn't have to give that much attention to any one group."

"That's exactly what we decided." Stella let out a groan of frustration. "I feel like I dropped the ball so many times that night."

Marilyn Kramer walked into the saloon then. She froze when she saw us at the bar, as though deciding if she should turn and go someplace else, but she continued to the far end of the bar and chose a stool.

"Pinot noir, Stella," she barked, "and don't be stingy with your pour."

Stella filled a glass to the top with red wine and then set it and the bottle in front of Marilyn.

"What's the matter with her?" Carly whispered to me.

Marilyn repeatedly winced and rubbed her neck as she drank.

"She's probably stressed because of what Nash did." My voice wasn't as low as Carly's, so Marilyn heard.

"Came to your defense." Marilyn turned stiffly toward us. "Henry is right. You did something to him."

Every disdainful word was laced with acid.

"Nash did what?" Carly asked, and I realized I hadn't told her yet.

"What kind of spell did you put on him?" Marilyn accused and then laughed. "No, couldn't have been you. What is it that you're claiming? You don't know how to use your powers?" She took a long drink of pinot, downing a third of the glass. "Guess you're not lying about that. Living in a non-safe town for all those years, we'd know if you tried."

"What does that mean?" I asked Carly. "Who's *we*?"

Carly shook her head and shrugged.

"As inept now as you were as a child." She hadn't had enough wine for that to be her excuse, so her nastiness was one hundred percent pure Marilyn. "Dusty Hotte is a gray witch who can't cast a proper gray spell. Aiming for all those kids and no one died."

Other patrons were listening now. Some had even moved to the doorway separating the bar area from the dining room when they saw her walk in. Guaranteed to be a show when a Kramer was around.

"I hear she's learning from her mother." Marilyn laughed, slapping her hand to the bar. "Have any of you seen Griselle Warren lately? No, probably not. She's been in hiding. You wouldn't believe how decrepit she is. Why the woman doesn't just drop dead, I can't say."

With the first word she spoke, anger and annoyance sparked in my gut. With that last line, the spark burst into an inferno. I squeezed my hand into a fist and the bottle in front of Marilyn exploded. Deep-red liquid splattered her light-blue denim shirt like drops of blood.

She turned toward me, and fear flashed in her eyes for an instant.

I set a twenty on the bar and thanked Stella for the information and the drinks. "Let's go, Carly."

My cousin remained silent, letting me mutter as we walked. I repeated my earlier question. "Who is *we*? Do they monitor Ordinary towns? They must. How else would they discover the witches there? Other than word from *concerned* citizens . . . Is Henry feeding her information? He's the Council rep for the Ordies. He must have access to all kinds of information . . . And how does she know Mom is helping me?"

I fumed, clenching and unclenching my hands as I stomped down Gala Street between the mall and the mall's parking lot.

"Can't cast a proper spell." I clenched my hands again, and a nearby garbage bin caved in like a crushed soda can. I stopped walking abruptly and stared at the bin.

"Did you do that?" Carly asked, stunned.

"I think so." A thrill ran through my body.

"Did you mean to break the wine bottle?"

"No. I was aiming for her glass."

Carly tilted her head side to side as though weighing that decision. "Probably for the best. The glass might have cut her hand, and she'd have you arrested for assault."

We started laughing so hard we had to prop each other up.

"Oh, my goddess." I put a hand to my now aching side. "Is this some new power manifesting all of a sudden?"

"Beats me." Carly wiped her eyes. "You told Mrs. Slayton you could make things happen and stop things from happening. Might be a gray thing. Either way, you need control."

I did. "Have to say, I think I understand the rush a little better."

"What rush?"

"The one that comes from doing the wrong thing for the

right reason. Not sure there was a right reason to crunch that trash can, but damn did it feel good."

"Better out than in," Carly quipped.

Granny Sadie's favorite saying fit so many aspects of life.

I frowned guiltily at the can that now looked like an hourglass. "I should probably pay to have that replaced, hey?"

"Nah. It's mall property. Marilyn will have to replace it."

And the day was getting better again.

CHAPTER 23

"We have to ensure things like that don't happen again," Carly scolded the aunts for the problems their releasing spell caused. Looking around the dinner table, she asked, "Any ideas?"

Emma had taken Cricket to the family room to see what the familiars were doing when the conversation turned to adult things. Sebastian went with them. Nina was at the diner. She had decided Wednesday was paperwork day. That way she could have two full days off on Sundays and Mondays. Alex was with Savannah.

In answer to Carly's question, I asked, "Can we limit the radius to the farm until we're sure new spells work properly?"

Jett was not in favor of this. "Far too dangerous, lass. What if they do something to the hedge?" Her brow knit. "If that's possible. Wonder if there's ever been an attack from the inside."

"Maybe," Maks began, "someone needs to review the spells before they activate them."

"Great idea." Carly thumped her fist on the table like a judge banging her gavel. "Dad and Jett, you are the review team."

The pair stared at each other, matching expressions of *how did that happen* on their faces, but they didn't object.

Granny Sadie drifted over to Jett and said something.

"Okay," Jett agreed. "She and Freddie have news to share."

Freddie's arms waved about as he spoke and passed right through Granny at one point. She swatted at him, her hand going right through him. They had a good laugh about that before he returned to his tale.

At one point, Jett asked, "Really?"

Freddie put his hand over his heart. Granny arched a brow as though wanting to know if Jett was doubting his word.

"Very good. I think I've got it." To us, Jett said, "The two of them overheard Dusty talking to Nash after he defended her honor this morning." Jett looked at me for confirmation.

I took a minute to explain what had happened.

"Points to Nash for being a standup lad," Jett approved with a crisp nod. "Our ghostly duo decided to do a little sleuthing of their own afterward."

"Sleuthing?" Comfort repeated. "Far as I know, Jett's the only one who can hear them."

"I can," Cricket called from the other room, and Emma shushed her.

"I stand corrected," Comfort said. "My point being, they can't sleuth if they can't ask questions. So you meant to say they did a little eavesdropping."

Granny Sadie swished her hand and spoke.

"*Toe-may-toe, toe-mah-toe,*" Jett interpreted.

"What did they learn?" I asked.

"They followed Nash," Jett continued. "Henry was having a bite in the diner when all this happened, and word spread to him quickly. He dragged Nash to Marilyn's office so he could chew him out in private."

"Was Marilyn there?" Pepper asked.

The ghosts shook their heads.

"What did Henry say?" Gwynne asked, worrying her hands together.

"According to Freddie, Henry said, 'Do you have any idea how much we did to protect you from fallout over that accident? How many people we had to pay off to get you a five-year sentence and make them *forget* the whole thing? No one remembered any of this until that witch came back to town. Just can't stop yourself from running your mouth, can you? You ruined everything.'"

We all sat and processed this revelation for a minute.

Folding and unfolding my napkin, I said, "Wish I could say I'm surprised by this. When I learned Nash got only five years, I knew there was some kind of under-the-table cover-up going on."

"Aside from the obvious," Maks began, "you know what stands out to me in all this? We've got a pair of sleuths who can slip in anywhere undetected. Unless there are others who can see spirits, of course."

There was a moment of silence followed by small cheers of excitement.

"Very handy," I praised.

"Good job, Granny and Freddie," Carly added.

The two attempted a high five and passed right through each other again.

TINY PLASTIC BAGS of camphor (for decreased sexual desire), vervain (banishing malevolence and inducing chastity), and datura (to induce hallucinations) lay on the table before me. Another held a pinch of belladonna (temporary paralysis). A fifth contained enough mala mujer to bring on a good long bout of stinging, burning, and itching. A small vial held lettuce juice (to induce sleep). On a parchment, I'd written the effects each item would produce and highlighted the potential lethal qualities of the belladonna and datura. I still wasn't sure I'd give her those.

I also set out an incense blend of lavender for stress relief and sandalwood for grounding.

With that, I'd done all I could think to do for Adrianna's spell. I was ready for my mother to check my work. When was the last time I'd needed her to do that? Sixth grade? Fifth? I gave Pearl a note and sent the little squirrel to find her.

Was this spell the only way for Adrianna to deal with this or the easiest? Her desperate young face appeared like a vision before me. She was so scared and angry. If I was being honest, I felt honored to create this spell for her. And right now, with her face clear in my mind along with the sickening knowledge she was not the only one to suffer at this man's hands, I felt a sort of responsibility to do what she asked of me as well. For her, the other woman, and his future victims.

Pearl returned to The Sanctuary; the note no longer clutched in her little mouth.

"I understand you're done." Mom had to stop and catch her breath after reaching the top of the staircase.

Her mind was still sharp, but her physical condition seemed to be getting worse by the day. That scared me. For years, since well before I left Blackwood Grove, I hadn't cared if she was alive or dead. But now that we'd formed this connection, I wanted more time with her.

"Come sit," I said, helping her to the rocking chair. "Tea?"

"Lemon would be lovely."

I went to the tea cart and found a mug already steeping. There was also a container of shortbread cookies, so I put a few on a plate.

"All right," she said after her first sip, "tell me what you decided."

I showed her the collection I'd assembled as well as the

handwritten explanations of what they each would do and instructions for how Adrianna could use them.

"I like that you are giving her choices," Mom approved. "I recommend you also include a tea light candle and four crystal chips—carnelian for releasing anger, garnet for reclaiming personal power, bloodstone to find the courage to proceed with purpose, and Apache tears for forgiveness."

"Forgiveness? You want her to forgive this man?" Memories of Micah's father flashed at me.

"That's up to her," Mom said. "I want her to forgive herself for whatever she chooses to do to him. For every request I received that involved anger or revenge, I included an Apache tears crystal to protect the person from negative emotions. None of those stones are for him. They're all for her. I encourage you to study them all and use them in all your spells."

I gathered each of the stones she mentioned from the one-hundred-drawer apothecary cabinet that held my crystal collection, then wrote their description and purpose on the parchment.

"She should choose a cardinal direction that means the most to her at this time." Mom pointed at the parchment, indicating I should add that. "North for earth and stability, west for water and cleansing, south for fire and passion, east for air and release. She should face that direction, make a circle with salt, eighteen inches in diameter, then place the candle in the center with the ingredients surrounding it and a crystal chip at each cardinal point. Doesn't matter which crystal goes where. Whatever feels right to her. Finally, she should create an incantation. It doesn't have to rhyme or include fancy words. It simply needs to be a statement of what she wants to achieve by casting this spell. Encourage her to take her time with that part because words are important, and as you know, intention—"

"Is fifty percent of a spell's effectiveness." I sat on the stool next to her and reviewed my choices and everything she had suggested. "I think I'm comfortable with this. Except for these two."

Unsure of how much was lethal, I removed the datura from the collection. Then I reduced the pinch of belladonna in the small plastic bag to half a pinch.

"Very good," Mom approved. "Text or call her and tell her it's ready. Make sure she's still okay with the price. If she's not, the deal is off. There should be no wavering on her part, and you must always stick *exactly* to the agreement. Nothing can change or you'll need to start over."

I checked the time as I took out my phone. I'd told Carly I would meet her by the pond at ten thirty, and it was already ten after. Twenty minutes probably wouldn't be enough time.

It's ready. I can meet you at midnight. Remember to bring cash. The price has not changed.

We're fine with the price. We'll pay anything.

We?

Me and the other woman. We want to make sure I was the last woman he touched.

"She says the other woman is involved."

Mom shook her head. "That's a change. You created the spell for Adrianna. The other woman can give her all the money and support she wants, but Adrianna alone must cast this spell, or it will not work."

I told Adrianna that.

I understand. I will cast the spell. Where should I meet you?

I typed the instructions for how to get to the gate.

"What's the code?" I asked Mom.

"Whatever you decide it should be."

I thought for a moment and then sent it to Adrianna. "How do I let the hedge know?"

"Tell the property," Mom said through a yawn.

"The password is *strong and powerful*. Please let Adrianna through the hedge at midnight when she says it."

Mom smiled. "I like it. There's one final thing you need to do. Roll up the parchment and tie it with a red string. Place it and everything else in a bag. Cast a circle on the table and then a pentagram inside it. Place your preferred incense and crystal at the center of the pentagram."

The hardest thing about that was drawing the pentagram with the applewood wand I found in one of the cabinets. The handle fit my hand perfectly so the moment I touched it there was no doubt it was meant to be mine. As for incense, I was a cedar and sandalwood girl all the way. At the apothecary cabinet, I opened the super seven drawer and raked my fingers through the stones until I felt one of them vibrate. That was my super seven.

Once I had everything in place, Mom instructed me to pass the bag through the incense smoke while speaking my intent for Adrianna and the spell. I did so and instructed that the magical potency of the herbs should be nullified after forty-eight hours. That would be enough time for her to cast her spell. Longer than that would indicate she didn't really want to do this.

When I had finished, Mom leaned back and closed her eyes. "Go deliver your spell, gray witch."

CHAPTER 24

With Adrianna's spell in hand, I made my way to the pond. Tomorrow was the new moon, so tonight there was only the tiniest possible sliver of the waning crescent visible. At the pond, I lay in the grass and stared up at the sky. The lack of moonlight put all the stars on display, and the sight took my breath away. I knew Micah couldn't see much from his cell. Could Josie see the stars wherever she was?

The sound of Carly's footsteps on the gravel driveway reached me before her voice did. "Hey. How long have you been here? I could have come earlier."

"It's only been a few minutes." I motioned at the spell bag sitting a few feet away and explained how Mom had helped me with it.

"I'd like to say I'm happy you're working with her on your magic, but I'm not sure you want to hear that."

"She's not doing well," I said after a beat.

"That's pretty obvious."

"I know. Guess I've realized it's time for me to stop being stubborn and face the truth about her and my life."

The hopeful look on my cousin's face tugged at my heart.

Does that mean you're staying? Fortunately, she didn't ask it out loud because I wasn't prepared to answer. I'd never in my life been so back-and-forth about a decision. Even though I was leaning strongly in one direction, I didn't want to promise anything and then change my mind. No wonder she'd been so standoffish and irritated with me.

"Ready to find her?" I asked.

Carly inhaled deeply. "I'm ready to try. It's a good night with the moon almost new. Minimal reflection. It would be best if it was cloudy because all those stars also reflect on the water, but tiny lights are easier for me to look past than a big orb." She looked at me, her expression serious. "I've been practicing, but I can't promise anything will happen."

"I understand, Carly. Do what you can. Any little thing might help."

She circled the pond until she found a spot she liked facing east—for release?—and sat with her legs in crisscross. Then she lay back and dug in her jeans pocket. "Almost forgot my crystal. Blue tiger's eye. It's great for communication and insight. It also enhances intuition and psychic powers."

"Perfect." I didn't know there was a blue tiger's eye. I definitely needed to learn more about crystals and stones. Between Carly, my mother, the aunts, and the dozens of other witches in Blackwood Grove, I was surrounded by all the knowledge and magical energy I should need.

I sat close enough to hear anything Carly might say, my notebook and pen at the ready, but not so close I'd distract her. She held the stone in her right hand and pressed her left into the grass, literally and figuratively grounding herself. With her eyes closed, she took deep, slow breaths. I found myself breathing along with her, giving her all the energy I could.

Softly but with determination, she said, "Show me Josie Santos. She's a twenty-six-year-old Filipina woman. Mother to

Cricket. Love to Micah. She was taken from her family, and they want her back."

She said these words over and over, pausing in between as though letting the Universe make the connection and then reminding it of who we were looking for when nothing came through.

This went on for half an hour, and I was starting to lose hope that anything would happen tonight. Then, halfway through her plea, Carly gasped. Either I became hyper-focused on her or the crickets and other creatures of the night really did go silent because all I could hear was Carly breathing.

So softly I had to lean forward to hear her, she asked, "Where are you, sweetheart?" Then, "Any little thing. Please." Finally, "We won't stop looking for you."

I sat frozen in place, desperate to ask if she'd found her but not wanting to break her trance in case something else came through. After what felt like forever, Carly's eyes opened, and her body slumped. She lay back in the grass, her chest heaving like she'd just finished running a marathon.

"What did you see?" I asked, crawling closer when her breathing slowed to normal.

"Her. I'm almost positive. You said she has a single dimple in her right cheek."

I pulled out my phone. Not wanting to influence Carly's vision at all, I hadn't showed her a picture of our beautiful Josie. "Right there." I lay down next to Carly, held the camera over her face, and pointed to the spot about an inch from the corner of Josie's mouth. "It looks like she was poked with a pencil."

Carly grasped my arm and looked from the picture to me. "That's who I saw. She's okay. As in, she doesn't appear to be hurt."

Was she scared? I didn't ask, too afraid to know if she was. "Any idea where she is?"

She pushed herself up to sitting, so I did too. "In a house or some kind of building. I think the walls were paneled with plain wood planks. That's all I saw. I'm sorry."

I threw my arms around her. "That's more than we've known for two months. She's okay. That's huge."

"You're really going to put that much faith in my rusty ability?"

"I'm putting that much faith in *you*. I asked you a few weeks ago if I could trust you, and you said of course I could. If you say you saw her, I believe you."

She swayed a little as she sat there.

"Are you okay?"

"That was intense. Completely wiped me out. Would you walk me home?"

I grabbed the spell bag and then helped her to her feet. The usual five-minute walk took ten. Her house was completely dark except for a dim lamp in the entry way. The kids must have left it on for her. I helped her upstairs to her bedroom then assisted with swapping clothing for her nightshirt. Then I kissed her on the forehead the way I did Cricket and tucked her into bed.

By the time I got back to the farm, a light was blinking on-off, on-off by the gate. I rushed over to find Adrianna there.

I echoed Carly's words from earlier. "You haven't been here long, have you?"

"Maybe two minutes." Her eyes locked onto the bag in my hands. "Is that it?"

"It is. And it's extremely important you do this exactly as I laid it out. Understand?"

She nodded, seemingly unable to tear her eyes away from the paper sack.

I went over the instructions for the spell again, and to be sure she was actually listening to me, I made her repeat them to me.

Tears filled her eyes. "I can't tell you how thankful I am for this."

I felt it. Her thanks was palpable. "I understand that you feel this is the only way—"

"It *is* the only way," she insisted. "There are so many layers to this, Dusty. You said you didn't want to know too many details."

My mother had explained that hearing too much about either the target of the spells or the caster's story could influence how I put the spell together. It was best, however, to have some kind of proof so I wasn't creating a spell that would harm someone unjustly. Adrianna had another woman backing her up with the same story.

"What if the person lies to me?" I had asked Mom. "What if they're simply trying to poke at someone they don't like for whatever reason?"

"Trust your instincts," she had answered. "Part of your power is that you will know when justice needs to be served and when it's a simple case of hurt feelings or sour grapes."

That made sense. I didn't ask to speak to the other woman, and Adrianna could have gotten those bruises from anywhere, but as we sat in Carly's car, and Adrianna told her story, I immediately trusted her.

"I still don't want details." I held my hands up, stopping Adrianna from saying anything. "If I'm meant to know more, I will. Take your time. Read the instructions carefully at least three times. Be sure of what outcome you want before you cast the spell. You've got forty-eight hours. After that, you've basically got bags of yard clippings."

She hugged me over the gate, handed me the cash, and took the bag as though it contained either a bomb or something precious. Funny how both things needed to be treated with the same level of care.

And now, I had enough money to pay my mortgage. Or to

hire a private detective to find Josie if necessary. Although a room with wood planks on the walls wasn't much to go on.

CHAPTER 25

*C*ricket woke me up the next morning. Not an easy task since I'd stayed up past midnight, something I rarely did. She jumped on my bed, jostling me, then dropped down by my side and traced a finger from the bottom edge of my nose around my mouth and down to my jaw. "What is that, Lola?"

I put my hand to my face and felt something there. Good question. "I don't know." In my bathroom, I discovered a deep parenthesis-shaped wrinkle that no amount of lotion would smooth. My consequence for giving Adrianna that spell, I assumed. The vain side of me would have preferred another ache or pain. I was used to those.

After dropping Cricket off at preschool, I drove to the police station to talk to Leezza about what Carly and I learned at The Paddle Wheel regarding the Triple Threat, as Stella called those guys.

"Welcome to the police station," the twenty-something young man behind the front desk greeted. His enthusiasm was . . . comical.

"Are you new here?" I asked.

"Just started last week," he announced proudly. "I graduated

from high school in the spring and haven't been able to decide
on my path yet.

"So you're thinking about police work?"

"Oh, no. Customer service. I love meeting people and
making their day better. How may I make your day better?"

I couldn't help but smile at him. "Is Officer Chapman
available?"

"She is. I'll ring her for you."

The officer came out a minute later and led me to the rooms
in the back. On the way, she asked, "What do you think of him?
Our new guy."

"He's very cheery." She waited for me to expand on that.
"Maybe a little too cheery for a police station."

"That's what I told Beau. He said we should give him time.
Says, 'the criminals will wear the shine right off him.'"

I chuckled. "I recall you being very smiley when I came here
to talk with Carly that day."

She frowned. "Guess Beau is right. I'm not so shiny
anymore."

"You've been tempered by two murders in less than a month.
You're still plenty shiny."

"Thanks." She indicated I should take a seat in the small
interview room and closed the door. "I assume you stopped by
for something other than to boost my ego."

"Have you spoken with Stella at The Paddle Wheel about
Tracy's death?"

"We did the day we found her body. Nash Kramer said he
went to pick her up at the saloon Thursday night, but she wasn't
there when he got there. We wanted to confirm his account
with Stella and the others who were on shift that night." She
took out the notebook she carried with her everywhere and
flipped through a number of pages. "She told us it was really
busy that night, confirmed Tracy started the fight with you, and
said it was then she realized Tracy had become intoxicated far

too quickly for the strength of the drink she gave her so presumed Tracy had been drinking before arriving at The Paddle Wheel."

"Did you check Tracy's blood for drugs?"

"We're waiting for the results. Why? Do you suspect something?"

I shrugged. "A hunch really. Everyone Carly and I talked to said Tracy was trying to cut back on her drinking. And like you just said, Stella mixed Tracy's drinks weakly, but when we saw Tracy, she was visibly intoxicated or appeared to be."

"You think there's another reason for her condition that night?"

"Did Stella tell you about a group of guys she calls Triple Threat?"

Officer Chapman flipped through the pages again. "I don't have anything in here about a Triple Threat. Who are they?"

"Keefe, Paco, and Marquis. Redhead, bald, and massive afro respectively. We think one of them might have put something into Tracy's drink."

"Ah." She tapped her notebook. "I've got those names here. Stella didn't refer to them as Triple Threat when I spoke with her. I've also seen them around. They work for the farms."

This was news. I immediately thought of the work gloves from my vision. "Which farm?"

"I guess they go from one to the next doing whatever needs doing. Things like replacing fences, planting, harvesting. Those kinds of jobs that aren't year-round."

Just like we did at Applewood Farm. "But they stay in this area?"

"I believe so, but I'm not positive. What did Stella tell you they did?"

"She basically said they get their kicks harassing women."

"Surround them and basically be pests," she read from her notes. "Stella said they were being especially obnoxious that night and were bothering Tracy. She didn't see if they followed Tracy after she took her outside."

I nodded. Her notes matched with what we found out. "Stella feels horrible about not paying closer attention to her."

"Not her fault," Officer Chapman insisted with a head shake.

"That's what I told her."

"So, what makes you feel one or all of these men are persons of interest?"

Her comment made my stomach turn.

"Are you okay, Dusty? You're kind of green all of a sudden."

"Thinking about how Tracy must have felt. To have one man harassing or following her is scary enough. Three would be absolutely terrifying, Leezza."

She didn't have to say anything. Her agreement was clear on her face.

"As for why," I began hesitantly, not wanting to reveal Adrianna's identity, "a local woman told me she believed someone put something in her drink at The Paddle Wheel recently."

"And what happened?" She prodded when I didn't say more.

"Whoever drugged her also sexually assaulted her."

"Why didn't she come to us? That's what we're here for. Let me guess, she's scared. I hate that women feel that way."

"I've encouraged her to come in and will continue to do so, but I won't tell you anything more because it's not my place."

"I understand. Tell her to come to me. I will listen to her."

I nodded, pleased by that. "For the record, she didn't specifically report any of these men. I thought the situations were similar in ways."

"Okay. I'll find these guys and talk to them."

Leezza Chapman was approximately Micah's age and not very big. The mother in me came out before I could stop her. "Bring someone with you."

"Probably not a bad idea." She flipped through her notebook

again and tapped her pen to the page she stopped on. "Harriet Wong."

"What about her?"

"She says she heard something the night Tracy was killed."

"She told us she heard a thump outside her boat."

"Right. I think she saw something too. When we spoke with her Friday morning, she started to say something about voices up river but cut herself off. When Beau circled back around, she insisted she didn't say anything about voices. I know she did; it was my job to take notes." She referred again to her notebook. "Beau was making small talk, putting her at ease, and asked if she felt safe living on a boat. She said it was as safe as a house and he shouldn't worry because she had a gun. Legally licensed. Then she said, 'I knew I heard a splash and voices. Then those men from upriver—' That's where she cut herself off."

"She heard the murder." My heart sunk. "Did they know she heard them?"

"I don't know. She refused to admit she made that comment. I think she knows a lot more but is afraid to say anything *to us*." Leezza held my gaze. "She might talk to someone else though."

"Wayne was afraid to talk too," I mused regarding the homeless man who had admitted to killing Ludo Beck.

Confused, Leezza asked, "You think Harriet killed Tracy?"

"What? Dear Goddess, no. I mean someone is working the puppet strings in this town. Whoever they are, they're scaring people into silence."

"That's what Beau thinks too." Suddenly, Leezza seemed to recognize she wasn't talking with a fellow officer, blushed, and ended our conversation. "Thank you for the information on this trio of men. I'll dig into this today." A small smile turned her mouth. "And I promise to have a partner with me when I interview them. Which will probably be out in the middle of a cornfield with my luck."

She escorted me back to the reception area just as Beau

walked in the front door. I hadn't seen him since the incident in the park where the townies were hurling verbal pitchforks at the witches.

"Dusty," he greeted stiffly. "Everything okay?"

"Everything's fine. I had some information about Tracy's death to pass on."

His eyes darted to Leezza and back. "Officer Chapman will have to fill me in."

He paused then and looked me straight in the eye. Something he hadn't done since before the park incident. There was something behind the look. Confusion, maybe. Like he wanted to say something but couldn't remember what.

"Have a good day, Dusty." He gestured toward the back rooms and indicated that Leezza should follow him.

Weird.

CHAPTER 26

*a*t four o'clock, Carly met me in the kitchen. There, Cricket was telling the aunts and me what happens if you have paste on your hands and don't wash it off before touching your hair.

"It wasn't me," she insisted. "Isabella got a big glob of it on her ponytail."

"Did Miss Autumn have to cut her hair off?" Pepper teased, straight-faced.

Horrified, Cricket clutched her own ponytail protectively. "No. She washed out the paste."

Carly chuckled as we waved goodbye to the group. "Where should we go today?"

I explained Leezza's silent plea that we talk to Harriet.

"Let's go, then. But let's stop at the teashop first. I need a caffeine jolt."

"You do look beat," I observed as we slid through the opening in the hedge. "Busy day at the barn?"

Carly yawned. "Still wiped out from last night. I don't remember scrying taking this much out of me."

"Must be because you're fifty."

She glared at me. "I assumed it was because I haven't done it in a while." She paused and then grinned. "Same thing is true when Kyle gets home from being on the road for a long trip."

"And you do things you haven't done in a while?"

She flushed and flapped the front of her shirt to cool herself.

On the way to the teashop, Carly told me she spoke with Nicola about picking up some hours at The Apple Barn now that farm work was winding down. "You were right, she seems perfect. I told her she can start tomorrow morning."

"I get her next growing season," I demanded. "And we still need her for harvest."

My cousin gave me a sly look. "We'll see. She might prefer retail to digging in the dirt."

I held out my hand. "Challenge accepted."

Inside So Mote It Tea, we found chaos. On a small scale. Sitting at a round table toward the back were three men who could only be redheaded Keefe, bald Paco, and Marquis with an indeed huge afro. Stella's Triple Threat. They were laughing loudly and telling vulgar jokes that were obviously offending the other customers.

"Hey!" Maggie yelled from behind the counter. "Enough of that. Last warning. I told you if you can't be good little boys, go sit outside."

The other customers clapped appreciatively.

"What can I get you, ladies?" She kept one eye on us, the other on the terrible trio.

"I'll try a hot apple chai," I answered after scanning the special seasonal menu.

Maggie gave a happy little moan in reply. "It's so good. The perfect autumn beverage. And you, Carly?"

"Black tea latte. Good and strong, please. No cinnamon."

While we waited, Russell came out of the backroom and said hi. Within a minute, the men ramped up again. Keefe said something that made Marquis's shoulders shake as he laughed silently. Paco brayed like a donkey, then silenced his too-loud laugh and slapped both hands repeatedly on his jeans-clad legs instead to illustrate how funny he thought the comment was. Then they noticed us. Or rather, me.

"What you looking at, witch?" Paco asked.

No matter how I responded, I would have gotten the same reaction, so I spoke my truth. "Taking in the show. I heard about you *boys*." Maggie's classification fit much better than *men*.

Keefe pushed his shoulders back and, in an Irish accent, said, "Been askin' about us, have ye?"

"Don't flatter yourself. I've been asking about a lot of people."

Out of the corner of her mouth, Carly grumbled, "What's the matter with you? Are you trying to cause a scene?"

"Trying to figure out which one of them followed Tracy and possibly assaulted Adrianna," I replied just loud enough so they could hear if they were listening. Apparently, they were.

"You don't want to be stirring up trouble, witch," Marquis taunted. "You might be the second person to end up in the river this week. And we all know witches don't float."

"That's it. All of you, get out." Russell strode around the counter. "Mags, call the police station. I want to make a formal nuisance complaint about these three."

"I'm not done with my drink," Keefe complained.

Inexplicably, Paco found that hilarious and did the leg slapping thing again. Since Paco was the first one Russell came to, he grabbed him by the back of the shirt and practically lifted him off his chair.

"Call the po-po, Mags," Paco hollered. He met my eyes as he passed by. "I want to make an assault complaint."

Holding firm to his shirt, Russell pushed him out of the shop.

Carly nudged me with her elbow, then nodded at a pair of yellow leather work gloves hanging from Paco's back pocket.

They were shoved in cuff first, so we only saw the fingers, but I assumed if we looked, we'd find a distinct logo imprinted on the leather.

"Total disrespect." Marquis stood. "Won't be coming back here again."

"Good," Maggie replied, phone to her ear. "That will save me having to tell you you're not welcome." Into the phone she said, "We're showing them the door now. She'll find them in the park."

As Marquis stormed past us, we noticed he had a pair of the same gloves.

Maggie set the phone back in its cradle and then pointed at Keefe. "You heard my husband, get out."

The redhead slammed back his drink and then stood, pushing his chair away hard. It fell into a nearby cluster of plants on the floor, breaking one of the pots. Keefe turned to leave, swayed as though struck by a massive dizzy spell, and fell onto a rather large shard from the broken pot. It had to be a one-in-a-million chance for it to precisely impale his genitals the way it did.

I turned to see if Marquis would respond to his friend's cries of agony and spotted Adrianna standing near the window, gazing inside. When she saw me, she inclined her head and held up a paper So Mote It Tea cup as though toasting me. In her other hand, she held the bag I'd given her last night.

I returned my attention to the scene inside where no one was going to Keefe's aid.

"Help is on the way," Maggie called out while setting the phone back in its cradle. "Stay still, they'll be here shortly."

"Just curious," I said, pointing at the broken pot, "what kind of plant is that?" The leaves looked familiar.

"It's a Dieffenbachia. Just got it. Isn't it great? Looks like it will need a new pot, though."

That's what I thought. Very interesting. "You know it's toxic, right? Eating the leaves can cause temporary paralysis of the vocal chords and swelling of the throat that can lead to severe breathing problems."

She frowned. "Probably shouldn't have it around my customers, then. Guess I'll bring it home."

"Or just put it up where kids and pets can't get at it." I glanced at Keefe, moaning in agony with his hands clutching his privates. "Not much we can do about adults' behavior."

At least, most people couldn't do much.

"Quit your complaining, you great arse," Maggie barked at Keefe, mimicking his accent. "The paramedics are on the way. And don't you pull that out. You'll bleed all over my floor."

We stayed with Maggie and Russell and watched while Leezza and another officer handcuffed Paco and Marquis. They led them around the back of the teashop, probably to their squad cars in the parking lot, and then Leezza returned to get details from Russell about his nuisance complaint. When she was done with him, she went to the counter to talk with Maggie.

Russell pulled Carly and me into a quiet corner. "I think the bald guy might be your killer. When I touched him, my psychometry kicked in."

"Really?" Carly asked.

"Well, the police couldn't make an arrest based on it," Russell admitted, "but I sensed rage in him, got a flash of a blond woman crying, and then water. Sorry I can't be more specific than that."

"No, that's great, Russell," I assured him. "We'll do what we can."

"I heard what he said," Russell added before we could leave. "About you ending up in the river and witches not floating." His nostrils flared with anger. "I know what you've been going through, Dusty. Don't think you're alone here. Ever. Me and the other witches, we're on your side. Even those who didn't seem to be before. They don't know you and didn't understand what happened with the boat. I set them straight. You need us, just say the word."

My heart swelled, and I hugged him close. "Thank you, Russell. You have no idea what that means to me."

Outside on the patio, Adrianna was waiting for me. She started talking the moment I was next to her.

"I followed them inside and stood behind them at the counter. He didn't even notice me. Or was ignoring me." She glared through the window at Keefe, currently being lifted onto a stretcher. Looked like the itching had started. "I listened for which drink was his and told Maggie I'd help her out by bringing their order to their table. When her back was turned, I add a little extra something to his cup, if you know what I mean. Just like he added something to our drinks at the saloon. Then I stood here and waited to see if the spell would work.

"It felt like it was taking forever, and I was getting worried I didn't do it right. I made the salt circle like you said and faced east for release, hoping that would help me move past this. For the incantation that you said I should write, I included a plea to the Universe to issue the proper punishment. Finally, the spell kicked in. Looks like I put in just enough to make him woozy and unsteady on his feet." Her smile darkened. "A power bigger than me took care of the rest."

"Which herbs did you put in there?" I asked, curious. I'd need to note the result in my grimoire.

She clutched the paper bag tighter, and two tears flowed down her cheeks. "All of them except the belladonna. I don't want him to die. Not until he's paid for what he did at least."

"In that case," I began, "I think now is the time for you to talk with Officer Chapman. The other woman should too."

"Okay, I'll ask her if she wants to go to the station with me." Adrianna held her head high. "Thank you, Dusty. Justice wouldn't have been served without you."

CHAPTER 27

*B*efore we went to the houseboat, I pulled Leezza over to the side and told her we were going to try and get Harriet to talk.

"I need ten minutes to wrap things up here with Russell and Maggie," she said. "Stall Harriet. I'll stand outside and listen."

"I'll do what I can," I promised.

Carly wanted to make a stop on the way and led us toward the diner.

"A pie?" I asked. "Why?"

"For Harriet. Nina's skills aren't quite to Mom's level, but she's pretty good. I'm hoping a little comfort will encourage Harriet to open up."

Brilliant.

When we got to the houseboat, Harriet was taking down the furniture she had out on the sundeck and was storing it in a cubby.

"You're not leaving, are you?" I asked.

"Not right now, it'll be dark soon. I'm planning to take off first thing in the morning."

She didn't seem as excited about her river adventure as she

was the last time we'd seen her. Instead, she looked frantic. Scared, maybe. Had Paco threatened her? Or Marquis or Keefe?

"We got here just in time, then." Carly held out the pie. "French apple. It's a boat-warming, *bon voyage* gift."

"One of Comfort's?" she asked.

"Nina's," Carly admitted, "but Mom taught her well."

Harriet hesitated, then smiled and set down the cushions in her arms. "Come on in and have some with me. I'll never eat a whole pie myself. Unless that's what I have for breakfast, lunch, and dinner."

"There are worse ways to blow a diet." Carly patted her narrow hips, as though she had any spare pounds on her.

I let Harriet and Carly go in first, waiting at the door until I saw Leezza cresting the hill across the street by the diner. She'd be on the dock and listening to our every word in less than a minute.

Inside the boat, Harriet dished up pieces for each of us. Her eyes closed with the first bite. She relaxed more with each subsequent mouthful.

"You're right. Comfort is a good teacher."

Loading my own spoon, I began, "You seem to be in a hurry to go. Did something happen?"

Harriet stared at the floor between us, past my shoulder, at Fluff . . . anywhere but at me. Still not quite ready to talk. The thing about a Warren pie was that after the first bite, the person would keep eating until they were content or had reached some sort of resolution. Even if that meant two slices. Or a whole pie. Knowing it could be a while before Harriet was ready to talk, I used the time to practice patience, something I'd never had much of.

After almost the entire piece, Harriet admitted, "Something did happen."

"To you?" Carly sat forward in her chair. "Are you okay?"

"Not to me," Harriet assured, so we waited. "I heard something. The night Tracy was killed."

"More than the thump against your boat?" I pressed but gently.

Despite the pie, she was still scared. Really scared. Her breathing was shallow, and she was blinking a lot.

"What did you hear?" Carly asked, matching my soothing tone.

"That morning," Harriet began, "after I found Tracy's body, I felt sick. I had no doubt she was dead before the river brought her to my boat, but to know she'd been out there the whole time I was in here sleeping . . ." Her body gave a single violent shudder. "I knew Nash would walk past early in the morning with Lady. He does every day. We wave, say hello, and he continues on. Friday morning, he was a little later than usual. Not much, only a few minutes, but it was enough to put me into a panic thinking he wasn't coming the one time I needed him to. When he finally showed up, I flagged him to come over."

"Why didn't you call the police?" Carly asked, no judgement in her voice.

"Because they would have asked me a bunch of questions I didn't want to answer." Harriet was getting worked up again.

"But they asked you anyway," I noted. "You told them everything, right?"

She shoved her last forkful of pie into her mouth, then went to the kitchen. As she dished up another slice for herself, she confessed, "I didn't tell them I heard splashing."

Carly and I exchanged a look, then she asked, "Outside your boat?"

Harriet shook her head as she sat again. "Upriver a bit. Couldn't have been too far because I could hear voices. Not their words, just that someone was talking."

"What time was this?" I thought of Leezza outside, probably

taking notes. She would want that information. "Do you remember?"

"No idea. I was trying to finish that editing project I told you about and was getting too tired to concentrate. I was shutting things down for the night and thought I heard voices. Then I heard splashing sounds."

French apple pie churned in my gut. She heard Tracy struggling while her killer, Paco, according to Russell, held her under the water. Gods, to realize after the fact what you'd heard . . .

"What happened after the splashing sounds?" Carly asked.

"Another voice. From a different place." Harriet's brow wrinkled as she thought. "Up by the road, I think."

"Was it a man or woman?" I asked, but Harriet just shook her head.

Was either Marquis or Keefe involved with the killing too? Were they right there watching? Did they follow Paco but get here too late to stop him? Any number of scenarios could be possible.

The crease across Harriet's forehead deepened. "This will sound crazy, but at one point, I swear I heard a donkey."

Paco laughed like a braying donkey. About having just killed a woman? Anger burned in my chest.

"Then," she continued, "there was a sound I couldn't identify."

I slapped my hands against my legs, over my pants, the way Paco had at So Mote It Tea.

Harriet gasped, and the color drained from her face. "That's it. You know who killed her, don't you?"

"I have a very good idea who it is, but Leezza and Beau will need proof. Did you *see* anyone?"

She ate another bite of pie and then whispered, "They were right outside. I was terrified. When I heard their voices and that slapping sound, I turned off all the lights and locked my door." She lifted a shaking hand and pointed toward the kitchen. "Then I sat across from the door with my gun aimed at it. I thought for sure they'd come for me. To eliminate a witness." She stared blankly at the spot where she'd sat. "Eventually I fell asleep right there with the gun in my hands. That could have ended horribly."

"You thought the second person was up by the road," Carly stated. "There are streetlights up there. Did you see them? Their silhouette? Can you describe them at all?"

But Harriet wouldn't say more.

Keeping my voice even, I said, "If you tell us who was out there, Beau and Leezza will lock them up, so they never hurt anyone again."

Harriet began to whimper like a wounded animal. Fluff climbed into her lap, attempting to soothe her while glaring at us.

"You're leaving, Harriet," Carly reminded her. "You can tell us, and no one will find you."

"I'll be floating down a river," she objected, flinging her hand southward. "Following me wouldn't be too hard."

"You told me there are hundreds of spots you could slip into and hide if necessary." I let my words fade away at the withering look she shot at me. "You can stay at the farm tonight if you're scared to stay here. And like I said, you tell us who did this, and they'll get locked up." I waited a few beats. "You're so brave, Harriet. Think about all that you've done with your life and all you still plan to do. You can do this."

She sat mutely for what felt like five minutes. Her mouth opened a few times, but nothing came out.

"Was one of them bald?" I finally asked.

Harriet closed her eyes and whispered, "I think so."

A gentle knock on her door nearly sent Harriet through the

roof. Leezza poked her head inside. "I've been standing on the dock listening. Can I come in?"

"Was she out there the whole time?" Harriet shot to her feet. "You set me up?"

"We didn't set you up," Carly assured. "We had a feeling you knew something and figured you were scared. I sure would be."

"So would I." I stood to look her in the eye.

Leezza stepped inside and held out a picture of Paco. "Is this the man you saw?"

Harriet shivered and looked away. "That could be him."

"He's currently in a jail cell being held on a nuisance charge," Leezza stated. "I promise he can't hurt you." She waited a moment, then asked, "You said there were two people?"

When Leezza showed her pictures of Marquis and Keefe, Harriet insisted it was neither of them but absolutely refused to name the second person or even confirm if it was a man or woman. That told me she knew but was too scared to say.

"Okay," Leezza said, "that's okay. Are you willing to make an official statement and repeat to me what you told Dusty and Carly?"

Harriet held her cat close. "I'm not leaving this boat. That other person is still out there. I'll talk to you here."

Leezza took a portable recording device out of a pocket on her belt. "I'll record it this way, then. Carly and Dusty, will you step out—"

"No. They stay. I want them here."

Leezza indicated the two stools by the kitchen bar and told us, "Sit there, please, and don't say anything." Then she sat near Harriet and turned on the device. She noted the date and time for the recording, indicated the crime in question, and who was present at the interview. "Go ahead, Harriet. Tell me what you heard and saw the night of September seventh."

Approximately half an hour later, Leezza concluded the

interview and thanked Harriet for her statement. "Is there any way I'll be able to contact you after you leave?"

"Email." Harriet dictated her address, twice in case she'd said something wrong. "I'll be here until sunrise, then I'm leaving. I've got a marina slip waiting for me."

"Will you come back?" I asked. "Maybe in the spring or next summer? You have friends here who care about you and would love to hear about your adventures."

She sighed and seemed to relax the slightest bit. "I don't know, Dusty. Something's wrong in this town."

There was. Maybe her leaving was for the best.

"Be safe," I begged. "I meant what I said about staying at the farm. Say the word if you want to use a guest room." I'd deal with the fallout of inviting an Ordie to stay in the house afterward. But Harriet refused the offer. "At least check in with me now and then so I know you're okay. Please."

She nodded. "I can do that. Until recently, this had been a great place to live. You work on cleaning things up around here."

I looked behind me, expecting she was talking to Leezza, but no one was there. Even Carly had stepped outside. "You think I can clean up the town?"

She smiled. "No doubt in my mind. Now deboard, please. I have to finish getting ready to leave."

Her words were brave, but I heard the tremor in her voice and felt it in her body as I hugged her goodbye.

Outside on the dock, Beau was congratulating Leezza for getting a positive ID on Paco. "She didn't give any indication who the other one was?"

"Not a clue," Leezza said.

"Sounds like Wayne," I offered for a second time. "He was terrified to admit who hired him. Said he'd rather go to jail."

"Whoever this is," Beau said with a scowl, "he's got a lot of power. Or has someone extremely powerful behind him."

Or her. Marilyn Kramer had a lot of pull in this town.

"I need to get home," Carly announced. "Dusty? You coming?"

"Thank you for your help, Carly." Beau stepped out of her way. "Actually, Dusty, can I talk with you for a minute?"

Carly and Leezza took off, leaving me standing there with a very confused-looking police officer.

"What's the matter?" I asked.

"I'm not sure. I've been having these dreams."

I waited for his eyes to turn glassy like they had every other time he talked about the accident, a condition of the spell my mother had put on him. This time, though, they remained mostly clear. Maybe this was about something different.

"Dreams about what?"

"The accident, I think. I'm not sure. I see bits and pieces . . ." Frustration grew thicker in his voice with each word. "Did you ever have a kaleidoscope?"

Where was he going with this? "Sure. Look through the tube and the little pieces of colored glass reflect on a mirror and make a picture." I smiled. "So pretty and never the same twice."

He nodded as I spoke, enthusiastic that I understood. Except I didn't.

"That's what my dreams are like. Fragments. I see blue and assume it's water. The river maybe. Then green which could be the trees next to the river." He ran a hand over his high-and-tight police haircut. "Then . . . Did you ever drop yours and break one of the mirrors inside?"

Seriously, was he okay? He acted wired, like he'd been awake for days and was running on adrenaline and caffeine. "Sure. I think they all break eventually."

"That's what the dreams turn into. What I see, I mean." He spoke faster while tapping his fingers to his forehead. "It's like the tube twists and the picture changes, but because the mirror is broken, the pretty picture becomes this mess that doesn't make any sense."

"Beau." I put my hands on his shoulders to steady him. "Take a breath. I know you're upset, but I'm getting worried about you."

I inhaled, encouraging him to match my breath, then again. And again. Finally, his shoulders dropped a little.

"Good. Okay, what makes you think these dreams are about the accident? You said you've spent a lot of time on the river over the years. Maybe they're related to something else." Besides, his eyes were practically clear.

His head bobbed in agreement. "Could be. Except I hear the sound of a boat engine revving full out and people screaming. Then . . . a crash. It's awful."

"I imagine it would be." Poor guy. I knew the truth was locked in there somewhere. Maybe his memories were unlocking because everyone was talking about it again. "Why are you telling *me* about this?"

He shrugged. "You asked about the accident and how my life turned out afterward. And it's not like I've got anyone else to talk to. I figured you'd understand. Sorry. Never mind."

He tried to turn and walk away, but I held him in place.

"I do understand, Beau, and you can always talk to me." Unintentionally, I moved a hand from his shoulder to his face. When I realized, I pulled it away again. "I keep a dream journal, and it helps." He listened as I explained that he should keep it next to his bed and write in it immediately upon waking in the morning or even in the middle of the night. "Don't question or edit anything, just write down whatever comes to mind. It might take a while, but hopefully something will start to make sense."

"Okay. I'll try that." He blew out a long breath. His blue eyes sparkled with gratitude. "Thanks, Dusty."

"Tell me if you have more dreams. Or if they change."

Like if he saw me standing on the shore. Far as I could tell, he still didn't know I was the reason he lost his leg. Or if he did, he was hiding it well. He'd surely heard about Nash's confession the other day. If his memories were returning, why now? Because people were talking about the accident or some other reason? Either way, what did it mean?

*a*fter the drama at the teashop and the intensity with Harriet, the rest of the night was blessedly uneventful. Once I'd read Cricket three stories and tucked her in, I took a long hot bath, then wandered around the quiet house with a mug of chamomile tea in hand. A few dim bulbs beneath the black shades of small lamps tucked here and there provided just enough light that I didn't step on anything. I did stub my toe on something furry, however. Wednesday the black cat lay like a speed bump on the floor in the family room.

"Why aren't you with Comfort?"

She replied by stretching to her full length and letting out a short *mrow.*

"Don't trip me. I could break a hip if I fell."

I circled the perimeter of the family room, the floors creaking with every few steps. At a built-in bookcase, filled with family photos, I paused to study their faces. Some I knew. Many only because someone had told me who they were. Which of these people created the voice I sometimes heard? Other faces were very familiar to me. My sister Brenda. Carly's siblings, Etta and Benny. They had disappeared from our lives. Where were they? Maybe Carly could locate them some day like she would Josie.

In the foyer, I came across what I assumed was a clock. Instead of the time, though, this clock displayed the current phase of the moon, its location in relation to the sun, and the positions of the planets. How had I forgotten about this? I'd been fascinated by it as a child. Right now, it reminded me that we were still within a new moon window.

New moons represented resets. The time for fresh goals for the upcoming cycle.

"A fresh start." I whispered out loud. "How do I do that?"

By clearing the slate, the voice of my ancestors told me.

"Or by clearing my name?"

A scuffling sound came from a shadowy corner. I expected to see Wednesday slink out, but a heartbeat later, Pearl appeared. I bent down to scratch her head, and she crawled up my arm and then draped herself over my shoulder. Normally she led me somewhere when she had a message to deliver. Her relaxed posture made me believe I was on to something and should stay right here. Okay.

"How do I clear my name?"

Across the room, something tipped over on one of the shelves. I picked it up to find a cross-stitch sampler that read simply: *Practice patience.*

"In other words, don't be in such a hurry," I said to Pearl and the house.

Pearl pressed her tiny paw against my cheek, and the house cheered softly.

THE NEXT DAY brought clouds and a fall-like temperature. A perfect day to spend in my sanctuary where the fireplace put out just enough heat to cut the chill. For lunch, the property gave me the most soul-satisfying bowl of minestrone soup I'd had in ages.

"That was perfect. Thank you." I felt like a queen when it took care of my needs that way.

"Talking to your ancestors?" Mom stood at the top of the stairs, catching her breath.

"It is them." I helped her across the room. "That's what I guessed."

She sighed as she lowered onto the rocking chair. "I heard there was a bit of excitement at the teashop yesterday."

I told her all about Adrianna's spell. "She was satisfied with the outcome, so I guess I did my job. And Russell was able to identify Tracy's killer with his psychometry."

"As a gray, it's easy to let yourself become isolated like I did. It's good that you have a coven."

A coven? Nice idea, but I didn't like the defeatist tone in her voice. "What's wrong?"

Before she could answer, my father appeared in The Sanctuary. The feeling his presence invoked was a little surreal. When was the last time the three of us had been together?

Dad looked like his standard *Nutty Professor* self, but there was something else this time. An urgency maybe. No, he always seemed to be rushing from thing to thing. Irritation? Anger? He was definitely distraught about something.

He crossed the room and placed an absent kiss on my mother's cheek, then mine.

"What are you doing here?" I asked.

"There's been activity going on in the town."

"All sorts of things are going on here." I retrieved a mug of lemon tea the property had prepared for Mom from the stand and set it on the table next to her. "Can you narrow that down a bit?"

He held up a hand, and a notebook materialized on it. He flipped through it, much the way Leezza did with hers. "Unrest between the witches and the Ordinaries. Another murder. A new gray spell was performed."

How did he know about my magic? I envisioned a massive map of Blackwood Grove on a wall at The Council building, wherever it was, that lit up with different color lights to indicate various activities or individual witches. Were they monitoring us?

He held up his hand again, and the notebook disappeared. A deep frown creased his forehead. "That's not the activity I meant, however."

"Why are you here, Dad?"

Granny Sadie joined us then and hovered behind her daughter. Dad's hand went to the back of his neck. He couldn't see ghosts but could sense them and hated the ants-crawling-over-his-skin feeling that came with the spirits. Pearl hopped up on the table. I reached out and stroked her head. Mom, Granny, and my familiar. A mini coven.

"I understand you're looking for help finding Josie."

Lucia told him. She did say she would. Or was Dad listening in on our conversations? What about The Council? No, not possible. Well, they could probably listen in when we were in town but not within Applewood Farm's hedge. Were they the ones who tried to break through the shrubs? And who were *they* anyway? Dad and Henry Kramer, I knew about, but who were the representatives for the witches and Ordinaries from the other safe towns across the Midwest branch?

"Why didn't you come to me?" he asked. "You know I'm always here for you."

"When did Lucia tell you?"

He swatted his hand about randomly. "The other day at the weekly Council meeting. She said a witch had gone missing and we needed to organize a team to look for her."

A team? That was encouraging. Except, Dad knew the day I asked for his help last month that Josie was missing. He probably knew she was a witch too. Why hadn't *he* organized a team?

And what did he mean he was here for me? He'd never once volunteered to help me before.

"What's the problem here, Dad? Are you upset I went to Lucia? Isn't it her job to help witches in need?"

"Well," he stammered, "yes, of course it is but—"

"Dusty? Are you up there?" That was Gwynne's voice.

"I'm here."

Seconds later, the others joined us. Gwynne, Comfort, Pepper, Maks, Jett, and Freddie. That should have been reassuring. Instead, I wondered why I needed this much backup.

"Oh," Gwynne exclaimed, "Jasper. Nice to see you."

"We didn't mean to interrupt," Comfort said in a way that made it very clear they did. "We've got news for Dusty."

Pepper held up a scrolled parchment. "We're ready to test the releasing spell again. Except we're calling it a revealing spell now."

"Revealing spell?" Dad repeated.

"To find Josie." Gwynne used her innocent little girl voice, but there was a wise old witch glint in her eye.

Dad turned to me, exasperated. And more than a little frantic. "You went to everyone but me?"

I shrugged, hating that I felt I couldn't trust him. "I've relied on you for so much over the years, Dad. The others wanted to help. Besides, you don't do spells."

He took me by the elbow and pulled me into a far corner. Pearl followed. So did Granny. "You need to be careful, Dusty. We don't know who took Josie, and I don't want any harm to come to you."

This time, I believed he was being genuine. "Cricket is safe here, right?"

"You know she is."

"That's all that matters to me right now. Josie and Micah could be in trouble. If you want to help, by all means, contribute to the collective. Otherwise, I'm not going to wait around for something else to happen."

He wanted to say more, I could tell by the way his mouth opened and closed, then his jaw clenched. What was he so worried about? And why wouldn't he just say it?

"Promise me you'll proceed with caution. We don't know what's going on, sweetheart. We . . . *I* would hate for anything more to happen to you." He motioned at the group across the room. "And use caution with any spells they give you. Remember why we wanted you here. Other than for your safety, of course."

To be their caretaker. "That's why we're testing their spells first."

"You'll be careful? In all areas, I mean."

"I have to. Until at least one of her parents is with her again, Cricket is my responsibility."

He left then, and I returned to my family. Mom was asleep in her chair, as I'd come to think of the rocker.

"What's going on, Dusty girl?" Comfort asked, fire in her eyes.

"I'm really not sure. For whatever reason, Dad doesn't like me searching for Josie on my own."

Pepper cleared her throat and arched an eyebrow.

"I mean without Council assistance. I couldn't do this without you all."

Pepper smiled at that.

"We're off," Gwynne announced as though going into battle, "to find Grampy's vase."

I asked Jett and Maks, "You're going to monitor this test run?"

"Yep," Jett replied.

"I'm ready," Maks answered.

"Let me know how it goes at dinner. Granny Sadie?"

She floated over and stood at attention in front of me.

"Do you know where The Council building is, and can you get inside?"

Her mouth moved.

"She doesn't know where it is," Jett translated, "but will find it. Why?"

"I'd like to know if I inadvertently got Lucia in trouble. Actually, there are a lot of things I'd like to know regarding The Council, but let's start with that."

Granny clapped and spoke.

"She's honored to be your mole," Jett reported. "And will take Freddie with her. Which is a good plan. He's very nosey."

As Cricket and I walked home from the playground, the cloudy sky darkened dramatically, and thunder rumbled in the distance. We ran the last fifty yards, which was a good decision because the skies let loose just as we got to the front door. The rain was still coming down and the thunder was all around us an hour later when I raced across the driveway to The Apple Barn.

"Dusty?" Carly checked the time on her smartwatch. It was just before four o'clock. "Did we have somewhere to go today?"

I shook my head and left my umbrella by the door. "No. I wanted to talk to you."

Then I noticed the changes she made to her shop. The most obvious being the mismatched wood farm tables scattered throughout the sales floor, each one piled high with goods. Tall wooden shelves lined the perimeter walls. She had thick, unfinished wood beams installed to mimic a ceiling and make the cavernous space feel cozier. Fairy lights wrapped around the beams added a touch of whimsy and charm. There was now a loft at the back of the barn where the clothing and housewares items were on display. And she had the stone floors smoothed out.

"They were a tripping hazard," she explained when I pointed them out. "It's still a work in progress, but it's getting there."

"It's fantastic. Really."

She turned off the *Open* sign and locked the doors. "What did you want to talk to me about?"

I went to a nearby round table encircled with chairs—a spot for customers to relax with a cup of coffee and a snack or simply chat with friends—and gestured for her to join me.

"The more time I spend with the aunts and my mom, the more I think about this last phase of life."

"Last phase? Who's dying?"

"No, I mean we've passed through maiden and mother—"

"I'm still in the mother phase," she said defensively.

"Carly, please. Let me talk."

"Okay, sorry." She sat back as thunder rolled across the sky. "Talk."

"*I* have passed through maiden and mother and am now securely into crone. You're not that far behind me. Spending time with the elder witches these past weeks, I've come to realize there are phases within this phase that have nothing to do with age." I tapped my forehead. "It's more about attitude, I think. The aunts are in what I consider to be the wise crone phase. They've had long lifetimes of learning and experiencing and are now passing that knowledge on to others. To us."

"If we don't wait too long."

"Very true. No matter how solid and secure any of us were in our younger years, our bodies and brains wear out with time. I've also observed Harriet this past week. I consider her to be in the confident and capable, slightly selfish crone phase. And I don't mean selfish in a bad way. She's living her life exactly the way she wants. I'm envious."

"Of Harriet?" Carly uncrossed her arms. "Why?"

"Not because of what she's doing. Trust me, I have no desire to live on a boat. I need earth beneath my feet. She's so confident with her choice and doesn't worry about what others think. That's what I admire most about all of them. They're living their lives according to their own plan. At least the aunts were until we made them quit their jobs."

Carly shook her head. "No, they're loving the freedom."

"You think so?"

"Totally. Every time I see them together, they're like kids again. Giggling and plotting."

"Yeah, we need to keep an eye on them."

"Agreed."

"And then there's us. Well, me. I won't speak for you." I paused and took a grounding breath. "I feel stuck. Have for years. I mean, I'm fifty years old and feel like I haven't *done* anything. Sure, I raised Micah, and that gave me great joy. But I haven't done anything for myself. I didn't belong to any clubs. Don't have any hobbies. I had few friends in the Ordinary town. No social life."

"You're starting to depress me."

I shook my head. "My point is the elder crones helped me realize I still have time to do something that's just for me. For the moment, I have to step back into the mother phase, but once we find Cricket's momma and free her daddy, I get to settle solidly into crone."

Carly sighed, becoming impatient with my cryptic speech. "What are you trying to say?"

A thunderclap shook the barn, and rain pounded on the roof.

"None of us gets to choose our powers. Once they manifest, however, we have two options. We can deny them or embrace them. I can't change that I'm a gray witch or do anything about gray magic involving doing the wrong thing."

"Dusty—"

"Mom and the property giving me The Sanctuary has sparked a fire in me. I want to embrace my magic. I want to become a powerful crone like the aunts are and our ancestors were."

A smile twitched at my cousin's lips as hopeful tears made her eyes glisten. "So you're staying?"

"I'm not going anywhere, I promise. Helping Adrianna with her problem gave me purpose like I haven't felt in . . . forever. I want to help others. Even if that means more of these." I ran a finger over my new wrinkle. "And then there are the problems in Blackwood Grove."

"Two murders in a month. That's unheard of." Carly shivered. "There's absolutely something big going on."

I told her about Dad's visit to my room.

"Well, crap. This isn't big, it's huge. We've got work to do."

"We do. Are you up for it?"

"Always. I am younger and sprier than you, crone."

"Six months," I pointed out with a laugh. "You'll be right here with me before you know it."

Carly grabbed a bottle of wine from the beverage section and got some plastic cups from the back room. She poured for each of us and held her cup up in a toast as another clap of thunder sounded. "To you, for making the best decision you've made in thirty years."

"I'll drink to that." A warmth spread through me that had nothing to do with the alcohol or a hot flash. Seeing the smile on my cousin's face solidified I was making the right decision. I held up my cup. "To us."

We drank again.

"If we're going to be crime solvers," Carly mused a minute later, "we need a catch phrase."

"The townies used to say, *The Warren girls, at it again.*"

"Nah, we're crones now. Mostly." She pondered, and then

her eyes went wide. "Oh, I know! *Hotte and Flasch, bringing the heat.*"

I choked as my wine went down the wrong way. "That's so lame."

"But you like it, don't you?" She waggled her eyebrows at me. "Nah, I love it."

Without a doubt, I was right where I was supposed to be.

ABOUT THE AUTHOR

Mystery and fantasy author Shawn McGuire loves creating characters and places her fans want to return to again and again. She started writing after seeing the first Star Wars movie (that's episode IV) as a kid. She couldn't wait for the next installment to come out so wrote her own. Sadly, those notebooks are long lost, but her desire to tell a tale is as strong now as it was then. She lives in Wisconsin near the beautiful Mississippi River and when not writing or reading, she might be baking, gardening, crafting, going for a long walk, or nibbling really dark chocolate.